Taryn pushed a hand into her stomach. "Ouch…"

"You okay?" He wasn't sure what to do. He just stared at her, his gaze flicking between her belly and her face.

"He's just kicking really hard," she said. "Don't look so spooked. Here—"

She took his hand, pressing it against her side, and he felt a powerful kick.

"Wow…" he breathed. That was a baby in there—a strong, active baby. For a moment they stood there, silent, his hand on her domed abdomen. This was his child…

Taryn released his hand and stepped away. She cleared her throat.

"Did you name him yet?" he asked, his voice low.

Taryn shook her head. "No. I want to see him first."

Noah nodded. There had been something in that moment of connection—and it was more than just the feeling of a baby's movements in utero. He'd felt babies kick before—his sister had four kids. But this had been different, almost electric.

Dear Reader,

I'm the mother of one child, and I can't have any more babies. But every once in a while, I fantasize about what it would be like to discover I was pregnant again. Normally, that daydream ends with the realization that as exciting as it would be, an unexpected pregnancy would turn my entire life upside down! And that is what happens to my heroine in this book—the shocking, wonderful, unexpected news that her life will never be the same.

I hope you enjoy this story, and that you'll check out my backlist for more of my books. If you'd like to connect with me, you'll find me on Facebook, Twitter and on my website, patriciajohnsromance.com.

Patricia

HEARTWARMING

Rocky Mountain Baby

—

Patricia Johns

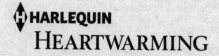

HARLEQUIN
HEARTWARMING

HARLEQUIN®
HEARTWARMING™

Recycling programs
for this product may
not exist in your area.

ISBN-13: 978-1-335-17986-9

Rocky Mountain Baby

Copyright © 2021 by Patricia Johns

This edition published by arrangement with Harlequin Books S.A.

For questions and comments about the quality of this book, please contact us at CustomerService@Harlequin.com.

Harlequin Enterprises ULC
22 Adelaide St. West, 40th Floor
Toronto, Ontario M5H 4E3, Canada
www.Harlequin.com

Printed in U.S.A.

Patricia Johns is a *Publishers Weekly* bestselling author who writes from Alberta, Canada. She has her Hon. BA in English literature and currently writes for Harlequin's Love Inspired and Heartwarming lines. She also writes Amish romance for Kensington Books. You can find her at patriciajohnsromance.com.

Books by Patricia Johns

Harlequin Heartwarming

The Second Chance Club

Their Mountain Reunion
Mountain Mistletoe Christmas

Home to Eagle's Rest

Her Lawman Protector
Falling for the Cowboy Dad
The Lawman's Baby
Her Triplets' Mistletoe Dad

Love Inspired

Redemption's Amish Legacies

The Nanny's Amish Family
A Precious Christmas Gift

Montana Twins

Her Cowboy's Twin Blessings
Her Twins' Cowboy Dad
A Rancher to Remember

Visit the Author Profile page
at Harlequin.com for more titles.

To my husband, the inspiration for all the romances that I write. I love you!

CHAPTER ONE

THIS BABY WAS A MIRACLE.

Taryn Cook had heard women describe their unplanned babies as an oops, a surprise, an accident…and this baby was definitely all of those things. Getting pregnant after her divorce at the age of thirty-nine, after ten years of struggling with infertility, having given up on a child of her own… This baby was a shock. But sometime in the future, when he got old enough to ask about how he came along, she was going to tell him that he was her miracle.

Taryn smoothed a hand over her domed belly and the baby stretched inside of her. She was only seven months pregnant, but even her maternity clothes felt snug. Maternity business casual was not an easy look to pull off, and anything Taryn wore lately made her feel rumpled. But today mattered—this was her first day of a new marketing project for Mountain Springs Resort, and this job was going to help her fund at least a few weeks of maternity leave. She hadn't had much time to plan. She had health insurance to pay for the delivery, but if she was going to get any time off after her son was born, her personal savings would have to cover it. So this job mattered—as did every other client she'd managed to squeeze in before the baby was due.

But taking this job in Mountain Springs wasn't only about the income. It was about spending time with her grandmother. Granny had been giving the family a hard time. She wouldn't accept help from anyone, and some of the family wanted to have her declared unfit to care for herself and put in a home. That felt heavy-handed to Taryn, and when she saw the posting for a marketing campaign in Granny's town, she bid on it, hoping it would give her some time with Granny. Maybe she could convince her grandmother that she needed more help than she realized. The problem being, Granny knew about Taryn's divorce, and about her struggles with infertility, but Taryn hadn't officially told her about her pregnancy. As old-fashioned as Granny was, Taryn wasn't sure that Granny would see the same joy in the situation that Taryn did, and she was in no mood to face anything less than sincere happiness at the prospect of her son's arrival.

The one thing that Taryn was particularly grateful for—and the thing that would likely scandalize Granny—was the fact that Taryn didn't know who the father was. He'd been a comfort on a very hard evening, and they'd both gone their separate ways afterward. She wasn't proud of that, but it did make things simpler now. The father was not her ex-husband, so she had no more ties to Glen, who was welcome to carry on with his new girlfriend without further complication. And the father wouldn't be asking for anything—a relationship, or joint custody— because she didn't know anything more than a first name…unless he'd been lying about his first name, as she had about hers.

Taryn was going to be a single mother, and at this age, after all she'd been through, she was glad of it. However, Granny wasn't going to be able to appreciate any of that.

Taryn sat in a visitor's chair in the office for the Mountain Springs Resort owner on the main floor, waiting for Angelina Cunningham to arrive. Angelina's corner office sported tall windows banking two sides of the room, giving a view of the pebbly beach and the sparkling water of Blue Lake. It was a stunning vista.

"Good morning!"

Taryn turned to see Angelina striding into the office with a bright smile. Taryn recognized her from a video chat they'd had a couple of weeks earlier. She was a tall woman with glossy blond hair tied up into a twist at the back of her head, and she was about Taryn's age, if not a couple of years older. She wore a linen pantsuit today, the sleeves rolled up to her forearms, and Taryn noticed her impeccable nude manicure.

"Good morning," Taryn said, and she half rose to shake hands before settling herself again. "It's nice to meet you in person."

"Likewise." Angelina circled around the broad white desk and sat down. "I'm sorry I'm late. There was a situation in housekeeping—one of my supervisors needed a hand with a guest who was upset that she emptied the garbage in his suite... It's taken care of, but there are times that some authority makes a difference."

"I can imagine," Taryn said with a nod. "Who did you side with?"

"With housekeeping, of course," Angelina replied, and they shared a smile. Angelina leaned forward. "But you aren't here to talk about difficult customers. I'm just glad to have booked you. I'm excited to see what you can do for an ad campaign. This lodge has boomed since I renovated and took over, but I feel like I've gotten as far as I can on my own, and I need some strategy here."

"That's where I come in," Taryn replied. "And you've done an amazing job with the place, I have to say. As we discussed over the phone, marketing has a lot to do with spinning a narrative that your guests will both connect with on an emotional level and want to share in. We just need to find the right story to tell."

"Do you have any ideas coming in?" Angelina asked.

"A few," Taryn admitted. "But I don't want to say anything until I've had a chance to look around and experience the lodge. Just because one narrative worked for another client doesn't mean it will work for you. What I need to find is your business's heartbeat, so to speak."

Angelina nodded. "I like that." There was a tap on the door, and Angelina looked up. "Come in."

The door opened and a tall man stepped inside. He was broad shouldered, lean and looked to be in his early forties with just a touch of gray at his temples. A pair of glasses set off his slate blue eyes. He wore a pair of gray dress pants and a crisp, white button-up shirt without a tie. His belt looked expensive. He hesitated when he saw her, and his gaze dropped down to her belly.

"This is our general manager, Noah Brooks," Angelina said. "I asked him to come by and meet you. You'll be working quite closely with him for the next couple of weeks, and he's a fount of knowledge for everything from operations to food and beverage."

"Of course," Taryn said, and she rose to her feet and shook his hand. "I'm Taryn Cook with Cook Marketing."

He didn't answer at first, meeting her gaze questioningly. "Right. Taryn. Just call me Noah."

Noah released her hand and gave her a nod. That seemed to be a common name these days. She'd met another Noah not too long ago...

"Let me show you your office, then," Angelina said, also rising. "I hope you'll be comfortable there. If you want any food or drinks delivered to your office while you're working, just give Janelle a call down at the switchboard, and she'll get you anything you need. It's all complimentary, of course."

"That's very kind." Taryn bent to pick up her leather tote, and scooped up the water bottle, too. She'd been advised to stay hydrated at this point of her pregnancy, and in the interest of allaying her obstetrician's worries, she was following her instructions to the letter.

Angelina led the way out of her office, and Noah gestured for Taryn to go ahead of him. He gave her another strange look. It was very likely her pregnancy. She garnered all sorts of reactions from people. It was amazing the personal questions complete strangers would ask a woman once she was showing. Whatever his opinions, he could keep them to himself.

Angelina headed up the hallway and paused a few doors down, gesturing Taryn inside. The office was small, but furnished with a desk, a lamp, an extra armchair in one corner and another bank of those beautiful tall windows that gave a view of a walking path, some green shrubbery and the clear lake beyond.

"I hope you'll be comfortable here," Angelina said. "If there is anything that might help out, just let me or Noah know and we'll make sure to get it for you. Noah's office is right next door."

"This looks perfect," Taryn said with a smile. "Thank you so much."

"Now, you mentioned wanting to see the lodge and what we have to offer," Angelina said. "I have an appointment in about twenty minutes, so I have to head out. But Noah will give you the grand tour. You'll be in good hands."

"Absolutely," Taryn said with a smile. "Thanks a lot."

Angelina left the office, leaving Taryn alone with the man. He stood in the doorway while she deposited her bag on top of the desk, then pulled out a tablet that was less cumbersome to carry around so that she could take some notes.

Noah said, "This is the key card for your office door. The only one who has access to changing your key card is me or Angelina, so you won't have to worry about security."

Taryn crossed the office and accepted the card from him. *No wedding ring.* She shouldn't be noticing these things. Less than a year postdivorce with a baby on the way, she wasn't looking for romantic connections. She'd already bumbled in that respect seven months ago—an evening at a pub turning into a romantic encounter that left her pregnant. And that evening had started with her noticing a hand very much like Noah's with no wedding ring, either. As if a man's confirmed single status was all that mattered. And ironically enough, that man had been named Noah, too... Except he'd been slimmer and had a rather impressive auburn beard streaked with silver.

"Have you been to Mountain Springs before?" Noah asked. "This is quite a popular tourist spot with that iconic mountain lake. You've probably seen pictures of it all over the place—"

"My grandmother lives here," she replied. "So I came up every couple of years growing up. I used to swim in Blue Lake with my cousins."

"Really?" Noah nodded at that. "Small world."

Was it? She eyed him for a moment. "Are *you* from Mountain Springs?"

"Yeah, I grew up here. I spent a few years in Denver and Montana, but I came back five years ago to take the job as general manager here at the resort."

"You probably know the area better than I do, then," she said.

"I might," he agreed.

"But I'm needing to see more of the lodge, not the town," she added.

"True." He nodded toward the door. "Angelina said that you'd be staying with us in one of our suites...unless you've got other arrangements?"

"I'll be staying here," she confirmed.

Noah paused again, eyeing her for a moment. She fiddled with her stylus and glanced away. There was something about this Noah Brooks that left her feeling a little off balance. He seemed to be expecting something from her in the way he looked at her.

"Did you want to get settled first, or did you want to start with a tour?" he asked.

"I can find my suite later," she said.

"Okay," he replied. "If you pick up your office phone and dial zero, it'll connect you with Janelle at switchboard. Let her know if you need a hand with your bags, and she'll arrange for someone to help you."

"Thanks. So, let's get to work. That tour would be perfect," she said.

"Great." He smiled. "After you."

As Taryn passed in front of him, she glanced up, and there was something about the look in his eye that made her breath catch. Noah. Tall and broad, with nice hands, no wedding ring. Noah Brooks didn't have the beard, but there was something about his eyes.

No… There was no way this was the same man! Was there?

Noah glanced down at the petite woman at his side. She came up to just past his shoulder, and she had thick, wavy brown hair that fell just past hers. She was a beautiful woman, close to his own age of forty. That was one of things he'd liked about her when they'd met in Denver before Thanksgiving— he didn't have to overexplain himself. She'd understood this stage of life, and that had been more than comforting; it had been incredibly attractive. She'd told him her name was Leigh, though, and right now, she had no idea who he was… Did he look that different without the beard?

Today, she was dressed in a clinging black dress and a pink suit jacket that brought out the blush in her cheeks, her belly domed out in front of her. She stood with a tablet in one hand, the other resting on top of her stomach.

It was weird to face her like this, remembering everything they'd shared that night, and she with no idea who he was. He'd held her close. He knew just how perfectly she fit into his arms and what her perfume smelled like…and now she was pregnant.

Noah did some quick math. He'd been in Denver in November when the leaves were bright orange and gold. Nevaeh had called off the wedding three weeks before Thanksgiving, and he'd gone to the city for a few days away from everything. He'd needed the time to himself before going back to Mountain Springs and telling all his friends and family to throw out the save-the-date. Besides, his best friend and the best man, Brody Walker, had gone to comfort Nevaeh, even though she was the one who'd broken up with him.

That night at the pub, he'd been awash in beer and his own heartbreak—definitely not at his best. When Leigh—or Taryn, it turned out—sat on the stool next to him, they'd started talking. She'd been heartbroken, too, but not soppy about it. Just deeply sad, and thoughtful. And she'd had a kind way about her. Add to that, she was stunning, and that wasn't just the beer talking. One thing had led to another, and they'd spent the night together. She'd left before he woke up.

If she'd stuck around, he would have gotten her number and given her a call. He'd wanted to take her out for dinner, at least, and have a real date. He'd wanted more conversation—and more of their romantic connection. It hadn't been purely physical. But when he'd woken up, he found a scribbled note saying that she was sorry to dash, but she'd never done this before and just wanted to forget it.

That was seven months ago...and he couldn't gauge how far along her pregnancy was just by looking at her. She could have met someone after him. She could be in a serious relationship right now, for that matter. She could have gotten pregnant by someone before him... If he remembered properly, she'd just signed her divorce papers, so maybe there had been a very brief reconciliation with her ex?

Or...was this baby his? His heart jumped at the thought.

"Noah?"

He realized that he'd tuned out, and he glanced down at Taryn. "Sorry, what did you say?"

"Can we start outside? I've been wanting to get down to the lake," she said.

"Yeah, for sure," he said with a nod. "The lake is our biggest draw, as you probably know. It's both glacier fed and from an underground spring, so there are two sources of the purest water. There are restrictions that don't allow for fishing or dumping, so it's stayed pristine. It's also nearly three hundred feet in the deepest spot at the mouth of that spring, so this is no lake to toy with."

"I remember that," she said. "I didn't know about the spring, though."

Noah escorted her to the front entrance, and he nodded at a waiter who was just arriving for his shift in the restaurant.

"Hi, Mr. Brooks," the young man said.

"Hi, Brian," he said with a smile. "It's busy today."

"Oh, yeah? I can't complain about that," Brian replied with a grin. Like all the servers, he made good money off the tips.

"All right, well, you have a good shift," Noah said.

Noah opened the heavy front door and held it for Taryn. She passed through, and he caught a whiff of that floral perfume as it mingled with the fresh outside air. It was a warm June day, but there was still a cool undertone to the mountain-scented breeze. He led the way to the sidewalk along the front of the lodge. His mind was spinning. Noah was in the running for a job in Seattle, and he was hoping to start fresh there...

if he could. Was his life about to get complicated again?

"Do you know all your employees by name?" Taryn asked, glancing up at him.

"Yes," he said. "We don't have that big of a staff, and most of our workers are locals, so you get to know who's working here pretty quickly."

"That's nice," she said.

"Yeah, we have a really low turnover rate here. When someone gets a job at the resort, they tend to hold on to it," he replied. "I'm proud of that, actually. Angelina and I have been working hard to improve morale and keep the workers we have. It's better to have happy, experienced staff and pay them a little better than it is to have a high turnover rate and be constantly retraining people at lower pay."

"That's smart," she said. "I noticed that Angelina sided with a housekeeping employee in a dispute earlier today."

"She would," Noah replied. Angelina was like that. She wouldn't do just anything for a paying guest. She had limits, and standards.

"What do you think this lodge has to offer that no one else has?" she asked.

Noah sucked in a breath, then shrugged. "Angelina."

"She's the one with the vision?" Taryn asked.

"She's also the one who won't bend her ideals," Noah said. "And that makes this place a cut above the rest. I'm proud to work for her."

They came to the side the building and he paused, letting her get the full impact of the lake scene before them. Blue Lake was nestled at the base of three jagged, snow-capped peaks. Clouds wisped around the tops of the mountains, and sun sparkled off the turquoise water. An eagle swooped down over the water and left a trail of froth with its talons, soaring back up with a fish in its grip.

"Did you see that?" she breathed.

"Yeah, it's untarnished up here," he agreed.

He watched her for a moment. *Leigh.* It was tough to adjust to calling her Taryn, even if it was her real name. This woman had been something to him—even though it was brief. He'd thought of her often since that night.

"Noah?" a voice called behind him, and Noah turned to see Brody Walker heading down the paved path toward him. Brody, former best man, former best friend. Noah's blood pressure spiked. Brody was a big reason why he wanted a fresh start in a new city. Too much personal history in a town could be a liability.

Brody caught up to him and gave him a tight nod. "Can we talk?"

Now? With an audience?

"I'm obviously working," Noah said curtly. "It's not a good time."

"It's never a good time. I'm tired of chasing you down. This won't take long." Brody jutted his chin toward a relatively private space a few yards off.

Noah's gaze flicked toward Taryn, who was watching them with undisguised curiosity. He lowered his voice. "Fine. You have five minutes." Noah turned to Taryn. "Feel free to head down to the water and enjoy the view. I won't be long."

Taryn glanced between them once, then wordlessly headed toward the water, and Noah rubbed a hand over his face.

"What's so important?" Noah demanded.

"How many times do I have to apologize to you?" Brody asked.

"An apology doesn't fix this!" Noah shot back. "That was betrayal. Nevaeh and I broke up, and you didn't stick with me. You were the best man, Brody! And you took off to comfort Nevaeh." He made air quotes around the word *comfort*. "We aren't friends anymore. I don't like you. How clear can I make this?"

"You and Nevaeh weren't right for each other," Brody said. "And don't make it sound crude. Nevaeh cried the night away. There was no *comforting* like that." Brody did the same air quotes.

"Yet the minute she breaks up with me, you run to *her* side?" Noah snapped.

"I always told you straight that I loved her," Brody said. "I told you from the start that if you ever let her go, I was making my move. I didn't hide that."

"And you did make your move. Congratulations. You got the girl—what the hell do you want with me?"

Brody's face paled and he dropped his gaze. "Look, I know I moved fast, but I wasn't giving up my chance with her. Nevaeh wants kids and you don't. You could have gotten her back if you wanted to give her what she needed—"

"Like you were," Noah said.

"Yeah, like I was," Brody replied. "I want the same things—and you don't. She wants a family, Noah. She wants kids! Is that so unforgivable? And I want kids, too. We love each other, and we make each other happy."

Noah stared at the smaller man. "And?"

Had Brody come to gloat?

"And I want to marry her," Brody said, and his voice caught. He cleared his throat. "I'm going to ask her to marry me, and before I do, I want to do my best to make sure that you and I are…okay. If that's possible."

Noah's blood felt like it had slowed to molasses in his veins, and he stared at the man incredulously.

"You're going to propose," Noah repeated.

"I already bought a ring," Brody said.

"And you want my bloody blessing?" The moment seemed to finally catch up, and Noah felt his blood heat to a boil. "You take advantage of everything I lost, and you want me to wish you well?"

"You and I were buddies—"

They'd had each other's back since they were kids. They'd hung out, defended each other, covered for each other a time or two. As grown men, they'd gone fishing together, talked about the deep stuff late into the night, and Brody was the one Noah had confided in before he'd proposed to Nevaeh a year ago.

Did Brody want some sort of absolution so that he could marry his best friend's ex-fiancée without a twinge of guilt? He wasn't going to give it.

"Go ahead and propose, but you aren't getting my blessing to make this any less awkward than it already is," Noah said.

"Okay," Brody said curtly. "Don't say I didn't try and make things right with you."

"I wouldn't dream of it," Noah said icily.

Damn it—Noah needed this job in Seattle. He couldn't stay in Mountain Springs and watch those two get married. He'd been through enough.

Brody turned and walked resolutely away. As Noah relaxed his fingers, his hands trembled. He'd wanted to give Brody the right hook he deserved. Not that he'd ever actually do it. He was civilized, after all.

Taryn stood on the lakeshore, and she bent down and picked something up from the pebbly beach. She was beautiful—rounded with the pregnancy, and he liked it, he realized. Gone were the days when long, lithe, young bodies were what he wanted. These days he seemed to be drawn to something different—a softer figure, a gentler face. He admired the way Taryn's eyes sparkled when she smiled.

Nevaeh had been ten years younger than him—young, bright, nary a gray hair in sight. And she'd wanted children…

Taryn turned as his leather shoes crunched

over the smooth rocks underfoot. She held a pebble in her palm.

"Forgive me, but that sounded a bit intense," she said.

He met her gaze, and for a moment he was tempted to brush the question aside and get their professional banter back. Except that she wasn't just the marketing expert, was she? He didn't have the energy to guess about something this important. He needed to know.

"Seven months ago, my fiancée, Nevaeh, called off our wedding," he said. "That guy who was so intent on talking to me is Brody, and he was supposed to be my best man. He just informed me that he's asking Nevaeh to marry him."

Taryn's eyes widened, and the color seeped from her cheeks. "Um—" She licked her lips and dropped her gaze to the black oval rock she held. "I met someone a few months back who had a similar situation—he and his fiancée broke up because she wanted children and he didn't. His best man moved right in on her…" She raised her dark gaze to meet his again, and he could read the question in her eyes. He'd told her about that at the pub—they'd talked for hours.

"Leigh," he said.

She swallowed, silent.

"I shaved," he added quietly. "And, um, the glasses are new."

Taryn swayed slightly. He put out a hand to steady her, and she took a step back, closing her hand into a fist around the pebble.

"That was you?" she breathed.

"Yeah. I shaved the beard off when I got home. A new-start kind of thing. But that was me. I recognized you right away."

She nodded, and she pressed her lips together. She seemed to be thinking, but she didn't say anything.

"Taryn, I'm going to ask you something," he said quietly. "And this might be really offensive…" He paused, and she didn't look up. "I have to know… Is the baby…mine?"

Taryn sucked in a slow breath, and some color came back to her face in a flush. "I was so stupidly, naively relieved that there was no father to make any claims on this child…"

What did that mean? He waited, silent, his breath bated.

"You didn't want to be a father, I thought," she said at last. "At least, that's what you said."

"I didn't," he said. "I don't. I just might not have a choice—"

Taryn was silent for a few beats before she

shrugged faintly. "Yes, you're the father. But you still have a choice about being a dad."

His heart thudded hard twice, and then it felt like it stopped in his chest.

CHAPTER TWO

TARYN FELT THE baby shift, and she put her hand on the side of her belly. Noah looked like he might pass out, and she eyed him for a moment, trying to figure out if she felt sorry for him. This wasn't planned, obviously, and it would be a shock…but no, he didn't get her pity. At their age, how babies came about was no surprise. Children were always a possibility with certain types of relationships, although in her defense, she hadn't thought she was even able to conceive. She and Glen had tried for a decade to have a baby—it had been the heartbreaking theme of their entire marriage.

"I don't want anything from you," Taryn added. "I'm perfectly ready and willing to raise this baby alone."

"We, uh…" Noah swallowed. "We used protection, though. Are you sure I'm the father?"

It was a valid question. "The only other man I was with was my now ex-husband.

And we struggled with fertility. We hadn't been together in a year by the time I signed those divorce papers. So trust me, I was as shocked as you are now," she said. "But I've had a few more months to get used to it."

"I feel like I'm going to regret how I reacted here," he said. "I don't mean to imply—" he glanced around "—anything. We don't really know each other."

"It's okay," she said. "No offense taken."

"Is it a boy or girl? Or do you know?"

"It's a boy," she said. "I've had enough surprises. I wanted to know the sex."

"Makes sense," he said. "And I know you say you don't want anything from me, but I'm not the kind of guy who just turns his back on his own child, either."

"But do you *want* to be a father?" she asked. "Because I wasn't even looking for you. This was…" She cast about, looking for a word to describe it. "This was some weird stroke of coincidence. Yes, you're the biological father, but I'm not desperate for help. I'm fine, and I'm perfectly happy to raise my son on my own. That hasn't changed. I certainly won't be advertising that you're the father. We can keep that between us. I'm giving you an out if you want it."

In fact, Taryn hoped he would take her

up on that, because while raising this child alone would be difficult, it would be less complicated than trying to juggle two families. And yet, when her son asked about his dad one day…would he be upset that she hadn't tried harder?

"An out?" Noah frowned.

"You weren't planning on this," she said.

"Neither were you."

So he wasn't going to take an easy exit. She wasn't sure if she should be impressed or irritated.

"I've wanted a baby for years," she countered. "This fulfills my deepest desires. It doesn't for you—and that's okay."

"Was this—" He swallowed. "Was this something you did on purpose?"

"No!" She shook her head. "No, that night together was just comfort, I guess. I was heartbroken, and upset, and…feeling very rejected. I wasn't trying to get pregnant with a stranger's child. Trust me, if I were going to take that route, there are more clinical ways to go about it. This was an accident."

"Okay, well, I'm not walking away from my responsibilities," he said, and for a moment, they just looked at each other. Then he sighed. "Is this going to make working together difficult?"

"I need this project," she confessed. "I'm a small business owner, and if I'm to get a maternity leave at all, I have to pay for it myself. So, I do understand how this might be awkward between us, but please don't ask Angelina to find someone else—"

"I wouldn't do that," he said. "Come on... I'm not a jerk. Not that you'd really know that. So let me just reassure you that I have no intention of ruining this job for you."

Taryn felt a surge of relief. That was a start.

"Thank you," she said. "And maybe we can get to know each other a little bit. I mean...just on a human level."

Because she'd just told this man that he was the father of her child, and she didn't actually know him. Was he a good guy? That might be wise to find out. He still looked a little wan, and he ran a hand through his hair.

"Do you wish you hadn't asked now?" she asked. "Or that I'd lied?"

Because she was starting to wish she had...

"No." He met her gaze and he smiled faintly. "I'd rather know the truth. It's better than a surprise in twenty years, right?"

"Maybe," she admitted. "But just to be

clear, I don't want anything from you. Seeing you again wasn't part of my plan. So no pressure."

"How are we going to do this?" he asked.

Taryn ran her hand over her stomach. "I don't know. Let's just…work. And we'll figure out the baby stuff later on."

"Okay," he agreed, and he looked around, then his drilling gaze swung back to her. "Did you want to continue the tour?"

"Maybe I'll head up to my room and get settled first," she said. She wouldn't be paying attention to the details that she needed to absorb, anyway.

In this moment, with a cool breeze coming off the water and the laughter of a nearby family filtering through the air, Taryn deeply wished she were a better liar. She'd always prided herself on her honesty and integrity, but everything would be a whole lot easier today if she'd just followed the knee-jerk reaction to lie to the man.

How many men lied to women? Glen had lied to her for two and half years about his relationship with another woman. Given the speed of her conceiving a baby with another man, she was also inclined to believe that Glen might have been the issue with their troubles conceiving, despite his insistence that he wasn't. The general population was steeped in lies, and yet here Taryn was at the age of thirty-nine, and her personal sense of integrity wouldn't let her do it.

One lie to Noah would have given this man a wild sense of relief, but that lie would have turned into a thousand more when her own child asked who his father was. She'd yearned for motherhood for too long to become the mother who lied to her child. Her marriage had broken, her life's path had gone awry, but she refused to mess this up. She might end up being one of the oldest moms at the playground, but she'd be a good one.

"Let me help you with your bags," Noah said. "It's the least I can do."

"Thanks," she said. "I appreciate it."

A few minutes later, Taryn used her new room card to let herself into her suite, and Noah followed her inside with her two bags. He put them next to the TV stand, and Taryn looked around the room. There was a king-size bed in the center, a small table and chairs, a love seat, a desk and, from what Taryn could see through the open bathroom door, a generous bathroom with a large Jacuzzi tub.

"Yours is one of our bigger rooms," Noah

said. "Angelina wanted you to experience the best we've got to offer here."

He headed across to the window and pulled back the curtains to reveal a generous balcony overlooking the lake. He pulled open the balcony door, and cool mountain air rushed inside, billowing the curtain.

Taryn followed him to the balcony and looked out. They were dwarfed by the towering peaks surrounding them, and from where they stood, she could see another eagle sitting high in a tree close to the shore. There were a few cottages around the lake, their wharfs pushing out into the clear turquoise water. A canoe cut slowly along on the far side. She could feel her stress seeping away.

"Wow," she murmured.

Noah shot her a smile. "Yeah, it's something." Then he sobered. "I'll let you settle in. I'll be in my office if you want, um, anything."

This was going to be awkward, wasn't it? There was no way to get back to a professional balance once you'd told a man he was the father of your child.

"Thanks," she said.

Noah shut the door softly behind him, and Taryn sank into the love seat, her mind spinning.

"What did I just do?" she whispered.

What would happen now? She'd hoped that Noah would take her offer and stay out of the baby's life, but she wasn't so sure he would now... Even in shock, he seemed pretty intent on being decent.

And Taryn had dealt with more than one devotedly decent man. Eleven years ago, she'd gotten pregnant by Glen, and he had magnanimously proposed and said he'd do the right thing by her. She'd lost the pregnancy two weeks before the hurried wedding. Taryn's father had sat her down and asked her point-blank if she still wanted to go through with the wedding.

But if she'd backed out then, it would've meant that Glen wasn't worth it unless they were bringing a child into the world. Glen couldn't have backed out at that point, either, without looking like a jerk. So they'd carried on with their thrown-together wedding, and for the next ten years Taryn had tried to conceive again—the one thing that might have made the marriage worth it—but hadn't had any success.

Glen hadn't been the right man for her, but she'd allowed his desire to do the "right thing" to make that decision for her, and she would never do that again. Whatever gallant ideals Noah had weren't her problem.

She'd learned her lesson. A man might want to do right by her, but it didn't fix anything else. Glen had cheated on her, and it wasn't with a younger, more attractive woman, either. He'd fallen for a woman five years older than himself who loved long-distance running and old movies, just like him. It hadn't come down to youth or beauty, or even a pregnancy. He'd simply fallen in love for the first time in his life.

Did that hurt? Hell, yes. It was like a knife to the gut when she saw her husband's eyes light up in a way that had never happened when he looked at her, not even in the early days. But for this other woman, he melted.

Men didn't give a woman direction. She would choose her own path. Taryn had made a mistake in marrying Glen—and she was perfectly willing to take responsibility for her part of that—but going forward, Taryn was choosing the path that was authentic, honest and self-reliant.

Except now she had Noah Brooks in the picture—another guy with a sense of responsibility toward her and this baby. She'd had quite enough of that.

Taryn sighed and sat up straight. The baby stretched, and she felt a heel, or a knee, or something push solidly downward.

"Well, now I have to pee, thanks to you," she said with a smile, rubbing the side of her belly, and she headed for the bathroom.

With a baby coming, life would never be simple again. And she had a job to do so she could have a few weeks of maternity leave, so she didn't have the luxury of emotional sidetracks. Maybe given some time, Noah would see the wisdom in backing off and leaving her to raise this baby in peace.

She could hope.

NOAH WENT INTO his office and shut the door, then he let out a slow breath. He scrubbed a hand through his hair. Okay...he could deal with this. That single, uncharacteristic one-night stand had gotten Taryn pregnant. She seemed like a reasonable enough person—but she didn't seem to want him in the picture. This was no plea for support as she gave birth to their son. In fact, he got the impression that she regretted telling him at all.

He'd thought about Leigh—Taryn—over the past few months, and he'd wondered if she was really as beautiful and interesting as he remembered. But no, his memory hadn't exaggerated it. She *was* gorgeous. And as smart as she'd seemed then, if she was running her own marketing company...

Sometimes a man didn't want to delve deep into his emotions. Sometimes he just needed to skate across the surface for a little while, because if he had to get brutally honest right now, he was terrified. And he had every right to it. He had chosen not to be a father up until now for a very good reason—he wasn't dad material. He knew that, and he wasn't going to make the same mistake other men in his life had made. He wouldn't inject himself into a family and then let everyone around him down.

For the next few minutes, Noah double-checked some numbers to make sure they were sticking to the budget, made a few notes for the accounting department to double-check and had finished some paperwork he'd been putting off when there was a tap on his door.

"Come in," he said.

The door opened, and Taryn entered, tablet in hand. For a moment they both looked at each other, and he was struck again by how beautiful she was. He could see her mild discomfort in the way she met his gaze. He was going to have to be able to work with her…and eventually, they'd have to discuss the baby, too.

"I was hoping I could get the rest of that tour," she said. "If you're free."

"Sure," he said. "I'm just about finished here."

Noah saved his work, then locked his computer. He took off his glasses and stood up. So, he needed to carry on with business as usual, even though his head was spinning. They headed out of his office together, and as they came into the foyer, he sucked in a breath.

"If there is anything I can do, any way I can make things easier—" Noah started to say.

"I'm fine, really," Taryn replied. "I was being honest before. I'd prefer to do this on my own. I'm newly divorced, and I don't want to be leaning on another guy. I'm prepared."

How long would she feel that way, though? How long was he going to sit here perched on an emotional ledge, waiting for her to need help…to *want* his help.

"Okay," he said after a beat of silence.

Taryn turned to face him, and she eyed him for a moment.

"Maybe we could make a deal," Taryn said.

"What sort?" he asked.

"Let's just agree to be honest from here on out," she said. "We have nothing to lose by it, and we won't be working together for too long, so I think some plain honesty between us will make all of this easier. I suggest we don't hide our feelings or agree to things that make us uncomfortable. We lay things out and we talk straight. We aren't romantically involved, so there's no fear of hurt feelings or drama. We're both professionals, and I think we can address our parenting relationship in a similar way."

"As professionals?" he said.

"It sounds…stupid. I hear that." She shot him a small smile. "But it's the best we have right now. We can treat each other with respect and honesty. And without being overly sensitive. You seemed to expect me to dissemble about my feelings—say I was fine on my own when I really wanted something from you."

"Yeah, I guess I do," he admitted.

"I'll promise you right now that I won't do that," she said. "I'll be honest. I'll say what I mean, so you won't have to waste your valuable time trying to figure me out. We aren't young lovers, or trying to manipulate each other into feeling anything. Let's just…opt out of the games."

Was that an actual possibility? He felt an unbidden wave of relief.

"That sounds kind of nice, actually," he said. "I'll do the same for you. Complete honesty. And I won't make you figure me out, either."

"Perfect." She cast him a smile.

The key here was that they weren't dating. There were no expectations to fulfil, and no real disappointments to experience. He'd been surprised before that she'd wanted to raise the baby on her own without a father in the picture, but maybe he could see why. His relationship with Nevaeh had always been a challenge—him always trying to figure out what to say, or how he'd upset her this time... If he and Taryn could skip that part, it would be a relief.

They came to the dining room, and Noah opened the glass door and led the way inside. The breakfast rush was over, but a few patrons were having brunch, mostly sitting around the edge of the dining room next to the windows with the lake view. A server came out of the kitchen with a platter of food balanced on one hand, and they waited until she'd passed before he led Taryn toward the kitchen.

"We have a Michelin-star chef who runs

our kitchen," Noah said. "His name is Albert Bertoni, and he will only work with the freshest meat and produce. Angelina was insistent that investing in the food would make this lodge more than just a place to sleep or to look at the mountains, and she was right. The restaurant costs us a fair portion of our budget, but she's hopeful that it will draw more guests from farther afield."

"Michelin star," Taryn said, raising her eyebrows. "That's impressive."

"Albert feels he was owed two, and he's sensitive about it," Noah said.

She smiled at that as they peered through the swinging door. Kitchen workers were chopping vegetables and prepping desserts. Albert was cooking a sauce over a flame, and he looked up at them. Noah waved him off—no need to distract Albert just now. Besides, he was a very focused man, and he got irritable when his routine was interrupted.

They stepped back out again and Noah paused while Taryn jotted down a few notes on her tablet with a stylus.

"Let's carry on," Noah said, keeping his voice low so as not to disturb the guests, and he led the way back out of the dining room and toward the fireside room. It was empty at this time of the morning, and the two tall stone hearths that flanked the room were cold and swept clean.

Taryn turned in a slow circle, taking in the space. Noah knew that this was the most impressive room in the entire resort. The log walls were burnished to a shine, and the artwork that hung there—light pastel water-colors of wildflowers—was in gilt frames, offsetting the rustic surroundings.

"Do you use the fireplaces often?" she asked.

"Not in the summer months," he said. "It just gets too hot in here for comfort. But once the fall comes and we get that chill in the air, we keep the wood bins full and the fireplaces lit whenever guests are in here… which is pretty much up until eleven, when we close the room for the night. It makes for a cozy, relaxed atmosphere."

Taryn nodded. "It sounds that way."

Taryn walked toward one of the water paintings and looked up at it, a thoughtful look on her face.

"This isn't a print," she said.

"No, those were commissioned by a local artist," Noah replied. "She's incredibly tal-ented. One of Angelina's friends owns and operates the Mountain Springs Art Gallery, too—Jen Taylor Bryant. So Angelina has been adding to the art in the lodge."

"Hmm…"

Noah stood behind her, and his gaze moved down her waves of hair. He could make out the faint scent of that perfume again, and the floral scent, combined with the paintings, felt almost surreal, like the flowers of the painting had somehow tumbled out and into the room with them. Taryn cocked her head to one side, and then she turned, catching Noah off guard. She was so close that the front of her dress grazed his shirt. She looked up at him, her lips parted and a look of mild surprise on her face.

"Oh…" she said.

He stepped back. "Sorry."

"I'm not used to my…shape," she said, and she laughed, her expression suddenly softening into a smile. "I feel like I need someone to wave me in." She moved her hands like an aircraft marshaler.

Noah chuckled. "You're fine."

But as she moved away from him, he felt an invisible tug toward her. Yeah—this was it, the attraction he'd felt for her all those months ago in that Denver pub. She was competent, funny, composed, but underneath it all there was a layer of melancholy.

He still felt that pull of attraction toward her, with the added complication that the baby she carried was his.

A boy. Noah would have a son out there in the world, and that thought was still rather numbing. He didn't know how he felt. Would this little boy look like him?

"Do you have any personal memories from this lodge?" Taryn asked, turning toward him.

"Not under the current management," he said with a slow smile.

"Before?" she prompted.

"I came here with my stepfather a few times when it was a hunting lodge," Noah said. "It was a real guy space then—animal heads on the walls, men hanging out and having cheap beer. Nothing like this..."

He used to love when his stepfather, Tom, would bring him along. He'd felt so grown-up. His mother hadn't liked it—it was no place for a child, she'd said. But Tom disagreed. He said it was a guy hangout, and that Noah needed to be around some testosterone. So whenever Noah came with Tom, he'd felt excited and rebellious, but also a little guilty, because they normally left his mother in an icy, disapproving silence.

Taryn nodded. "I'm asking because I need

a personal element—the human connection—for this ad campaign. And it needs to be linked to the lodge at present."

"There have been a few weddings," he said. "Birthdays, anniversary and graduation parties. What are you looking for, exactly? If you could conjure it up, what would it be?"

"I'm looking for a picture," she said. "Nothing posed. Something that tells a story about a beautiful mountain lodge overlooking a crystal clear, glacier-fed lake, and the heart-stopping moments that make us want to come here for our own milestones. And it can't be fiction, or look too shiny. This has to be an authentic story, or it won't get clicks. This has to be something that people will comment on and share on social media—that's where the most successful advertising happens."

"A couple of Angelina's friends have gotten engaged or married here," he said. "There might be some personal aspect to their stories that people might find engaging…if they were willing to share."

"I'll ask her about it." Taryn looked down at her stomach and pushed a hand into her side. "Ouch…"

"You okay?" He wasn't sure what to do.

He just stared at her, his gaze flicking between her belly and her face.

"He's just kicking really hard," she said. "Don't look so spooked. Here—"

She took his hand, pressing it against her side, and he felt a powerful kick.

"Wow…" he breathed. That was a baby in there—a strong, active baby. He was so close to her that her perfume enveloped him, and he could feel the warmth of her body. For a moment they stood there, silent, his hand on her domed abdomen. He felt another movement, then a tap. This was his child…

Taryn released his hand and stepped away. She cleared her throat.

"Did you name him yet?" he asked, his voice low.

Taryn shook her head. "No. I want to see him first."

Noah nodded. There had been something in that moment of connection—and it was more than just the feeling of a baby's movements in utero. He'd felt babies kick before—his sister had four kids. But this had been different, almost electric. That was *his son* inside of her, and for the first time in his life, he felt the weight of that particular responsibility settling onto his shoulders. His son would need more than his financial support, and that was where Noah knew he was destined to fail.

"I feel like I should tell you that I'm not good with kids," he said slowly. "In the spirit of honesty and all that."

"Okay…" She eyed him cautiously. "In what way?"

"In every way. I've spent years sorting this out, so this isn't some shallow male aversion to commitment or something. When I was a kid, my mom married a guy named Tom. I liked him, but he and my mom constantly fought about parenting. Tom just didn't have a sense of what was good for kids and what wasn't. The problem was, I really connected with him. So when he and my mother split up, I was really torn."

"That sounds tough," she said.

"Well, for years I thought I was a lot like Tom—not cut out for family life. But I worked through a lot of that. It stood to reason that I had a lot in common with him since he was the father figure in my life, and I was about ten when he left, so it was a really formative age. And when Tom left, I lost that male influence, which was tough. I missed him a lot, and I was shredded with guilt because he'd make my mother cry a lot, too, and there I was missing the source of my mother's misery. She was a lot happier after he'd gone. She was like a different person... Anyway, I had more in common with Tom than I did with my mom or sister. So I could understand that about myself," he said. "I worked through my issues surrounding kids, and I even ended up dating a single mom about a decade ago."

"It didn't work out?" Taryn asked.

"Things were great when it was just Shelby and me," he said quietly. "But when we added her daughter into the mix, I couldn't be the guy they needed. It turns out, I *am* a lot like Tom. I don't have a sense of what's good for a kid. I didn't know how to connect with her, and she never did warm up to me. I felt like a failure. Her mother and I broke up because she needed to put her daughter first, and I wasn't good at the kid stuff. I fully understood—my mom had done the same with Tom, since she'd had to prioritize us kids..."

And he'd remembered how his mother had come back to life again after Tom left... Had it been the same for Shelby? It sure seemed to be the case for Nevaeh... She'd broken up with him and dropped into what seemed like a very happy relationship with his best friend. Noah looked at Taryn uncomfortably.

"I have to prioritize my son, too," she said.

"Of course. And I'm glad you will," he said. "I just want you to understand that when I say I'm not good with children, it isn't because I haven't worked through underlying issues or looked deep enough inside myself. I've done the work, and I've made peace with who I am. It was why I stood firm with my fiancée about not having children."

"That's fair," Taryn said. "I get it."

He was silent for a moment. "But I'm still here for you—for whatever that's worth," he said. It felt like very little to offer. He sighed. "Let me show you the rest of the main floor."

Taryn eyed him for a moment, not moving.

"I meant it when I said I don't need you to step in and be anything to this child," she said. "I'm not asking for anything."

"Yeah, I know, but I still feel a responsibility toward this little guy," Noah replied. "He's my son. And he's going to need a dad, of some sort. I sure did. I guess I'm just saying…lower your expectations."

"I have zero expectations," she said, and she smiled faintly.

How many women had tried to tempt him into the family life? What he needed was a woman who could join him in his ordered, streamlined world and appreciate the other pleasures in life, like music, art, books… Taryn wanted to raise their child alone. Maybe he'd be wise if he simply let her do that. But his moral compass was accusing him—a real man didn't just walk away from his son. Before today, the right thing to do was to be honest about his shortcomings and stick to his strengths.

But with a baby already on the way, what was the right thing now?

CHAPTER THREE

LATER THAT DAY, Taryn sat in front of her laptop in the office next to Noah's. This lodge was almost antique, but it had been redone to sparkle with new life. The very logs of the walls seemed soaked in history, and while the offices downstairs were modern and neatly arranged, the fireside room in particular had made her feel the spirit of the place.

This was a lodge where anything felt possible.

She ran a hand over her belly. The baby must be sleeping, because he was still at long last. But there had been a moment there, with Noah's hand on her stomach, that she'd felt this relative stranger's connection to her. He was the dad...and it was more than a biological fact. When she'd looked up at him and seen the haunted look in his eyes, she'd known that she wouldn't be able to sweep this man aside. He was connected, whether either of them wanted him to be.

But Noah had been honest about what he could give. She'd felt his sincerity back there in that rustic fireside room—he'd been opening up. And while she was glad to know that he was being straight with her, she wondered what this would mean for the future. *Was* she connected to this man for the rest of her life? Or would he eventually lose interest and leave her to raise the baby alone?

An email notification on her monitor caught her eye, and Taryn flicked over to check it. It was from Granny. Taryn sighed. Business was easier to focus on than her personal life right now, and a visit with Granny wasn't going to be easy.

Hello, my dear Taryn.

Your mother said you should be in town today, and I wanted to see if you are here. I don't know why you'd stay at a faceless lodge when you could come to stay with me. You used to stay with me when you were a little girl. I have the same bedroom all made up and ready if you decide you want to use it. But no pressure, my dear. I realize that if I make demands, you'll become incredibly busy and I won't see you at all. So all I will ask is that you do come by for a visit just as soon as you can. I have some old pictures you might like to see, and my sister sent a letter so there is all sorts of news about the East Coast family. And I want to see your face. Everything is better in person.

Was it, though? Taryn had managed her relationship with her grandmother through email and good old-fashioned greeting cards for the past few years. She hadn't even had a phone conversation with Granny about her pregnancy yet, although she guessed that Granny would have heard through the grapevine by now. The East Coast family consisted of Granny's sister and cousin and their children and grandchildren, none of whom Taryn actually knew. But her grandmother still shared vivid tales from the lives of these virtual strangers and strung out her offers of gossip like breadcrumbs to lure in visitors.

Pregnant at nearly forty, the father some stranger from a bar… She could already hear the rendition in her grandmother's voice. Granny was old-fashioned and particular. She liked things to happen in the right order—love, marriage, babies and then the eventual death of a spouse. Nothing else. Keep it simple. So Taryn's life of accidental pregnancy, marriage, divorce and then a baby conceived with a stranger wasn't going to be easy for Granny to swallow.

"Taryn?"

Taryn had left her door open a few inches, and Angelina eased it open the rest of the way.

"Hi," Taryn said, putting a smile on her face.

"I'm sorry I had to duck out there," Angelina said. "I trust you had good tour with Noah?"

"Yes, and the lodge is stunning," Taryn replied.

"Is there anything you need?" Angelina asked.

"A bit more information, if you don't mind."

"Sure." Angelina crossed the room and sank into the easy chair that flanked the window.

"We discussed my plans for clickable, shareable social media content that will focus on your lodge, but I need actual people—stories that have happened here," Taryn said. "It needs to be as authentic as possible for people to connect with it, and for it not to come off as advertising."

"Like...weddings?" Angelina asked. "We've had a few."

"That's definitely a start," Taryn agreed.

"We've had about thirty weddings here," Angelina said. "Two of them were my friends. Gayle and Matt got married here last year. This was a second marriage for both of them, and Gayle was just stunning." Angelina flicked through her phone, and then held it up so Taryn could see a picture of a striking couple, the bride in cream lace, her hair silver white. They looked elegant, regal, even.

"Like that…" Taryn breathed. "That's the kind of couple that people can relate to…or they want to relate to!"

"Gayle is wonderful," Angelina said. "And this is Melanie and Logan."

Angelina held up a photo of an attractive couple—about forty. The bride had one arm around a strikingly beautiful teenager who was dressed as a bridesmaid and was obviously pregnant.

"Did they meet at your lodge by any chance?" Taryn asked with a smile. "Or is that too much to ask for?"

"Mel and Logan dated as teens, but they did meet up again right here at my lodge." Angelina met her gaze with a twinkle. "They got engaged here, too."

"And the girl in the photo?" Taryn asked,

looking at the shot again with the lovely teenager.

"Her stepdaughter from her previous marriage," Angelina said.

"Do you think either of these couples would be willing to be featured in some online content?" Taryn asked.

"I could ask," Angelina said. "We get together for a dinner club every few weeks, and we're actually dining tonight."

"Dinner club?" Taryn asked. "That sounds interesting. What sort?"

"We call ourselves the Second Chance Dinner Club, and we offer emotional support to women who've just come out of painful divorces. It started out as a casual thing—I just wanted to help out a friend of mine who had gone through a nasty breakup. But then I met more women who needed that emotional lift, and it became…a thing, I guess."

"And these women are from the dinner club—the ones who got married here?" Taryn asked hopefully.

"Yes."

"Perfect!" Taryn leaned forward. "That's exactly what we need. It's definitely relatable, and it's the kind of thing that people might share to encourage each other. If I could do some content on the Second

Chance Dinner Club, have some stories of women who've found love after heartbreak, some candid photos of the couples now—"

"No." Angelina shook her head. "The dinner club is private. You can ask the women if they'd allow their weddings to be featured, but our club is a living, breathing thing. We rely on each other, and I'm not going to commercialize it."

Of course, it was too good to be true. But at least they were finding the right sort of element that could work for this campaign.

"I understand that," Taryn said. "I would never try to use any information that you aren't comfortable with. You have full control. I'd love to meet the women, though."

Angelina folded her hands in her lap. She was silent for a moment, then said, "You could come."

"You mean...to the dinner club?" Taryn asked. "Would they be okay with that? I don't want to intrude on a private event."

"It would be a perfect time to meet them," Angelina said. "They're busy women. I'll tell them who you are, but you'll have to be discreet about the club and anything said there."

Taryn couldn't help but like the idea of a dinner club of supportive female friends. Every woman had a point in her life when she needed that kind of solidarity to keep her moving forward.

"I'll be discreet," Taryn said. "Thank you for the invitation. You know, I could have used something like that in Denver. I can appreciate what you're doing here."

"Are you divorced?" Angelina asked quietly.

"Recently." Taryn smiled faintly. "He, um, left me for another woman."

"Younger?" Angelina asked. "That seems to be the pattern."

"Older," Taryn replied, and she heard the bitterness in her tone. "He just loved her more."

Angelina's gaze softened. "I'm sorry. My husband didn't leave me for another woman, and I almost wish he had. We just didn't work out. I wasn't what he or his family needed, and his life was better without me. A divorce because of another woman is easier to explain, you know? It might even be easier on my ego. But there it is."

"Yeah." Taryn shook her head. "I know the feeling. If he'd left me for a pert and bouncy twenty-five-year-old, that would be easier to explain, too."

They exchanged a smile. So Angelina understood...that was comforting. She'd felt judged on all sides this past year.

"Men can be cads," Angelina said.

"It was for the best...probably." Taryn shook her head. "Sorry, I didn't mean to get into that. I just wanted to say that I think what you're doing is admirable. I really do."

"Well, then..." Angelina nodded. "You might just belong with us, after all. Tonight at seven in the dining room."

Taryn felt a little welling of hope that had nothing to do with this job or even her future plans. It would be nice to have an evening with some women who understood. How often did that come along?

"Is there a dress code?" Taryn asked.

"We tend to dress up," Angelina said. "It's an excuse to feel gorgeous for a night, but there's no pressure. What you're wearing now would be just fine."

Taryn glanced down at her black dress and pink blazer. It was business attire, but she could do better.

"I'll see what I can do," Taryn replied.

She did have one formal maternity dress from an awards event last month. She'd gotten a bad cold and hadn't been able to attend. But she'd packed it for this trip, just in case it was needed...

She might like to feel gorgeous for an evening, too.

NOAH CHECKED HIS email one last time, and then shut down his computer and pushed back his desk chair. He took off his glasses and put them on the desk. He was waiting to hear back from the job he'd applied for in Seattle. It was a plum position—general manager of a luxury hotel. He'd been told that they'd get back to him in a week or so. It was still a couple of days early, but at this point he didn't have much he wanted to stay in Mountain Springs for.

He'd been honing his skills over the past several years with Angelina, with no plans to leave. But after his best friend and his ex-fiancée got together, he knew that Mountain Springs couldn't be his future. That was painfully obvious, and he was thankful for how much this job had developed his résumé.

It had been a long day. He'd noticed when Angelina and Taryn had left for the evening together—their offices now closed and locked.

He'd received a dinner invitation from his sister, Laura, a couple of hours ago. Apparently, they were barbequing tonight, and the kids wanted to invite Uncle Noah. Honestly, he was pretty sure that Laura invoked the kids whenever she felt sorry for him, and for the past few months, Laura had been including him more often in their family events. They'd all liked Nevaeh a lot, and the end of the engagement had been a blow to more than just Noah.

So tonight, Noah would drive up to his sister's acreage outside of town, and he'd eat burgers and make awkward conversation with his nieces and nephews, and remind himself that he had a family who loved him.

The light through the windows was getting soft and golden. The light faded a little earlier in a deep valley like theirs, shadow enveloping the town while the sky was still light overhead. He grabbed his suit jacket from a hanger on the back of his door as he headed out of his office.

"Have a good night, Lisa," Noah said, passing one of the housekeeping employees who was pushing her cart down the hallway to start her evening cleaning. Lisa Dear was a local writer who worked at the resort for her day job.

"You, too, Noah," she replied with a smile.

Taryn had been busy with Angelina for most of the afternoon, and he'd seen her in passing a couple of times, and after that he'd been swamped with his own work. But he'd been thinking about Taryn…

The irony here was rich. He hadn't wanted to be a dad—he didn't trust himself in that role—and he'd been willing to let his fiancée go in order to stick to that. So how was this going to look if he ended up with a son in his life, after all? Was Nevaeh going to be furious? She'd broken up with him, so she couldn't fairly hold this against him. It didn't mean that she wouldn't, though.

Because while Noah might not have wanted to be a father, he couldn't just let a kid think his dad had never cared. Noah had experienced that—his biological father had left his mother when he was too young to even remember him, and then Tom left, too. When Noah was a boy, he used to lie in bed at night imagining that Tom had come back and told him that he loved him—that Noah was the son Tom had always wanted, and that now they could be a proper family.

And Tom wasn't even his biological father. Noah's throat got thick even remembering it. He wasn't letting his own son make up stories like that to self-soothe. His son would know that he cared...if he could figure out how to do that much right.

Noah glanced up at the stairway that led to the suites above as he walked past—an instinct mostly. He saw Taryn's dress before he even realized it was her—it was deep, rose red, with a draping skirt that swung around her curves, and with lace sleeves and bodice. She came down the stairs slowly, one hand on the banister, and he stood there watching her cautiously descend. She looked up as she reached the bottom, and color bloomed in her cheeks.

Wow. Noah crossed the foyer and felt the smile tickling his lips when he reached her.

"You look great," he said. "What's the occasion?"

"I've been invited to dinner," she replied with an arched eyebrow.

"Yeah?" He had no right to feel that hint of jealousy.

"With Angelina's dinner club," she said, and she smiled. "Apparently, they dress up."

"I've seen them," Noah replied. "And they do dress up."

Taryn licked her lips, and he noticed her makeup—understated except for her eyes, which were smoky and dark. She glanced up at him.

"Are you only leaving now?" she asked.

"I had some work to finish up," he said. "And my sister invited me for dinner at their place tonight, so—" There was something that was holding him there, and he felt her gaze locked on him expectantly. "You look really beautiful."

Shoot. That was too blunt. He wished he could take it back, but it was too late.

Taryn looked down. "I feel a little foolish, actually. Dressed to the nines like this, pregnant out to here." She put a hand at the front of her stomach.

"And looking amazing," he said. "Trust me on that. I'm not the kind of guy who says stuff he doesn't mean."

Apparently, he wasn't a guy who kept his mouth shut, either.

Her smile deepened. "Thank you. It'll have to do."

He chuckled and took a step back. "Have a good night, Ms. Cook."

"Enjoy your family dinner, Mr. Brooks," she replied, and she shot him a smile over her shoulder as she headed toward the dining room. His gaze lingered on her retreating form until he noticed Susan at the front desk watching him with undisguised curiosity.

He cleared his throat, gave her a nod and headed for the front door. The last thing he needed was for the staff to see him ogling the marketing specialist.

As he headed out to his truck, he pulled

out his cell phone and called his sister. She picked up on the second ring.

"Hi, Noah," she said. "Don't you dare cancel."

"I'm not canceling," he said. "I'm on my way. I'm just running a little late."

"How is work?" she asked, and then said in a more muffled voice to the side, "Aaron, if you don't take your hands off your brother—"

"It's fine," he said. "Do you need to go?"

"They'll be fine," his sister said. "They're in a fighting stage—like physical battles. There are days when I understand why you don't want smaller versions of yourself. They're a handful."

"About those smaller versions of myself," he said, opening the driver's side door and hoisting himself up into the seat.

"Are you changing your mind about having kids?" his sister asked with a laugh. "Don't get everyone's hopes up."

"Not exactly," he said, putting his phone on speaker and dropping it onto the magnetic holder. "It's… Look, Laura, I'm only telling you this because I don't have anyone else I trust with it. But you have to keep this between us."

"Of course," she said, growing serious. "What's going on?"

"It looks like I'm about to be a father…"

There was a stunned silence.

"Laura?"

"Am I allowed to react?" she asked, her voice low.

"No. You are sworn to secrecy," he said.

"Is it with Nevaeh?" she asked.

"No…it's a little more complicated…"

Noah told a very short version of what had happened. This wasn't the kind of tale a man normally felt comfortable telling his sister, but she needed to know the broad strokes, at the very least.

"And she wants nothing?" Laura asked.

"That's what she says," he replied.

"Does she even want you in her life?" Laura asked.

"Um, we still have a lot to talk over," he replied. "Quite honestly, she wasn't looking for me, and she said she'd wanted to do this on her own. Less complication, I guess."

For her, at least. This was going to be complicated for Noah regardless.

"Are you sure she wasn't looking for you?" she asked. "I have to tell you, raising a child alone would be expensive. Women bring the fathers to court to get child support, and that isn't them being petty. They need the money!"

"She didn't know my last name," he said. "And she didn't even recognize me. She wasn't looking for me—I'm sure about that."

"Does this change anything for you?" Laura asked. "And you know what I'm talking about. You and Nevaeh loved each other, and I'm not convinced you're over the breakup."

"I'm over it," he said.

"Noah, I know you—"

"Brody came by the lodge today," Noah interrupted her. "He's going to ask her to marry him."

There was a beat of silence, and then his sister sighed, "Oh, Noah…"

"Quit feeling sorry for me," he snapped. "I'm fine."

And truth be told, when he'd had time to mull things over in his office, he hadn't been agonizing over Nevaeh marrying Brody. He'd been thinking about Taryn and the fact that after all his careful dodging of fatherhood, he was going to be a dad anyway. That was the more life-changing news.

"I know you hate to hear it, but Brody does love her," Laura said softly. "He has for years."

"Yeah…"

Nevaeh was ten years younger than he was. She wasn't tarnished as he was. Most guys liked that. Heck, he'd liked it, too. He'd never really identified the age difference as a problem before today, but there was something oddly alluring about a woman his own age.

An image rose in his mind of Taryn as she'd been in the pub, an untouched beer in front of her and her elbows resting on the bar. She hadn't been weak, but she'd been sad. And when he said hi, and she looked over at him, he'd seen a depth in that dark gaze that had drawn him in.

"Is this about a guy or a job?" he'd asked, nodding to her beer.

She'd given him a faint smile. "A finalized divorce. You?"

"Broken engagement," he replied.

She'd lifted her beer in a salute. "Here's to heartbreak."

He'd moved over to the stool next to her, and they'd talked a little while. Then they'd moved to a booth and talked for hours. People milled through the pub, left for the night, but they'd kept talking. It was just such a relief to have someone understand him. And listening to her stories was an unexpected balm for his own pain. He'd told himself it was because she was a stranger, since he'd never talked to Nevaeh like that before…

"Noah?" his sister said, pulling his thoughts back.

"Maybe I'd better focus on the road," he said. "I'll be there in fifteen minutes."

"See you soon," his sister replied, and Noah hit the button to disconnect the call.

A long time ago, in a very age-inappropriate discussion about women, Tom had told him that there was nothing more attractive than a long, honest conversation with a woman. Noah had no idea what that had even meant at the time, but it looked like he'd reached that phase of life when a woman with dark, soulful eyes and a sharp wit could catch him on a level he'd never experienced before…and a long conversation had been just what his aching heart had needed.

CHAPTER FOUR

THE MOUNTAIN SPRINGS RESORT dining room was full that evening as Taryn stood at the double doors, scanning the room looking for Angelina. She spotted her when Angelina stood up and beckoned her over to a table on the far side of the room next to tall windows. Quiet music played inside over the murmur of voices and the clink of cutlery. She glanced up at the tall, sloped ceiling with thick wooden supports that shone burnished in the low light.

This was one extraordinary dining room, and she'd have to feature it in the ad campaign…but tonight wasn't about work entirely, and as she wove her way through the tables, she scanned the women who sat with Angelina. They were all dressed up—gowns, jewelry—and they looked toward her curiously. She immediately spotted Gayle, the woman with the gorgeous silver hair twisted into an updo. She recognized Melanie from the other wedding photo, as well—

she wore a midnight blue, off-the-shoulder dress. Her makeup was understated, and her skin was flawless. There were three other women at the table besides Angelina, and they all looked companionably cheerful together.

Taryn felt a rush of nervousness. She'd never found making new friends easy, and somehow tonight, even after Noah's compliments, she felt exposed. She hadn't been joking when she said she felt a little silly doing this. She'd almost changed into something more casual before leaving her suite, but something about dressing up appealed to her. Besides, she wanted to enjoy the last few weeks of this pregnancy. She might not ever be pregnant again, and if she never did wear this crimson dress, she'd regret it. She knew that much. So why not step out looking her best tonight?

"Welcome to our dinner club," Angelina said, gesturing to an empty seat between herself and Gayle. They both sat down at the same time, and a passing waiter helped scoot her chair in underneath her. Taryn smiled her thanks over her shoulder.

"Everyone, this is Taryn Cook," Angelina said. "She's the marketing pro who's doing an ad campaign for me."

Taryn smiled at the women. They all murmured their hellos, and Taryn smoothed her hand over her belly. Her son was squirming at her new, seated position, and she let out a slow breath as she waited for him to calm.

"Okay, first of all, some ground rules," Angelina said. "Melanie and Gayle both said they'd be happy to talk to you about their weddings."

"Thank you for that," Taryn said with a smile. The women smiled in return.

"And for anything else said tonight," Angelina said, leaning forward, "there is a strict confidentiality policy. We're here as friends, and anything that's said at this table doesn't leave it."

"Absolutely," Taryn said quickly. "This is really kind of you to let me join you this evening."

"Oh, there's always room for one more," Gayle said.

"I let everyone know that you're recently divorced, as well," Angelina added. "So we all have that in common. Let me just introduce you to everyone." She gestured to the tall, lithe beauty sitting next to her. "This is Belle Villeneuve. She was a model and married to her agent."

"Until I put on some healthy weight and

he dumped me for a younger version. I'm *almost* over it," Belle said with a wink. "But I'm having more trouble moving on than the other women here."

Even with those stunning looks. But moving on wasn't always about attracting a fresh mate—it was about being ready for it. And Taryn could understand that all too well.

"Sorry…" Taryn said.

"No need," Belle replied. "At this dinner club, we don't have to be polite or offer condolences. We just…understand."

"This is Renata." Angelina gestured to a shorter, plumper woman who had beautiful eyes and a lovely smile. "She has three kids, and one ex-husband. She also has a rather sweet boyfriend we all like a lot."

"Can I ask what happened?" Taryn asked hesitantly.

"Of course," Renata replied. "I caught my husband cheating on me, and he figured it was a good solution for us to stay married, and for him to move his mistress into the family home."

"Oh… Yikes…" Taryn winced. So there were women who had it worse than her. At least Glen had been willing to make a clean split and hadn't tried to make it worse than it was. "That's really low."

"Yeah. So... I'm divorced," Renata said, but she shrugged then. "It's for the best. I've met a really nice guy. Life does get better... I promise."

Sitting next to her was Melanie, the one Taryn recognized from the photo with the beautiful pregnant teenager. Melanie looked even better now than she had in her wedding photo—a little plumper, too. Was it just some extra weight and some marital happiness that made the difference?

"I'm Melanie McTavish," she said "As you know, I'm remarried now, but I was married for fifteen years to my first husband, and I found out he'd been cheating for most of that time. I raised his three kids from his first marriage, and then, of course, had to leave him."

"That's hard," Taryn said softly. "Are you still close to the kids?"

"Actually, yes," Melanie said with a nod. "I'm grandma to my youngest stepdaughter's little girl. She's a year old now, and just adorable." Melanie looked down for a moment. "I'm also pregnant—I'm four months along. So my granddaughter and my own child are going to be pretty close in age. It's going to be interesting."

"I think it sounds wonderful," Taryn said.

"You look great, by the way," Melanie said. "But don't get me sidetracked on babies. Meet Jen and Gayle, first."

"I'm Jennifer Bryant," the next woman said. "I own the art gallery in the old mansion up on the hill."

"Noah mentioned you," Taryn said. "That's really impressive."

"I bought it with my divorce settlement," Jennifer said, and she fiddled with a wedding ring on her left hand. "I wanted to be smart about my restart. I met my first husband at college—he was my professor. No big cheating drama for us. We just grew apart. He likes young, adoring students. I grew up. What can I say?"

Taryn nodded. "Understandable. But you're remarried?"

"I am." She stopped fiddling with the ring. "We got married last month. I hired him to do renovations on the old mansion, and… one thing led to another, I suppose."

"As they do," Gayle said with a chuckle.

"This is my aunt Gayle," Jen said, nodding to the woman next to her with the elegant, silvery updo. She wore a pale pink dress and a slim wedding band on her left hand.

"My husband came out as gay after thirty-five years of marriage," Gayle said softly.

"And he left me for his best friend. I was crushed…but it was the best thing for both of us, really. Stu deserved to live his life honestly, and I deserved a chance to be truly desired."

To truly be desired… Funny, Taryn could identify with that the most at the table tonight. That had been missing in her marriage with Glen. They'd both been so determined to do the right thing that they hadn't stopped to consider if it was worth it. And maybe that was partly her own fault, focusing so exclusively on getting pregnant again. But still…

Taryn felt tears mist her eyes. "You seem to have taken the high road."

"Well, it's a lot easier now that I'm married to Matthew," Gayle said with a low laugh. "I wasn't always this graceful."

The other women laughed good-naturedly. There was obviously a lot of shared history between them.

"But who is graceful all the time?" Melanie asked. "I mean, we get our hearts torn out, our hopes dashed, our egos flattened… And we're supposed to smile through it all? How can we? This is what this dinner group is for. We remind each other that we're not alone, and that it gets better."

"Which brings us to you," Belle said, turning toward Taryn. "What's your story?"

Taryn smoothed her hand over her belly again. "I married the wrong guy." She shrugged. "I think that's what it comes down to. Glen and I weren't dating very long when I got pregnant the first time. He was all gallant and said he'd marry me, and I...went along with it. I'd always wanted children, and I suppose I liked the idea of a wedding and a nursery...you know."

The other women nodded.

"So, we started planning the wedding. But just before the wedding, I lost the pregnancy," Taryn said.

"And you went through with it anyway," Gayle said softly.

"We did," Taryn said. "I never did get pregnant again with Glen, though. And I tried everything. The doctors couldn't see anything technically wrong with either of us, but... Anyway, I think I can identify with Gayle a bit, because I wasn't the right one for Glen, either. He met a woman he adored a couple of years ago—and she wasn't younger or prettier than me, either. She was just...right for him."

Gayle nodded and dropped her gaze. "I know that feeling..."

"We got divorced," Taryn said. "And I'm not saying I wasn't bitter, but we weren't happy, Glen and me. This is probably better."

"You said you and Glen never did manage to get pregnant again…" Melanie prompted.

"Yeah…" Taryn felt her cheeks heat. "This is harder to explain. I had just signed the divorce papers and I went to this bar in Denver to just…process, I guess. And I met this guy."

"Enough said," Renata said with a sympathetic nod. "After all those years of trying for a baby, was this good news?"

Taryn felt some of her nervousness melt away. Maybe there wouldn't be as much judgment as she'd feared. But she wasn't going to live her life in shame for having an untraditional family, either.

"This was excellent news!" Taryn replied firmly. "I wanted a baby so badly, and now I'm going to have one. It's a boy. And I couldn't be happier. Besides, I don't have to stay connected to Glen with this child, either. And I get to be a mom."

"A truly fresh start," Jen said as the other women nodded.

"Exactly," Taryn replied. "How many of us get that?"

"Did Glen wonder if the baby was his?" Gayle asked.

"No," Taryn replied. "We'd been separated for a year by the time we signed the papers and I...conceived. So there was no question about paternity there."

"I know what that's like to want a baby and not be able to have one," Melanie said quietly. "In my first marriage, it wasn't a fertility issue. My husband already had three kids and didn't want more. It's hard—and it's the kind of thing you don't feel like you can talk about."

"Yes!" Taryn reached for her water glass and took a sip. "That's the thing—I felt like I couldn't really talk about it. And I had to be happy for my friends who were having kids and growing their families, and I had to pretend that this was part of the plan— double income, no kids."

"I know, it's a matter of pride," Melanie agreed. "You have to appear happy, because heaven forbid any of us be less than blissful. It's as if we're judged on our happiness level. A happy woman is a successful woman. A woman who has some heartbreak has somehow failed."

Taryn understood that pressure all too well, and the other women nodded in agreement.

"Even if things are terribly wrong, you smile brilliantly," Gayle said softly. "I did that for thirty-five years. And everyone believed me. I was a great actress."

"We did believe you," Jen said. "You were our ideal couple—the ones we aspired to be like."

"Ironic," Gayle said and she shook her head. "You never know what's happening behind closed doors, do you?"

"I think we all need to agree that even in our current relationships, we stay honest with each other, at the very least," Renata said. "Here, in this circle, we tell it like it is."

The waiter came with menus then, and after a few minutes of perusing her options, Taryn chose the yam tortellini with a cream sauce, and Angelina ordered some white wine, as well as some sparkling apple juice, for the table.

"At least two of us aren't drinking tonight," Angelina said with a smile.

When the waiter left again, Taryn took a sip of her water and settled back into her chair. She had a direct view outside, and the entire lake was submerged in shadow from the mountains. The baby had settled, and she could feel him hiccup, which always made her smile. She was looking forward to holding him, looking into his face…but she couldn't picture what he'd look like.

"So how is everyone?" Angelina asked.

"I have…a situation," Belle said, and Taryn pulled her attention back to the table.

"Oh?" Renata said. "What's going on?"

"So you know how I've been dating Philip?" Belle said. Everyone murmured assent. "The thing is, he doesn't want me to meet his parents. I'm not sure why! He says it isn't me and that his family would love me. But…" She paused. "He says I'm too beautiful to stay with him."

"What?" Angelina shook her head. "What does that mean, exactly?"

"He says that he's not the kind of guy who can keep a woman like me interested for the long haul," Belle replied.

"He's managed to keep you interested for the last six months," Gayle said.

"That's what I told him," Belle replied. "But he says he wants to wait. So… I guess we wait."

"What does he think you'll do?" Jen asked.

"Leave him, presumably," Belle replied. "You know this isn't the first time I've had this problem. I find a really nice guy, and he gets intimidated. I don't want some cocky rich guy with a Porsche. I've dated them be-fore—they're horrible. They treat you like another acquisition. I want a real man with a real heart. That's what I want, but Philip has this whole insecurity that I'll be swept off by someone richer and better looking."

"*Is* he a nice guy?" Taryn asked.

"That's a good question," Gayle mur-mured.

"No, he really is," Belle insisted. "He's a kindergarten teacher at the elementary school here in town—" this was said to Taryn "—and he's got this wonderful way with kids. He's kind and funny and sweet… He's a good one, I promise. He's just…in-secure."

"Sweetie, if he isn't superexcited to have you on his arm, he's an idiot," Renata said. "Look at you! You're stunning. You're a lit-eral model."

"Ex-model," Belle corrected her.

"Oh, semantics!" Renata shot back. "You know what? Of all of us, you're the one who can walk into a room and just shut it down with your good looks. And I don't think you should have to dull your shine for an inse-cure man."

Taryn had to agree there. Just then the

wine and sparkling juice arrived, so they all had their glasses filled accordingly, and when the waiter left, Angelina lifted her glass.

"To second chances," Angelina said, and turning to Taryn, she added, "and to new friends."

They all clinked their glasses, and Taryn couldn't help but smile as Renata turned back to Belle, not to be so easily put off.

"Belle, I think you need to let us set you up with a man worthy of you," Renata said earnestly. "Seriously. Philip is just a dear, I'm sure, but you need someone stronger than that."

"I need someone sweet and ordinary—"

"You're only one of those things," Angelina added with a laugh.

This group of friends was like a breath of fresh air, and Taryn took another sip of sparkling apple juice and listened to the women debate Belle's problem.

If only she'd had something like this in Denver…but a dinner club of divorced women who completely and sincerely supported each other wasn't exactly easy to come by. She could see why Angelina was protective of this group.

PATRICIA JOHNS 87

But it was this kind of support and sincerity that needed to be shown in Taryn's ad campaign. Because if anything would draw people to this gorgeous mountain lodge, it would be a stunning glacier-fed lake, and this kind of heart. As Taryn could attest, it was hard to resist.

NOAH PULLED INTO his sister's driveway, and all four kids were at the living room window to wave at him while he got out of his truck. The sky was dusky, and he could smell the aroma of barbecue coming from behind the house. Henry, his sister's husband, would be out there cooking up a feast.

The front door flung open and Aaron, his eldest nephew, came outside to stand barefoot on the steps.

"Hi, Uncle Noah!" he called.

"Hey there, Aaron," Noah said, and he locked the vehicle with a blip and headed up toward the door. "You're taller. Come here. Let's measure."

Noah always measured the kids against his side, every single visit. And honestly, they grew pretty fast, but he made a much bigger deal about it. Noah measured the top of his head against his torso.

"Holy smokes, kid," Noah said. "You're huge. What happened? Did you eat your vegetables or something?"

"No," Aaron said, and laughed.

"No? What? You've got to be eating your spinach and brussels sprouts and broccoli, and—" He cast about, looking for more veggies his nephew hated.

"I don't eat any of that!" Aaron retorted. "And I grow anyway. That's a hoax."

This was a new development since Noah had last visited. He shot his nephew a look of surprise.

"No, it isn't," he said. "I got muscles because I ate my veggies."

"You were lied to by the Man," Aaron countered, and Noah couldn't help but laugh at that.

The other kids came tumbling outside, and Nicholas, the five-year-old, had to be measured, too, and told that brussels sprouts were key to his growth and muscles. And then came the twins, Micah and Libby, who were only three, but who still tried to be involved in everything. He always told the twins that they needed more cake, which was the big joke, of course, because they were the babies of the family and therefore got favored in every way. Noah scooped up

Libby in his arms and kissed the little girl's cheek as he headed into the house, where his sister waited with a smile. Her hair was pulled back in a ponytail, and her face was flushed from the heat. She wore an apron that read "Baking is better than punching people," which just went to explain his younger sister's sense of humor.

It was hot inside, all the doors and windows flung open to capture some breeze, and Laura reached out and gave him a hug as Libby reached for her mother. Laura scooped the toddler up and set her down next to Micah.

"Okay, let go of your uncle," Laura said. "Aaron, go outside and see if Daddy needs anything, and Nicholas, go into the garage freezer and get me three cans of lemonade, okay?"

While his sister marshaled the kids, Noah let out a long breath. He was comfortable with being the uncle, but that was because Laura and Henry did all the actual work. Noah called a hello to his brother-in-law, who was flipping burgers at the barbecue, and when the kids had been sent on various errands, Laura leaned against the counter and fixed him with a serious look.

"So, you're going to be a dad," she said.

"I don't know about the dad part," he said. "She might not want me terribly involved. I'll be a father, though."

Laura's expression turned mildly incredulous, but she didn't say anything.

"I'm in shock, honestly," he said. "But I've told her that I'll do whatever I can. I mean, I don't want my son growing up wondering if his dad cared, you know? Like we did."

"Our father was a horrible person," Laura replied. "Good riddance."

And that had always been Laura's stance. Their father had refused to marry their mother after they'd been living together for about five years and both Noah and Laura came along. Laura was an infant when their father left and never came back. Noah had tracked him down once, just out of curiosity, and he'd found a guy who wasn't working, did a lot of drinking and pot smoking, and when he discovered that Noah was his son, the first thing he did was try to borrow money.

"Yeah, I know," Noah replied. "I agree. But you know who I do miss? Tom."

Laura rolled her eyes. "Tom was terrible with kids. Do you know what Mom said about him? She said he was part of her pattern in choosing the wrong guys."

"Yeah, I guess…" Tom wasn't exactly exemplary father material. He'd put Laura on a long leash attached to a spike in the lawn so that she wouldn't run off when she was about four. He'd let Noah start the car for him when he was only about six. Tom had taught him how to light matches, and he'd let him watch his first knock-out boxing match when he was seven or eight, and Noah had had nightmares for years afterward.

"I heard from him, though," Laura said. "He's on Facebook now."

"What?" Noah blinked.

"Get on Facebook with the rest of the world, and you could reconnect with people, too," Laura said with a short laugh.

"Maybe I should," he admitted. "What's he doing?"

"He runs a dog rescue," she replied. "It looks like it's a pretty big setup, too."

"Did you talk to him at all?" Noah asked.

"Briefly. He's the one who found me, actually. I asked how he was. He's married again, but no kids—no surprise there. I told him about Henry and the kids—that was about it," she replied.

"Oh…"

"He asked about you," she said.

"What did you tell him?"

"Oh, that you're a general manager now, and doing really well." His sister pulled out her cell phone, flicked around on the screen and then passed it over. "Those are the pictures on his Facebook profile."

Nicholas came back into the kitchen with the frozen lemonade cans—six of them, and two dropped from his grip onto the kitchen floor.

"How many did I ask for?" Laura asked, taking them two by two from her son's arms and lining them up on the counter.

"I don't know."

"Think. How many?"

"Eight."

"No…" She held up three fingers.

"I don't know."

"Three, Nicholas. I asked for three. Now, how many did you bring me?"

While his sister tried to explain some basic math to her five-year-old, Noah tuned them out and flipped through the pictures. It was a strange relief to see Tom's face again. He hadn't changed that much. He was grayer now, and a little heftier, but he had the same easy smile, the same creases around his eyes. A few pictures showed Tom sitting on the front steps of an old house, his feet bare and a beer in one hand, a large dog sitting next to him, tongue lolling out of the canine's mouth. There were other photos of him at his dog rescue—standing with big bags of kibble, and squatting next to various dogs, a reassuring hand on their backs.

"So you bring these ones back to the freezer, okay?" Laura was saying to Nicholas. "And close the freezer!" Nicholas ran off in the direction of the garage, and Laura hollered after him, "I mean it! Make sure the freezer is closed!"

Noah looked down at Tom's familiar grin. He was the closest to a dad that Noah ever got.

"I miss him," Noah said, his voice low.

"We had Mom, Noah," Laura said. "She worked her fingers to the bone to take care of us and make sure we could get an education. The men came and left. They weren't worth much."

"I liked Tom, though," he said.

Laura sighed. "Mom deserved the credit. Tom was like an extra kid in the family. She needed a partner, not a liability."

Those were his mother's words.

"I know." And he couldn't argue with it, either. Their mother had been fierce, hard-working, devoted. She'd always put Noah and Laura first. They'd never lacked anything, and even now he wasn't sure how she'd done it all. She'd been a great mother… And they missed her deeply.

Would Taryn be like that—the protective, determined mom who made sure that their son got everything he needed? Would his son grow up with no reason to complain, but with some hollow feeling inside of him all the same because of the dad he never knew?

"With Mom gone, you don't ever think about Dad or Tom?" Noah asked.

"No," Laura replied. "I think about *Mom*. That's who I think about—the one who raised us."

Right. Laura had always been the loyal one. She'd sided with Mom on everything.

The door opened, and Noah looked up to see his brother-in-law come into the kitchen, Aaron in tow.

"Hey, how are you doing?" Henry said. Henry was tall and lanky with a generous smile. "Good to see you, man."

"Hey, Henry," Noah said with a grin. "I've been promised burgers, I think."

"I've got some ribs going, too," Henry said. "They'll melt off the bone, guaranteed."

Noah handed Laura her phone, and the family moved into dinner mode. Laura handed a wooden spoon to her husband and pointed to a juice jug.

"You mind, Henry?" Laura said. "We need to make the lemonade."

"Sure," Henry said, accepting the wooden spoon and heading to the counter.

"Aaron, I need you to get the carrot sticks from the fridge," Laura said, turning in a circle, and scooping Micah up as he reached for a plate of barbecued burger patties.

"I'm not eating carrot sticks," Aaron muttered, heading toward the fridge.

"Of course you are," Laura replied. "Didn't your uncle tell you that veggies build muscles?"

Aaron rolled his eyes and Laura froze, pointing a finger at her son. "Watch the attitude, young man."

"I *hate* carrots," Aaron retorted.

"Since when?" Laura said.

"Since now," he shot back. "I'm not eating that. You eat it if you think it's so great."

Noah saw the color drain from his sister's face. That kid was playing with fire.

"Come on," Noah said, forcing a smile. "Muscles, remember?"

"Hoax, remember?" Aaron retorted, meeting Noah's gaze defiantly.

The kitchen fell silent, and Noah eyed his sister, wondering what she'd do. Aaron had always been relatively easy to handle from what Noah could see, but this was a whole new stage.

"Aaron, you want to try that again?" Henry's voice dropped an octave. "Apologize to your mother."

"Sorry…" Aaron muttered.

"Like you mean it!" Henry barked.

"Sorry, Mom."

"And apologize to your uncle for being rude," Henry said.

"It's okay," Noah said quickly. "Don't worry about it. Just kids being kids, right?"

This was uncomfortable enough as it was. Henry ignored Noah and eyed his son meaningfully.

"Sorry, Uncle Noah." The boy's gaze flickered toward him and then to the floor.

"Good. Now get the carrot sticks like your mother asked," Henry said.

Aaron went off to do as he was told, opened the fridge and pulled out a plastic tub.

Laura looked across the kitchen at her

husband. They exchanged a smile and they each mimed a high five.

Laura and Henry had it under control. Noah was just the uncle, and apparently, fooling around with the kids wasn't enough to get compliance anymore. Aaron was nine now—the attitude was starting.

Aaron's ears were red, and he carried the carrot sticks to the table, refusing to look up at anyone. Noah watched him go, but didn't say anything. This sort of thing made him feel awkward. He was used to being the uncle the kids would make nice with. What happened now if they started to get defiant with him, too?

"I want a hot dog!" Libby announced, running into the kitchen, her twin brother behind her. "I want a hot dog!"

"How about a hamburger?" Henry said, scooping her up.

"Hot dog," Libby said seriously.

"Hamburger." Henry tickled her, and she squealed, then he put her back down next to Micah, who seemed less interested in dinner than he was in the cat's water dish.

These were parents—people who knew how to handle this group of kids. Henry was good at being a dad—the right mix of serious and fun.

And Noah was going to have a son of his own…one who'd get just as defiant as Aaron one day. Would Noah even be around to tangle with the boy, or would he be a biological fact in the background somewhere?

He had a suspicion he'd end up more like his stepdad—fun, well-intentioned and not much use to the mother. He'd tried this before, and he couldn't help but remember that last talk Tom had had with him before he left.

They'd sat on the porch together, Tom's bags already loaded into his pickup truck.

"I'm just not good at this, Noah," he'd said.

"Yes, you are," Noah had pleaded. "You're good with me."

"Your mom disagrees there," Tom replied. "And…maybe I'm not so good with your mom."

Noah hadn't been able to argue that. Tom hadn't made Noah's mom happy, and they all knew it. Mom had cried an awful lot the past few years. There were too many arguments, too many words neither of them could take back.

"I'm sorry, buddy," Tom had said, pushing himself to his feet. "I tried."

And Noah had known that Tom had

tried. He'd done his best. It just hadn't been enough. The best of intentions weren't enough. It was the follow-through that mattered.

CHAPTER FIVE

WHEN TARYN GOT back up to her suite that evening, she'd left the Second Chance Dining Club still at the table talking and sharing some leftover ice cream the servers had brought out for them. That was one of the perks of being friends with the owner. But Taryn was tired, so she'd said her goodbyes and headed upstairs.

She stepped out of her heels, which was an immense relief for her poor, swollen feet, and flicked her phone's ringer back on. She'd missed a text from her mom.

Hi Taryn. Your grandmother called. You haven't visited her yet, and she wanted to know if you were dead, or just ignoring her. So…maybe visit Granny? We're all hoping she'll listen to you.

Right. Listen to her about the old folks' home. Granny was nearing ninety, and it wouldn't be terrible for her to have people around her who could take care of her. But she was a handful, and she knew how to push people's buttons a little too well.

Taryn pulled her hair out of the twist at the back of her head and texted her mother:

I'll drop by in the morning. Just got in from a long dinner and I'm wiped. Work is going well. I'll talk to you tomorrow, okay?

Then she flicked the ringer off, tossed the phone onto the thick bed and reached for the zipper behind her back. She was exhausted, but she'd enjoyed herself. This was probably the most pleasant evening she'd had in the past year...besides one rather memorable evening with Noah.

Strange how therapeutic it was to just be understood.

THE NEXT MORNING, Taryn grabbed a bagel and cup of tea in the dining room before heading out into the morning cool. Mountain Springs Resort was located on the far edge of Blue Lake, with the town of Mountain Springs proper on the other side. The drive to town around the lake was a leisurely one, and Taryn enjoyed the sparkle of the water that she could see through the tree line as she drove.

Granny's house was located on a quiet tree-lined street in the heart of Mountain Springs. A couple of houses had sprinklers going, including the house right next to Granny's, and Taryn had to park on the street to avoid getting sprayed when she got out of the car. The house was quiet and still, though one window upstairs was open and a curtain fluttered out in the breeze.

Would Granny even be up yet? Taryn hoped so. When Taryn was young and would visit her grandmother with her cousins, Granny had always been an early riser.

Taryn got out of the car. She was wearing a pair of formfitting coral capris and a floral top. She had plans to go experience some of the walking trails at the resort later that morning.

She headed up the walk toward Granny's front door, the mist from the neighbor's sprinkler giving her goose bumps. Before she could knock, however, the door opened, and Granny pushed open the screen.

Granny was a slim old woman with white hair and veined hands. She moved tremulously, and she squinted at Taryn for a moment.

"Come in, come in," Granny said. "I wondered what was taking you so long to come and see your own grandmother. My goodness." Granny paused and reached a tentative hand out toward Taryn's belly. "And what have we here?"

"A baby," Taryn said with a deep breath.

"I know that," Granny replied. "I heard months ago. I was waiting for you to say something."

Right. Would this have been easier over the phone?

Taryn licked her lips. "I'm sorry, Granny, I've had a lot going on."

"I'll say. I've been told you don't know who the father is," Granny said.

Taryn didn't answer that. If Granny already knew the details, there was no point in rehashing it. She'd have already formed a few opinions, too.

"Are you hungry?" Granny asked, and without waiting for an answer, she headed toward the kitchen. Taryn ambled through the familiar old house after her, glancing into the living room as she passed by.

It was the same—almost. There were a few more school pictures on the bookshelf from Taryn's cousins' kids, and the couch was different, but it was in the same place in the room with the same faded imitation Persian rug on the floor in front of it. She followed her frail grandmother into the kitchen, where there was a steaming pot of tea on the table with one teacup ready. Granny went to the cupboard and pulled down a second cup, which trembled and tinkled against the saucer in her grip.

"Can I help you with that?" Taryn asked, stepping forward.

"No," Granny said flatly. "I'm perfectly fine, and I will give you no excuse to go back and report to those vultures that I'm some feeble old woman in need of help. I'm fine."

Taryn stepped back and waited until her grandmother put the teacup on the table and gestured to a chair.

"Don't wait on ceremony. Sit down," Granny said. "So, when are you due?"

"Beginning of October," Taryn said as she sat. She smoothed a hand over her belly, feeling her son squirm in reaction to her touch.

"And you're doing this alone?" Granny asked, raising her eyebrows.

"Yes," she replied.

"Is that wise?" the old woman asked.

"Granny, this isn't up for debate," Taryn said, trying to keep her voice calm. "I'm almost forty, and I'm a grown woman. I'm not asking for advice or permission. I'm happy about this baby—I wanted a child so badly, and I'm not apologizing for him."

"I didn't ask you to," Granny replied. "I'm asking you to do the math."

"What math?" she asked with a sigh.

"You're forty—or you will be a couple of months. You'll be almost sixty when that child graduates from high school, and nearly retirement age when he finishes college."

"Yes," she replied with a sigh.

"That's expensive, my dear," Granny said.

"They all are," she replied curtly. "There's no going back now."

"You need a *husband*," Granny said. "And you're no spring chicken. This was downright stupid."

Her grandmother's words sank beneath her defenses, and Taryn felt them as keenly as a knifepoint. Stupid. She wasn't stupid; she was infinitely lucky! How many childless women dreamed of falling pregnant the way she had? She might have lost her marriage, but she'd gained her deepest desire to become a mother!

Taryn pushed her chair back and rose to her feet. "Granny, this is why no one visits you," Taryn said curtly, and she headed for the door. She wasn't doing this. If Granny wanted to sit by herself, then let her. But with every step toward the door, her conscience was already stinging her for the sharp words.

"Excuse me?" Her grandmother's tremulous voice behind her made her stop. Taryn turned. "Are you that thin-skinned that me pointing out a few basic facts has you running out of here like a petulant teenager?"

"My pregnancy wasn't planned," Taryn said. "What would you have me do?"

"In my day we didn't toss husbands out the door quite so quickly," Granny said.

"Glen was cheating!" Taryn snapped.

"They all do!" her grandmother shot back.

"And he was in love with another woman." Taryn's voice shook. "Deeply in love. He wanted *her*, not me. He's the one who moved out."

"After you caught him," Granny said. "He was happy to stay married until then."

Taryn stood in the narrow hallway, the scent of yesterday's cooking in the air. But her mind was still spinning and catching up to what her grandmother had said...

"Wait—" Taryn lowered her voice. "You said they all cheat. Granny, did Grandpa cheat on you?"

"What?" Granny batted her hand through the air.

Taryn shook her head. "You said in your day you didn't toss husbands out quite so easily."

"We didn't."

"*Do* they all cheat?" Taryn pressed.

"Fine. Your grandfather…stepped out on me. That's what we called it. But he always came back, and he always paid the bills."

Granny lifted her chin just a little, and the earlier confidence seemed to waver.

"Oh…" Taryn's heart gave a squeeze. Her grandfather had been a gruff old man, but he'd been kind. He used to let her watch him fix the car. He'd been unfaithful? That hurt…

"Was I angry?" Granny asked. "Yes! Did I sometimes think about smothering him in his sleep? Of course! But I wasn't foolish enough to toss aside a breadwinning man for my own ego. I had children to raise and feed, and I had my own old age to consider. We outlive them most of the time, you might have figured out! If I'd kicked him out, do you think I'd be in this house today?"

"Is that why you won't leave this house?" Taryn asked. "You…earned it?"

"It isn't the house—it's the town. Your

grandfather moved us all over the place working in those mines, and when we came here after his back injury, I swore to heaven or anyone else who'd listen that this was my new hometown. But since you bring it up, maybe I did earn this house. Regardless, I'm not moving. Not out of this house and not out of this town. I intend to die here. You can come collect me then."

"That's what we're scared of," Taryn replied.

"What do any of you care where I die?" Granny asked. "As you so aptly pointed out, no one visits anymore. Where I die is my business."

"*I'm* here, aren't I?" Taryn said.

"I was under the impression you were on your way out, righteously indignant about something," Granny replied.

Taryn sighed. "You push buttons, Granny."

"You're overly sensitive," her grandmother said, but her tone had softened. "Come back and sit down. The tea is getting cold."

But this time, Granny looked over her shoulder a couple of times to make sure that Taryn was still following her back into the kitchen.

"Tell me about Grandpa," Taryn said, sitting down at the table once more.

Granny poured some tea into Taryn's cup, and then served herself. She nudged a bowl of sugar toward her, and it looked old and lumpy, so she declined and drank it plain. Granny did the same, and for a moment they sat in silence, looking out the back window at the overgrown lawn.

"Your grandfather and I were born in a different time," Granny said. "A divorced woman was a scandal. You just...put up with it."

"Did he love you?" Taryn asked.

"In his own way," Granny replied. "We were too busy making ends meet and stretching a penny to worry too much about other things. No one expected fireworks."

"I don't believe that," Taryn said.

Granny shrugged faintly. "I stopped expecting fireworks. I adjusted my expectations. And that's my advice to you—you can still make things work with your husband."

"We're divorced," Taryn said quietly. "It's over, Granny. He's moved in with the other woman. They're...happy."

"Ah." Granny nodded. "I'm sorry."

"I'm not sorry," Taryn said quietly. "Was it hard? Yes. Did I think about smothering him with a pillow? Also yes."

Granny smiled at that. "Do you think you'll be okay on your own?"

"I'll have one little boy," Taryn said. "You had eight. It won't be as hard for me."

"My houseful of boys..." Granny sighed. "And they were always hungry, always fighting and always needing something from me."

"I get to be a mother," Taryn said. "I know the order this all happened is off, but I don't exactly have a lot more time to have a baby. That clock is running out. And I've been trying for a decade. I'm not sorry at all. I'm very, very happy about this! I'm not going to worry about how it all works out. I'm just going to enjoy it!"

"Can I give you some advice?" Granny asked.

Taryn eyed her grandmother. She wasn't sure that she did want that advice.

"About raising boys, I mean," her grandmother said.

"Sure..."

"If they can reach it with a stream of urine, they will pee on it," Granny said soberly. "And that is no exaggeration. They will pee in corners, on trees, in toy boxes and in beds. They will pee into cupboards, into pots, into teacups and into pretty much anything that is even slightly concave, just to prove that they can."

Taryn laughed in surprise.

"I'm not joking," Granny said. "It will last much longer than you think it will, too. And then on the very day that you stop worrying about someone peeing on your begonias, that's the day you start worrying about them getting someone pregnant."

Granny took a sip of tea and pressed her lips together. Her gaze turned inward, and she was silent for a few beats.

"Oh…" Taryn rubbed her hand over her belly. Her son stretched toward her hand, and she felt that wave of love toward this little boy she knew inside and out, but hadn't yet properly met.

"Don't say I didn't warn you," Granny said, and then nudged a bag of cookies across the table toward her. "Would you like a cookie?"

NOAH CAME BACK to his office after a meeting with the financial committee and tossed a file folder onto his desk. Angelina had been there, as well as the financial controller, and they'd been tackling some budget issues that needed to be sorted out before the next board meeting.

How easy would Angelina find it to replace him if he got this job in Seattle? He hadn't told her he'd applied for it. He figured if he got the job, he could talk to her then, but there was no reason to worry everyone if he wasn't leaving.

He pulled off his suit jacket and hung it behind the door, then loosened his tie. The problem was, he loved this job. He loved this resort, and the lake, and the town. But he couldn't build a life here. Whatever future he'd envisioned in his hometown didn't work anymore.

Brody had been on his mind this morning, too. Dating Nevaeh was one thing, but marrying her? That hurt, and not because he thought that he'd be better for Nevaeh. He wouldn't be. This hurt because Brody had done the one thing that undercut all their years of friendship—he'd swooped in on Nevaeh mere hours after she'd canceled the wedding. Hours!

Was Nevaeh right for breaking it off? Absolutely. If she wasn't happy at the prospect of a childless marriage, then she'd done the right thing. But it was painful. He'd still thought they were planning a future together, and he'd already started writing the vows. He'd even called on their mutual friend

Gabe, the one who was married with kids already, to help him out with some wedding-vow wording since he was the married expert. Was Gabe going to support Brody in this? Was there any loyalty left in those old friendships?

Noah had lost his best buddy and his fiancée, all in one weekend. At first, he hadn't known which one hurt more, but after a few months' distance from it, he knew. Nevaeh had made a decision for her own happiness, and ended a two-year relationship. Brody had taken advantage of Noah's lowest point and betrayed a thirty-year friendship. Brody won that one—he'd done more damage.

And Brody had wanted his blessing. …that thought still angered him. His blessing! He wanted Noah to say that this betrayal was fine—no biggie. Well, he couldn't do it. He could wish Nevaeh well with anyone else—just not Brody.

Whatever. That was life, and Seattle was starting to look really appealing.

There was a tap on his door, and he turned to see Taryn standing there in a pair of capri pants and a soft, short-sleeved, floral-patterned shirt that hung down just below her collarbone, exposing the soft, creamy skin of her neck. Her hair was pulled back away from her face, and she stood there, hesitating at the doorway. She held a DSLR camera in one hand and had some sturdy running shoes on her feet.

"Am I interrupting?" she asked.

"No, not at all." A lie, but his brooding wasn't helping matters. It actually felt good to see her. "How are you?"

"I'm fine. You look stressed-out."

"I am," he admitted. "But that's not your problem."

"I was hoping you'd point me in the direction of an easy trail," Taryn said. "I want to take some pictures to use for the campaign, but I'm not up for any exhausting climbs in my state."

"That's probably wise," he said, and he paused. She'd be alone out there—easy trail or not, he didn't feel right about sending her out by herself. "You want company?"

"In dress pants and a tie?" she asked.

"I have some clothes to change into," he said. "I don't know if I want to send you up any trail alone right now. There are a couple that are easier to walk, but this is a pretty steep mountainside, regardless."

"I'm happy for the company," she said. "Maybe I can take a few shots with you in them—you know, a human being enjoying the view."

He smiled at that. "We'll see. I'll meet you at the front doors in ten minutes."

Noah always kept a change of clothes at the office in case he wanted to hit the gym or something after work. He put on a pair of casual pants, a T-shirt and running shoes and headed out of his office. He poked his head into Angelina's office on his way past.

Angelina was at her desk, the end of a ballpoint pen stuck in her mouth as she frowned at a spreadsheet. She looked up when he cleared his throat.

"Hey, boss," he said. "Taryn wants to see the trails, so I'm going to show her what we've got. I have my phone on me. And don't worry about the budget. I'll stay late tonight and fine-tune it."

"Thank you," Angelina said. "I'm not worried at all. And I appreciate you showing Taryn around. This ad campaign could bring us a lot of business if she's able to find the right tone."

"No problem," he said.

Noah always got the work done, and maybe that shouldn't be surprising. At least these days, he didn't have anyone to distract him—no personal obligations. In fact, some evenings, he kind of liked staying at the office late when he could hear the guests enjoying the dining room or the fireside room, and he could watch the night fall outside his office window.

That would be his fate tonight, it seemed, so he might as well enjoy the time on the trails with Taryn this morning.

Noah grabbed some bottles of water and bug spray from behind the counter—they were there for staff use. He dropped them into his backpack. Taryn was waiting for him at the front doors, and they stepped out into the morning sunlight together.

"Am I dragging you away from anything important?" she asked.

"Nah." He smiled. "This is top priority right now." The campaign was Angelina's priority, of course, but Taryn was his, he realized. He felt a drive to protect her—keep her out of harm's way, at least while she was here in Mountain Springs. That was more than he'd say, though. "The trails are this way."

They headed together around the resort, away from the beach and up a gravel walk in the other direction. He pulled the bug spray out of his bag and gave it a shake.

"You'll want this," he said.

They paused, and she lifted some stray tendrils of hair away from her neck and he sprayed the back of her neck, then her arms and the lower parts of her legs.

"Are the bugs bad this time of year?" she asked.

"It's the mountains," he replied. "There's always bugs."

He sprayed himself down, too, then tossed the bottle back into his bag.

"Do you come out here often?" she asked as they started walking again. "On the trails, I mean."

"About two or three times a month," he replied. "The funny thing is that you can get used to anything, and here I am living in a town that people pay good money to vacation in, and I probably should have taken more advantage of it than I did."

She glanced over at him. "That sounds... past tense?"

He sighed. He didn't want to talk about this, but of all people, maybe Taryn deserved to know a little bit about his plans.

"I'm not talking about this yet," he said. "It's delicate. And I'm not ready to discuss it with my boss."

"Are you quitting?" she asked with a frown.

"Not necessarily, but I've applied for a job in Seattle."

"What's in Seattle?"

Space. Distance. A fresh start.

"A better-paying job and a new city," he said, and when she met his gaze in silence, he added, "and an excuse not to see people I'd rather avoid."

"Right." She nodded. "I hadn't realized you had plans to move."

"I didn't know about you and the baby when I applied," he said.

"I don't see how knowing about the baby should change anything," she retorted. "You know about us. That's a good thing, and you should live your life. I'll live mine."

He nodded. "Yeah, of course."

"I'm actually glad you have plans in place," she added. "It makes it easier for us both to simply live our lives."

But suddenly Seattle didn't feel quite the same. A bit of the shine had come off.

"Like I said, I'm not telling anyone about applying for the job," he said. "I don't even have the job yet." He nodded at some hikers coming down the path toward the resort, and he stayed silent until they were well behind them. "I love this job—I really do. But I've got a little too much history around here."

"I know the feeling. I have a fair bit of my own…"

They started slowly up the trail together, and he shortened his steps to match hers.

"You're talking about your grandmother," he concluded.

"I went to see her this morning. I'd been putting it off. I really didn't feel like facing her judgment," she said. "My grandmother has no filter, and while that was fine when we were kids coming to visit for a week, she's alienated a lot of people in recent years."

"I know the type," he said.

"Anyway, as it turns out, Granny had more heartache than any of us knew."

"Can I ask what happened?" he asked.

"My grandfather had been cheating on her," she said. "I had no idea—I don't think anyone knew. If they did, it stayed a very well-kept secret. Granny only told me because she figured I should have stayed with Glen for financial security. Turns out that's what she did with my grandfather—she put up with it. They had eight boys to raise, and she didn't feel like she had a choice."

The shade from the overhanging trees seemed to be calling as Noah looked down at Taryn, trying to read her emotions in her face. When they got to the shade, they slowed down again, and he noticed how her shoulders relaxed in the dappled cool.

"That's not right," he said after a beat.

"No, it isn't," she agreed. "But it was a different time, I guess. Women had fewer options. Granny never went through the pain of a divorce."

"It might have been worse living through that marriage," he muttered.

He didn't think he'd said it out loud, but Taryn laughed. "Maybe! There's a weird sense of freedom when you just let it go, though. When you let him love someone else, and stop trying to make him love you…"

"I've never been divorced," he said. "But I can understand the sentiment. When someone is happier away from you, what can you do?"

Taryn looked over at him, and he was reminded of that night in the pub and the draw of a too-honest conversation.

"Do you miss her?" Taryn asked. She didn't need to say Nevaeh's name. They both knew who she was talking about. Her voice was soft, and he felt his own tensions start to melt away.

"I miss…" He sighed, casting about inside

of himself, looking for a way to describe it. "This is going to sound strange, but I miss my life before the breakup. I miss the friends we had together, and the feeling that everything had a place. I actually miss hanging out with Brody and how stupidly excited he was about the bachelor party…"

He came to a stop at a wooden sign that read Elm's Trail. He was talking too much again… There was something about Taryn that brought things to the surface. "This trail is the easiest climb."

"Is the friendship over?" she asked.

"Yeah. Pretty much."

Taryn took out her camera and snapped a picture of the trail's wooden sign, looked down at the display screen, then raised camera again, adjusted the zoom and snapped another one.

"How about you?" he asked. "Do you miss Glen?"

She looked at him over her shoulder. "Most days no. But there are times when I wish I had a husband—like when I got to find out the sex of the baby and I was alone for it, or when I'm traveling by myself and I have to get the kind general manager to carry my bags."

He smiled. "Happy to do it."

"That might have sounded—" She shook her head. "I don't know how that sounded. But I'm mostly just glad to be doing this on my own, because I think it would be infinitely harder to be looking at having a baby and trying to make my husband love me at the same time. That's too much work."

"Yeah, that's one of things I found to be a lot of work with Nevaeh," he said. "I felt like I was always trying to make up for the kids I wouldn't give her."

"Are you relieved at all?" she asked.

"Yeah, a bit," he admitted. "I had a feeling that this was coming—before the wedding, or after. I'd rather do it now, when there's less at stake."

She nodded.

"Add to that, Nevaeh is ten years younger."

"Men like that, I thought," she said. "All that youthfulness and tight skin." She cast him a teasing smile. "It makes them feel younger."

Noah and Nevaeh had listened to different music, had different memories of childhood TV, even saw politics differently. He'd mellowed a bit—not a huge amount, but enough to be noticeable.

"Or it makes them feel old," he chuckled. "A decade makes a bigger difference than you'd think—in the way you see things, measure things. I don't know."

Maybe it was his age difference with Nevaeh, or maybe it was just that they weren't meant for each other, but in that pub with Taryn he'd felt more understood than he had in the entire two years of his relationship with his fiancée.

"Let's go," she said, and Taryn shouldered the camera strap and cast a smile over her shoulder. "Maybe we should just enjoy all this emotional freedom. No one to impress."

Noah caught up and they continued along the rocky path.

She might not want to impress anyone this morning, but he felt a testosterone-driven desire to make sure that she respected him, at least, by the time she was done here in Mountain Springs. He'd settle for that. Taryn was going to be in his life now for...the rest of his life. A child bound people together more tightly than an engagement. That was a sobering realization. And if they were going to be connected through this baby, at the very least he could be a man she could speak well of.

He didn't want a woman to look at him the way his mother had looked at Tom. He had to do better... Ironically, it might take him keeping his distance to make that happen. He wasn't going to try to be something he wasn't again.

There was only so long a man could hold his breath. And right now, in the cool shade with this woman who tugged at him in ways he couldn't quite name, this woman who wanted nothing from him, and yet made him wish he could give her more, it felt so good to finally exhale.

CHAPTER SIX

AS THEY WALKED farther up the trail, the trees closed in and the sound of wind rustling through the leaves and birds calling to each other made Taryn's muscles relax. She'd been carrying more tension than she'd realized, and she let out a slow breath. Noah walked beside her, keeping his pace slow to match hers, and she couldn't help but notice that he was in good shape. His arms were bronzed from the sun, and his muscles were defined. He obviously spent time at the gym.

Their footsteps crunched along the path in unison, and Taryn spotted a squirrel on the side of a tree staring down at them with glassy little eyes. She knew her camera well enough to not even bother trying to take the picture.

They'd only been walking for about fifteen minutes, and she was already starting to tire. Nothing was easy at this point of the pregnancy, but her doctor had told her that staying active would help in everything from prenatal health to delivery to recovery. So she was doing her best.

"Is there any family medical history I should be aware of?" Taryn asked.

"Um—" Noah paused for a moment. "My mother died of breast cancer a couple of years ago. My maternal grandfather died of a heart attack at ninety. I have a cousin with type 2 diabetes."

"I'm sorry about your mother," she said.

"Thanks."

"What about your dad's side?" she asked.

"We never really knew them," he said. "My dad left when my sister was a baby. He had a really fractured family, and his mom died a long time ago in a boating accident in Italy. There wasn't anyone to even look up. Believe me, I tried."

Raised by a single mom—it wasn't a bad life. A devoted mother could give a child everything he needed, or almost everything. Did Noah miss having a father? She wanted to know but was afraid to ask—she didn't want to come across as asking for more from him than she was. Back when finding this baby's biological father wasn't even a possibility, she'd had a good excuse to not worry about it. But now?

They came to a break in the foliage, and she

looked down a tumbling ravine to a stream. The scene came upon them so suddenly that she stopped short, breathing quickly from the exertion. Brambles and vines covered the jagged descent, and the stream rushed over rocks, frothing and splashing. A cool breeze wafted from the icy water toward them. But even with the grandeur of the Colorado Rockies, her mind wouldn't be diverted from the question that worried her.

"Did you ever resent your mom?" Taryn asked after a moment. "I hate to even ask this—it's in no way my business. It's just—"

"You want to know if this little boy is going to resent you for raising him alone," Noah said, and he met her gaze evenly. She waited—looking for judgment in his clear gaze, but there was none.

"Yeah." That was exactly what she wanted to know.

Noah sucked in a slow breath. "I think we all universally resented my biological father," he said. "He left us, and the couple of times I did try to make contact over the years, he wasn't really happy to hear from me and seemed relieved when I went away again. The one I missed was Tom—my stepdad."

"He was different?" she said.

"Maybe I just remember him differently." Noah rubbed a hand over his jaw. "And I was mad at Mom for a few years because she was the one who kicked Tom out."

So there was *some* resentment…

"Why did she break up with him?" Taryn asked.

"Mom always said he was like having an extra kid. She needed a partner, not a dependent."

"He didn't work?" she asked.

"No, he did. He just…didn't know how to parent, because he was too much of a kid himself. He wanted to be the fun one, and he always took things too far. I guess she didn't trust him with us, and that eroded their relationship. I can see how that would be a problem now. At ten, I was less understanding. On this side of forty, I can see why my mom was as frustrated as she was."

And yet, Taryn could see something just under the surface—deeper emotion he was holding back. Had he loved that stepfather?

"Did you stay in touch with him?" she asked.

"No. They got divorced, and he went his own way. We weren't his kids."

"Biologically," she said.

"He hadn't adopted us. He had no rights."

She nodded. It wasn't like she blamed a woman for keeping her kids close. They were her children, after all.

"How about you?" he asked.

"My parents are still married," she replied. "I have a massive extended family. My grandmother here in Mountain Springs is on my father's side."

"So our son—um, the baby—will grow up with a lot of family," he said.

"He will," she said with a nod.

"That's good," he said. "I missed out on that."

She looked up at him and, standing there with the sun dappling his features, the leaves and sky behind him, she took her camera off her shoulder and looked through the lens.

"Hold on," she said, and she backed up a step, then snapped the picture. "Perfect."

"For what?" he asked.

Taryn looked down at the image on her camera's screen. His good looks had been captured exactly—the first picture she had of her son's father. Should she keep it for later on, for when he asked about his dad? She felt a lump rise in her throat, and she forced back the melancholy.

"You're very rugged and outdoorsy," she said, holding the screen so he could see it.

"Am I?" He sounded amused. "Just say it. You think I'm handsome."

She chuckled. "Does it matter?"

"Maybe not. I mean, I know you saw *some*thing in me back in Denver, but…do I lose all allure with no beard?"

"I did like that beard," she said, and she shot him a grin. "But this picture is strictly business. I need pictures of faces like yours."

"What's special about mine?" he chuckled. "My smoldering good looks?"

She chuckled. "I'm not saying you aren't good-looking, but that's not what I'm looking for in this campaign. I need people who look accessible. Customers should want to hike with you."

Noah caught her gaze for the first time, and a slow smile spread over his face. She looked down at her camera. What was it about this man that made her stomach flip when he looked at her like that? He was supposed to be an isolated mistake from one stupid night, not…so real.

This picture had something in it, though— something deeper than an attractive man in the woods. There was an openness in his gaze, a vulnerability, even. People might look twice at a handsome guy, and she wouldn't blame them, but it would take something more to make them stop and mentally put themselves with him on this trail.

"Um…" She glanced around. "Go over there—up by that big tree—just up there."

She pointed in the direction she meant. Noah climbed up a small incline, slapping at a bug on his arm, and then turned. She took another couple of shots, then nodded, satisfied.

"Yeah, this is good…"

Noah came back down to the trail and looked over her shoulder as she perused the photos.

"Your turn," he said, and his voice was close to her ear.

"Oh, no, I'm the one behind the camera," she said with a short laugh.

He was close to her, close enough that she could feel the warmth of him, even though they weren't touching.

"Not for the campaign," he said. "For your son. Some pictures of you when you were pregnant with him, looking happy, and—"

She turned and he stopped talking. She almost regretted having broken the moment.

"Um," he said. "Here, give me the camera. Just stay right where you are."

Noah slipped the camera out of her hands and looked through the viewfinder. She looked down self-consciously and heard a couple of clicks. He backed up a couple of paces.

"Taryn—" His voice was low, insistent, and the same tone she recognized from that one reckless, stupid night together. She looked up, there was a click and he grinned.

"There—" He came back toward her and handed over the camera.

She looked down at the view screen, and she saw a photo of her looking significantly more pregnant than she realized she did...but it was more than that. She did look happy. She looked relaxed, too, and maybe it was the pregnancy hormones, or just a hike in the woods with this brawny, good-looking man, but she looked feminine, too. Glowingly.

"Beautiful," he murmured, and she felt goose bumps at the word.

Her gaze still on the photo, Taryn took a step forward, and her shoe caught on something. Her heart jumped and she felt the camera drop from her fingers when Noah's arm slid behind her, and he pulled her hard against him. She caught her breath as her body pressed against his, the side of her belly against his stomach. Even the baby inside of her seemed to be frozen in surprise.

"You okay?" he murmured.

As she looked up at Noah, his face was only a whisper away from hers—so close that she could see an eyelash that lay on his cheek. She swallowed.

"Yeah. Thanks…"

The baby gave a little squirm, and she put her hand over her belly protectively. Noah held up the camera—he'd caught it, too— and she smiled, feeling heat on her face.

"Anytime." His voice was still that bass rumble, and when she glanced up again, he was still looking at her.

"How come you're looking at me like that?" she asked.

"I'm remembering you that evening in the bar," he said. "You weren't like any other woman I'd seen."

She didn't answer.

"You were funny, and smart, and quick-witted," he said. "And you were…gorgeous."

Was that what he'd seen in the bar that night?

"I figured it was just a tough night," she said.

"Nah," he replied with a shake of his head. "I thought it might have been the alcohol or the heartbreak, or some fatal combination of the two, but seeing you again, I realized

I was right. You're as beautiful as I remembered."

"And you're as smooth as I remember," she said with a laugh. He'd cast a few well-timed compliments her way that night, too.

"I'm actually not smooth at all," Noah said. "Not usually. I'm honest, and most times that works against me. Besides, I'm not hitting on you."

"Good, I'm pregnant," she said. "I have bigger things to worry about than how to let a guy down gently."

He chuckled. "Ouch. But no, you're safe there. It's just nice to know I wasn't wrong."

"This is about you being right?" she asked with a laugh.

"What can I say?" he said. "It feels good."

She pulled out her phone to check the time. "Maybe we should head back."

"Sure. The really amazing views are up there—" He pointed beyond the trees to a sheer cliff that rose up farther on."

"What's up there?" she asked taking a step closer and raising her camera again.

"A waterfall," he said. "And a view worth every grueling minute of the five-hour hike to get there."

Five hours—she wasn't getting near that view at seven months pregnant. She nodded. There seemed to be an awful lot that was out of reach these days. It was probably best to make the most of what was right here in front of her.

NOAH HAD WONDERED what it would feel like to hold her in his arms again, and his fingers still tingled where he'd touched her. Even pregnant, she fit perfectly into his arms, and he let out a slow breath remembering her curves and the swell of her belly against his hands.

She smelled good—something faint and feminine—not perfume, exactly, but some scented product she was using. Even the bug spray was associated with pleasant memories for him as a kid growing up in the Colorado Rockies. As soon as the weather was warm enough for hiking, it was also warm enough for bugs.

The walk together down the trail was easier, and he noticed that Taryn was still moving slowly, cautiously. She couldn't see her feet, could she?

"There's a root," he said.

"Thanks…"

He pulled out his phone and flipped through his photo roll, stopping at a few pictures from last year's hike up to the cliff.

"This is the view," he said, and he passed his phone over to her. They stopped again on the trail, and she flipped through the photos.

"Wow…" She got to the end of them and flipped once more, stopping at a picture of his nephews and niece. It was a picture from last year. All of the kids were a little bit smaller, and they were sticky from melted ice-cream sandwiches. "Whose kids?"

"My sister's," he said, accepting the phone back. "She's got four."

"Uncle Noah, huh?" Taryn said, casting him a smile.

"Yeah… I'm good for a bimonthly visit and a birthday card with cash in it. Can't say the kids appreciate it yet, but they will eventually."

Taryn rolled her eyes, and he found himself putting his arm out as they came to a dip in the path. Her fingers grazed his arm, then she pulled her hand away.

"I'm fine," she said.

"Just making sure," he replied. "We've got an image to maintain here of a safe and fun resort. It'll be hard to explain if you take a tumble."

She smiled, but he did notice that she moved in closer to him, and a couple of times she caught his arm as they made their descent.

"So, even with your nephews and niece, you weren't willing to change your mind about having kids for your fiancée?" Taryn asked.

"No, I wasn't…" He sighed. "Look, I know how awful this is going to sound considering that I got you pregnant, but I think there's a difference between the ability to make a baby and the ability to raise one. I'm not good with kids. I've tried. Like I said, even dating Shelby about ten years ago, but it only proved what I already knew—I'm not good dad material. And I don't have this deep yearning to have a houseful of kids. I like my quiet. I like order. I like a quiet evening in front of my fireplace or out on my balcony with a good book. And there are a few men out there who should realize the same thing and stop creating kids that they aren't going to be able to raise either financially or emotionally."

Taryn was silent.

"Maybe I should haven't said all that," he said.

"No, it's fine," she said. "And I'm different—I'm not asking you to be a dad. I think it's good that you say what you mean."

She might not be asking, but it didn't change facts. He was going to be a father, whether he wanted to be one or not. She hadn't asked for his help on this hike, either, and she'd needed it. Just because she didn't ask him to help her with their son didn't mean she wouldn't struggle without him.

"What can I do for you?" he asked as the bright sunlight from the trail's entrance came into sight.

"What do you mean?" She caught his arm again as she stepped past another root.

"I mean—obviously, you've made it pretty clear that you want to raise this child alone, and I respect that." He swallowed. "The thing is, I can't just let go of any responsibility toward this little boy, either. I was part of bringing him into this world, and I should provide…something."

"Like what?" she asked.

"Financial support?" he asked. "That only seems fair."

Her cheeks were already pink from the exertion, but the color deepened.

"Maybe contribute to a college fund?" she said.

"I could do that. Anything else?"

"I'm not thinking terribly long-term right

now," she said. "I'm working to afford some maternity leave. That's about it."

Maybe he could assuage a bit of his guilt if he got this job in Seattle—because if he left Colorado, he'd be across the country from his son, and he'd likely not see him as often as he should. But if that better-paying job could give his son a better life because of the financial contribution he'd be able to make…

"Look—" He stopped short, just where the trail widened onto the gravel path that led back to the lodge, and he caught her hand to stop her. "What if I helped you with the maternity leave?"

"How?" she asked with a frown. "I'm not asking—"

"I *know* you're not asking," he said, interrupting her. "If I get this job in Seattle, it comes with a pretty good signing bonus. I could hand it over to you, and it might give you a few months of not worrying about an income after he's born."

"You'd do that?" she asked with a frown. "What about you?"

"It would have been nice to have, but I don't need it. I'd rather give it to you now and know you'll have less pressure for a few months while you settle in as a mom."

Taryn stared at him in surprise for a moment, then let out a breath. "I don't know what to say. It's generous, but..." She licked her lips. "I wasn't looking for you, Noah. I wasn't looking for help."

"I'm this baby's father," he said, dropping his voice. "When he asks about me one of these years, it would be nice if you had something good to say about me. Besides, giving you some time and lowering your stress after the baby is born is good for the baby, too."

"I'll give it some thought," she said.

And that was all he could really ask.

When they got back into the lodge, Taryn headed up to her suite to change, and Noah went into his office to do the same. Once he was back in his dress pants and a tie, he felt a little more confident and in control.

He wasn't sure if Taryn would accept money from him, and maybe offering it the way he had was crass. But if he wasn't offering himself as a romantic option, or as a dad figure for this kid, then what else was there to give? Besides, it would help—he was willing to bet on that. And what better gift to give his newborn son than uninterrupted time in his mother's arms?

Noah opened up the budget file on his

computer and stared at it for a couple of minutes, but his mind wasn't cooperating. He picked up his glasses from his desktop and put them on, then he clicked shut the spreadsheet and opened an internet browser instead. Ever since seeing Tom's profile on his sister's phone, he'd thought about setting up a Facebook profile. It didn't take him long, and he had a couple of photos on his computer from various work events to use as his profile picture. He gave very little information otherwise.

Then he typed in Tom's name, and his profile popped up immediately.

Was this a good idea or an impetuous mistake, like a drunk dial late at night? Maybe he'd put too much emphasis on Tom when he was growing up—for Tom it was a four-year failed marriage to a woman who already had kids. What was Noah even expecting here? That Tom would be overwhelmed with emotion? That wasn't likely.

Noah's phone rang, and he saw Angelina's cell number.

"Hi, boss," he said.

"Hi, Noah, how were the trails?" she asked.

"Great. It's beautiful out there. Taryn took a few pictures, and she seemed to really like what she saw. I can give her a few of my own personal photos from the top of the cliff, and that should get her started."

"Perfect," Angelina said. "I have some of my own, too. So you're back now?"

"I'm back," he said. "I'm just opening up the budget now."

"Do you have time to step into a meeting about our food orders? Apparently, there's a complication with the meat delivery, and—" She paused, there were some muffled voices, then she came back on the line. "In about ten minutes in my office, if you're free."

"Of course," he said. "I'll be there."

"Thanks, Noah," she said, and hung up.

Noah's gaze moved back to Tom's smiling face on the screen. There was a button to message him, and he didn't have a lot of time. He could delay this and put a whole lot of thought into a message later on, but that wasn't a good idea. He'd just overdo it. It was better to send off a quick message and forget it. He clicked on the text button, and before he could talk himself out of it, he started to type:

Hi Tom. It's been a few decades. My sister said she'd connected with you again, and I just wanted to say hi. I'm general manager at the Mountain Springs Resort now. You took

us up on the trails around here a few times when we were kids, I remember. Anyway, my sister filled me in about your dog rescue—that sounds great. It would be nice to catch up.
Noah

He paused with his mouse over the send button, and then he exhaled and pressed it.

Whatever. His emotional hopes all set on one guy who'd only been part of the family for four years was ridiculous, and he knew it. Maybe it would help to chat with him a bit, and bring Tom right back down to size in Noah's own head.

Noah locked his computer screen, and then reached for his suit jacket and pulled it on.

He had work to do—thankfully. The last thing he needed was to overthink personal issues.

CHAPTER SEVEN

"You're looking for Lisa Dear?" Janelle was a middle-aged woman who sat at the front desk, glasses perched on the end of her nose and a computer screen in front of her. She had a streak of white through one side of her hair blending into an ash-blond.

"Yes, the writer. Noah mentioned that she was a published author—"

"Yes, she's brilliant," Janelle said. "We're very proud of her. Have you read her stories? My daughter studied one of her stories in her college English class."

"Wow. That really is impressive," Taryn said. "I haven't read her work yet. I'd like to. But I was hoping to chat with her a bit. I don't want to interrupt her day, and this wouldn't take too long."

Janelle typed something into her computer, clicked a couple of times, then nodded. "She's working today. Her shift is just about done. She's probably down at the laundry room."

"And where would I find that?" Taryn asked.

"Take these back stairs—the basement is pretty much laundry and storage. You'll hear the machines," Janelle said with a smile. "Ms. Cunningham told me that you could go anywhere you liked."

"Thank you." Taryn smiled back, and headed toward the back stairs.

She'd been focused on the experience of the guests, but having an employee who was also a celebrated writer was impressive in itself, and who knew? There might be some aspect that could be used for the campaign.

The lodge basement was clean and well lit. While upstairs it was all polished wood and glittering crystal, downstairs the floors were white tile, and the hum of washing machines and the muted laughter of people chatting echoed. There were elevator doors in the center, and the door to the laundry room stood open. When Taryn poked her head inside, she saw three women and a young man, all in housekeeping uniforms, chatting next to a table that held piles of unfolded, clean sheets.

"Hi, can we help you?" an older woman asked, looking up.

"I was hoping to speak to Lisa Dear," Taryn said.

One of the women gave a farewell smile to the others and came in Taryn's direction. She looked to be in her early thirties, and she had long dark hair that was twisted up into a bun at the back of her head.

"Hi," Lisa said. "What can I do for you?"

"My name's Taryn. I'm working with Angelina Cunningham on an ad campaign for the resort," Taryn said. "And I've heard about you from a couple of different people now—you're a writer, aren't you?"

"Yes, I am." Lisa led the way out of the laundry, and they headed for the stairs. "Are you looking for a writer to work on ad copy? Because I'm not really that kind of writer."

"No, I need a face," Taryn said. "I need real people. I'm creating shareable content that will feature the lodge and encourage people to click over and learn more about it, but it can't feel like an ad. So that's the sort of thing I'm trying to dig up."

"And you wanted to feature…me?" Lisa said.

"I'd like to talk to you about it," Taryn said. They made their way upstairs, and Lisa gestured toward another back hallway.

"We can go to the break room and talk there, if you want."

"Perfect."

The employee break room was on the far end of the lower level, across the hall from the gym. It was furnished a little less extravagantly than the rest of the lodge, but it was a beautiful room with the same broad windows the rest of the lodge sported. There were several couches, an open kitchen with a high-end coffee maker on one counter and blinds that let in a generous amount of sunlight. One wall had some lockers, and Lisa headed in that direction and opened one, pulling out her purse.

"So what would you like to know?" Lisa asked.

"I was hoping you could tell me what Mountain Springs Resort means to you personally," Taryn said.

Lisa was silent for a moment. "This job started off as just a job. It was a regular paycheck. I'm a single mom—I need the benefits. But over time it became more than that. The morale is high, people help each other—they encourage each other. When I get a story rejected, or I hit writer's block, it's often a work friend who hears about it first."

"Does this resort inspire any stories?"

"A few." A smile touched Lisa's lips. "I'm careful, though. When you use people you're close to, or say, a job you really want to keep, you don't want to offend anyone. I made a few mistakes with that in my early days. But please don't mention that…"

"Of course not," Taryn murmured. "This is meant to promote the resort, not dig into uncomfortable details."

"That's a relief." Lisa smiled faintly. She turned to look out the window. "The lake, though… I grew up in Mountain Springs, and for years I took this scenery for granted. But I don't anymore. There's just something about this lake, and the mountains—you feel small, you know?"

"Does Mountain Springs feature in any of your stories?" Taryn asked.

"Every single one." Lisa glanced back. "When you grow up in a place like this, it seeps into your bones. These mountains, this lake… It's home. The place that formed you comes out your pores. It's reflected in your language. Short stories are meant to dig deep, and the deeper you dig, the closer to home you get. It's like following a vein of silver in a mine…"

Taryn's breath caught, and she met Lisa's gaze.

"Do you know what I mean?" Lisa asked.

"I think I do," Taryn said. "My grandmother lives here. I used to visit as a girl."

Her difficult, opinionated, filter-free grandmother. Despite all of her shortcomings and her stubbornness, Taryn couldn't leave Granny here to face her last years alone. She had to find a solution...

"Then there's a vein of Mountain Springs inside of you, too," Lisa said.

There was... And the more time Taryn spent here, the more it seemed to seep into her. Except, Taryn didn't want to dig deeper to find out what it all meant. What she needed was some financial security for her maternity leave, and some emotional calm. She didn't need old pain or long-buried hopes coming back to the surface.

"Could I use that line?" Taryn asked, "The vein of Mountain Springs inside of us?"

"Sure," Lisa said. "Feel free."

"Could I take a few pictures of you—maybe out by the lake?" Taryn asked.

"I should probably get changed, then," Lisa replied.

"No, no, I'd love to have you in your work uniform," Taryn said. "The color really suits you, and it connects to the resort in such a real way. If that would be okay. The thing is, you're a real woman with your own family and responsibilities, yet you're creating this beautiful artistic life for yourself, and I'd like to show both of those sides of you. You're…" Taryn paused, then smiled hopefully. "Frankly, you're inspiring."

"I suppose a few pictures would be okay," Lisa said. "Then I have to pick my son up."

"I won't take long," Taryn promised. "Thank you."

Taryn's feet hurt, and the baby stretched out, jabbing her just under the ribs. But this moment was too perfect to let pass. She was uncovering the heart and soul of this place, and it started with Angelina, and the divorce that had rocked her life, and moved out like ripples in the lake. How many dreams and accomplishments started out the same way?

This resort deserved more than guests; it deserved to be seen for the cradle of rebirth that it was. Because this was a lodge that had been rebuilt by a woman with a vision, and in return it had become a place of hope and inspiration for many others.

And there was something about looking out over that glacier-fed mountain lake, sunk into the shadows of the looming, jagged peaks that surrounded it… It whispered of untested depths and unfinished business.

Noah sat in his office late that evening, the budget tweaks completed. He always made sure the work got done—that was part of why Angelina trusted him. He cared about making sure this place was run well, too.

He'd seen Taryn out his office window several times that day—taking pictures of the lake, of Lisa Dear, of Angelina… She'd been busy, and so had he. But a couple of times he'd glimpsed her standing out there by the water staring out over it with her hands cradling her belly. He'd been transfixed looking at her—she was beautiful… and even thinking about her now was making it hard to focus.

Noah pulled his mind back to the task at hand. He saved the various files on his computer, and then emailed the most recent versions to Angelina so that she'd have them in her inbox first thing in the morning. Then he opened Facebook. He'd looked at it a couple of times in the past few hours, and he told himself he'd check once more, and then be done with it until tomorrow.

This evening, there was a message from Tom waiting for him, and his heart sped up as he opened it.

It's really nice to hear from you, Noah. I wanted to contact you over the years, but your mom was pretty adamant that you guys just needed to be allowed to live your lives. Besides, I wasn't great stepdad material. Anyway, enough years pass, and it just gets harder to think of what to say, you know? But I'm glad to see you've come out on top. I always thought you would—you were smart, and you had this way of stopping to think that I admired.

Anyway, I'm doing well. The dog rescue is a passion of mine. It doesn't make me a fortune, but the work is really rewarding. If you're ever wanting a dog of your own, we have all sorts of loving pooches up for adoption to the right home. No pressure—just putting it out there.

Are you married yet? Do you have any kids? I'm remarried. My wife and I work together at the rescue. She also paints—she's really creative. No kids for us—just the dogs.

It's really great to hear from you, Noah.

Tom had included a picture in the message—Tom with his arm draped around the shoulders of a plump woman at his side. She was smiling into the camera and leaning toward him. She had a puppy in her arms that was chewing on her fingers. A plain wedding band was visible on both their hands.

How long had they been married? he wondered. Was this something new, or had Tom found someone who would last with him? He'd worried about Tom as he'd grown up, wondering if he was alone or if he had anyone to care about him. So seeing him with a wife at his side was a sort of relief.

Should he answer the message? He wasn't sure what he'd say, either. He didn't have a wife or kids to show off as proof of his happy life. He didn't have a picture of a smiling fiancée anymore. Besides, the old guilt about bonding with Tom was simmering under the surface. It felt like betrayal to his mother… still.

There was a tap on his office door, and he looked up. "Come in."

The door opened to reveal Chef Bertoni. He held two cardboard clamshells and he lifted them with a smile.

"We have some leftover appetizers. Crab puffs, miniquiches and Brie-pomegranate cups," Albert said. "You're the last one here. I thought you might want them."

"Thanks, Albert." And he was about to

turn them down, when another thought occurred to him. "Sounds delicious. Have a good night."

"You, too," Albert said. "Good night."

Noah accepted the clamshells and then pulled out his cell phone. He wouldn't be so bold as to go upstairs to Taryn's suite. Maybe she was sleeping already…but he could call, right?

He selected her number and dialed. It rang twice, and Taryn picked up, sounding alert.

"Noah?" Taryn said.

He liked the way she said his name.

"Yeah, it's me," he said. "I got tonight's leftover appetizers—and they smell amazing. I was wondering if you might want some."

"I'm ready for a break, so absolutely," she replied. "At this point of the pregnancy, I'm always hungry."

"Still working?" he asked.

"Yes… I've got some great ideas, and some great shots, and I wanted to start putting it together while it was fresh," she said. "What about you? You're still working?"

"Just finishing up," he replied. "So…are you coming down, or should I come up?"

"Why don't you come up?" she said. "My feet are sore. I had a big day."

"Deal," he said. "See you in a minute."

When he knocked on Taryn's door, it opened almost immediately. She was wearing a pink sundress that swung around her calves, and her feet were bare. Her hair was twisted up into a bun, and her face was now makeup free. She looked fresher than he felt right now. A smile broke over her face, and she angled her head, inviting him in.

"This is good timing," she said. "I was going to order room service when I realized the kitchen was closing and I was too late."

Taryn's laptop was set up at the desk, and he could see some photos she was working from—one of Lisa, and one of Angelina, both of them standing on the pebbly beach at the edge of the lake.

"I'm working on a new angle," Taryn said. "Have a seat."

She gestured to the little table by the window with the lake view, and he headed over there and put down the food. He opened the two containers, and the aroma burst out to meet them.

"You sure I'm not intruding?" he asked.

"You brought food," she said. "You're forgiven."

Noah chuckled and sat down. He watched

her run a hand down her belly for just a moment, outlining her round form. She sank into a chair opposite him and reached for a miniquiche.

"Mmm…" She chewed slowly, then swallowed. "These are great."

"Albert's the best," Noah said. "So you've got a new angle?"

"I'm going to include employees, as well as guests," Taryn said.

"Yeah?" He raised his eyebrows.

"People like to know that the place where they spend their money treats its people well," she said. "And you have some interesting people here."

"Lisa, the writer," he said.

Taryn reached for a Brie-and-pomegranate cup. "Angelina is an absolute force of nature, too," she said. "And you're rather interesting—"

"Me?" He chuckled. "I don't know about that. I'm a workaholic."

"You used to come here with your stepdad, you said," she replied.

"Yeah, I did," he answered. "He took us hiking, and said he'd use up our energy so we'd sleep and he'd get time alone with our mother." He used air quotes around the last words.

"And you had no idea what that meant," she said with a low laugh.

"Not a clue," he replied, and he laughed, too. "I really liked Tom, though. He was the stepdad who'd let us jump in the mud or make a mess. He didn't care. So he'd take us out in the trails and we'd climb all over the place. He'd let us climb trees if we could get up them ourselves, and if we got stuck up there, he'd tell us that if we got up, we'd better figure out a way down."

"Which you did," she said.

"Once I fell out of the tree and broke my arm," Noah replied. "My mother was furious. She was the cautious one, and because Tom wasn't our real dad, she was the one who laid down the law."

"Sounds like you had fun all the same," she said.

"Yeah, I loved it up here. It was fun, and the air just felt fresher, you know?" Noah paused for a moment. "Maybe it's part of a Colorado upbringing, but the outdoors gets into your blood."

She nodded. "So when you came to work here as general manager…"

"It was like coming home in a way," he admitted. "Except that Angelina had improved everything. But yeah, I had a personal connection to the place."

"Would you be willing to be quoted saying that?" she asked.

"Saying what part?" he asked, narrowing his eyes.

"That you used to come here with your stepdad, and that taking the job as general manager was like coming home."

"It'll fall a little flat if I take a job in Seattle, won't it?" he asked.

Taryn took a bite of the Brie cup and chewed thoughtfully for a moment. "If you leave, that doesn't negate what you experienced here. You're allowed to grow and move on. No one expects you to retire at Mountain Springs Resort."

"I suppose so," he said. "And if it helps Angelina, sure."

"Thanks." Taryn held his gaze.

"You have your own memories here, too," he said.

"Not at the resort," she said. "My grandmother lived in town. We came to the lake once or twice, but she was afraid of us drowning. Apparently, we weren't terribly obedient."

Noah chuckled. "You were wild, were you?"

"Well, when you get three or four cousins together..." She licked some cheese off her finger, and they fell silent for a moment. Taryn looked toward the lake through the open balcony door, and he noted the way her eyes shone in this low light. She was silent for a few beats, and he noticed the way her pulse fluttered at the base of her neck... That was one thing he'd noticed that night together—the tender beat of her pulse.

"Can I ask you something?" he said quietly.

"Sure." She turned back, and her warm gaze met his easily.

"How come you left before I woke up?"

Her cheeks pinked and she dropped her gaze.

"I'm sorry if that's over the line to even bring up," he said. "I don't want to make you uncomfortable or anything, but I've been thinking about it. I was thinking about it before I even saw you again. You didn't let me say goodbye."

Taryn shrugged faintly. "I'd never done that before—hook up with a stranger like that—and I was embarrassed."

"Oh..."

"I mean, did you ever do that before?" she asked hesitantly.

"No, never," he replied. "But if you'd stayed, I would have gotten your number. I would have wanted to see you again."

She shook her head. "Your fiancée had just broken up with you. I wasn't going to be anything more than a rebound."

"What makes you so sure?" he asked.

"Because my divorce was just finalized. You weren't going to be anything more than a rebound for me, either."

He felt the sting in those words, but she was only being honest.

"That's fair," he said.

"I wasn't looking for a relationship," she said quietly. "I'm still not. I need to focus on my son—" She swallowed and dropped her gaze. "Our son."

He froze, her words sinking down into him. Our son...

"For the record?" he said after a beat of silence. "I would have called you. I'm not the kind of guy to just hook up and move on."

"See, that's the thing," she said, and she adjusted her position. "You're a noble guy. And that *is* a problem."

"How?" he laughed.

"I married a noble guy," she said. "He proposed because I was pregnant. It's possible to ruin your life over doing the right thing, you know."

"And you think I'd do that?" he asked.

She shrugged. "Maybe. You would have married a woman who you knew was incompatible with you, just to keep from breaking her heart."

Noah sucked in a breath. Did she have a point? "I loved Nevaeh."

"Over a decade, that can change," she said softly. "I loved Glen, too. He was a good man in the beginning, and he deserved good things. He deserved a wife who was grateful for him, whether or not there was a baby in the picture. But we got married for the wrong reasons, and even ten years of marriage wasn't going to erase that."

"So you blame Glen's nobility?" he asked.

"No... I blame my own naivete, which made me think that a chivalrous man was the answer. I wasn't the right woman for him. And no matter how sweet and well-intentioned he was, he wasn't right for me, either."

Noah picked up a crab puff and popped it into his mouth. "So you're done with nice guys, then?"

She laughed softly, her eyes suddenly

sparkling. "No, I'm not done with nice guys, but like you, I've become incredibly difficult to nail down."

"I'm in good company," he said.

"You are."

Noah reached behind him and grabbed a complimentary bottle of water off the counter and he passed it over to her. Then he took one for himself.

"Here's to being hard to catch," he said, and he cracked the bottle open and took a sip.

Taryn smiled and did the same. "I didn't want to like you."

"No?" He raised his eyebrows.

"I think you'd be easier to brush aside if you were some shallow guy who didn't want anything to do with this baby," she said. "You'd be easier to explain." Her expression saddened. "It's easier to be the woman done wrong than the woman who made a choice. Especially when your child might be angry about it."

"Hey—" he licked his lips "—Taryn, I honestly think it's possible to be two decent human beings who aren't romantically linked."

"Do you?" she asked uncertainly.

"I really do. It's called being friends."

"Friends don't make babies together," she said.

"Strangers might," he replied. "And strangers become friends all the time. I'm serious. We can do this."

"You really want to be in the picture?" she asked.

His heartbeat stuttered in his chest. If anyone had asked him if he wanted this a year ago, he'd have laughed at them. But now... now, he couldn't imagine letting her raise his son without him in the picture in some way...

"Yeah, I want to be part of raising him."

She met his gaze seriously, and it seemed like she was considering something.

"If you end up being a jerk, I'll cut you out completely," she said, her voice low. "I'm telling you that straight. If you play games with either of us—"

"I'm not playing games," he said. "And it's a deal."

They regarded each other soberly for a moment, and he wondered what she was worrying about when she looked at him. Was it comparing him to her ex-husband, or could she sense his potential to disappoint her?

"You have my cell number," Noah said. "And if you need anything, day or night, you text me. This wasn't planned for either of us, but I really do think we can be decent to each other."

"It's good we're platonic," she said. "When hearts get involved, it gets messy. We have a little boy who's going to need better than that."

"Better than parents who love each other," he said with a rueful smile.

"Exactly." She smiled faintly in return. "It sounds crazy, doesn't it?"

Except it wasn't. He understood what she meant. When hearts got entangled, people got hurt, got disappointed. His mom had gone through that with Tom, and Noah didn't want to be the guy who let his son's mother down.

He put the lid back on his bottle of water.

"I should get going," Noah said. "It's late."

"Crab puffs for the road?" she asked, nudging a container toward him.

"Just one." He plucked one out. "The rest are yours."

"Thanks." She adjusted her position and rubbed a spot on the side of her stomach. Was the baby moving in there? He was starting to wonder things like that, he realized.

"I'll see you in the morning," he said instead.

Taryn rose to her feet and followed him to the door. He opened it and when he turned back, she looked so vulnerable standing there with one hand on her belly and her dark gaze meeting his uncertainly.

"Taryn?" he said softly.

"Yeah?"

"You might not really know me yet, but I'm not a jerk," he said quietly.

She didn't answer, and he wasn't sure what he would even expect her to say, but he did need her to know it. She was the mother of his child, and he wasn't going to hurt her. She met his gaze with those dark, clear eyes, and before he could think better of it, he bent down and let his lips brush across her cheek.

He didn't wait for her response before turning and tugging the door shut behind him. Maybe he shouldn't have kissed her, but whatever. He wasn't going to be some selfish cad who promised more than he could give, or who jerked her emotions around. Because as much as Noah had liked Tom, he'd never forgotten that Tom used to make his mother cry.

And maybe that was part of what held him back from answering that Facebook message.

Tom had been the only dad that Noah could remember, but he'd also watched Tom break his mother's heart. And Noah wasn't going to do that to his own son.

CHAPTER EIGHT

THE NEXT MORNING, Taryn drove back down to her grandmother's house and parked out front. During the first visit with her grandmother, they'd had a good talk, but they hadn't gotten down to the reason why Taryn had taken this job in Mountain Springs— to talk her grandmother into moving somewhere safer for a woman of her age.

Maybe to Denver…

And yet somehow, even as she thought it, she was reminded of Lisa Dear, and how she described the call of those mountains and the lake. Would her grandmother ever leave willingly? And if she didn't want to, was it fair to tear her away from this place?

Even from this little house-lined street, Taryn could see the mountain peaks glistening white in the morning sunlight. There was always snow there—and the time of year could be marked by how far the snow had moved down toward the valley. On a bright June day like this, the snow was relegated to those jagged peaks.

Some things could be counted on, like the mountain snow, and glacier chilled air that surfed down the mountains into the valley...and the irritating family relationships that both frustrated everyone and gave them roots at the same time.

Taryn knocked on the door, but there was no answer, and Taryn shaded her eyes to try and see into the living room window. She could see the piano, the couch... That was about all. The morning was warm and a little humid. The neighbor's sprinkler was spraying again, a mist falling on Taryn's bare arms, and today it felt refreshing. She was wearing a sleeveless black dress that fit her figure perfectly right now—but wouldn't for long. Another couple of weeks, and this dress would be too small.

She sighed.

Last night Taryn had lain in bed feeling strangely softened by Noah's kiss on her cheek. She still wasn't sure what to make of him. He was determinedly noble—and as she'd told him, she found that trait suspicious now. She knew how far nobility could take a man, and it wasn't quite far enough.

And Noah was very clear about how he

felt about kids. That was a good thing—wasn't it? Getting to know him was supposed to make this easier, but she'd been seeing a side to him that she hadn't anticipated—the tender, well-intentioned side of him. And it was making it harder to hold him at arm's length.

Taryn moved away from the door, and headed back down the front path just in time to see her grandmother coming around the corner. She was wearing a pair of walking shoes and pastel green polyester pants with a floral shirt that matched. She was moving slowly, but steadily, and when she saw Taryn, she smiled.

"Just taking my morning constitutional," Granny said. "What are you doing here?"

"Do you walk every morning?" Taryn asked.

"Oh, a few times a week. I just go around the block—that's a marathon for a woman my age. I deserve credit."

"Of course!" Taryn grinned. "You're almost ninety. I'm impressed."

"Good." Granny headed slowly up toward her front door. "Did you come for breakfast?"

"No, I ate already," Taryn said. "I came to visit."

"Oh?" Granny cast her a quizzical look. "I wasn't sure you'd be back after our last talk."

Taryn followed her grandmother into the house, and she noticed that the old woman had left the door unlocked.

"Shouldn't you lock up when you leave?" Taryn asked.

"Oh, no one would come in," Granny said. "I know everyone on this street."

"You don't know everyone in town," Taryn said. "Granny, that's dangerous. You could be a target for burglary."

"What would they take?" Granny asked, spreading her hands. "Doilies?"

"Har-har," Taryn replied. "Look—" this was a good segue anyway "—Granny, you're vulnerable."

"So are you," Granny replied. "And you know my opinion of the usefulness of husbands."

Granny was doing what she did best—jabbing back. This was why most people stayed away these days. If Granny didn't want to hear it, she'd make sure the messenger was miserable.

"We aren't talking about me," Taryn replied.

"I am."

"Granny!" Taryn pulled a hand through

her hair. "I'm not the only one who worries, you know. Everyone is worried about you living alone. If you were to fall, it could be days before anyone found you!"

Granny looked up. "And?"

"And that would mean horrible suffering?" Taryn said incredulously.

"If I'm going to die, I want to die on my feet," Granny replied.

"It might not be so immediate—" Taryn pressed her lips together. "Look, there is a seniors' home where nurses check on you, and with friends your own age and activities planned for you—it would be like a cruise."

"Friends my own age die," Granny said. "And being condescended to by a nurse or given silly games to play with plastic balls isn't my idea of a good time. That sounds a whole lot like hospital to me."

"It would be safer," Taryn said.

"It would be lonely. No one visits me now. They'll start once I'm in a home?"

Taryn felt the prick in those words. "People are worried. That's all."

"People haven't come to see me themselves," Granny replied. "Look around you—am I suffering? Can I not care for myself? I'm fine!"

Taryn glanced around and nodded. "You're

doing well. I guess we're just afraid that it won't last."

"Well, check in on me from time to time, and if I'm in trouble, you'll know it. But the way I see it, you all just want to lock me away with nurses who can take your place in giving a damn."

That was strong language coming from her grandmother, and Taryn felt a smile tickle her lips.

"You have a point, Granny," she said.

"Do I?" Granny looked surprised.

"Yes," she replied. "I'll tell my mother that you're doing well and maybe we should check in more often. But Granny, can you promise not to hide it if things do get hard for you?"

"I'm still reeling from being told I have a point," Granny said with a chuckle. "But yes, I could agree to that."

Taryn glanced at her watch. "I have to get to work, though. This campaign is important. I need to save up for my maternity leave, and that's coming up quickly. I can't force you to do anything, and I don't have the energy to try. But I'll talk to the family."

"Taryn," Granny said softly. "We come from a line of strong women. We endure a lot, but we keep going. And I will not, under any circumstances, resign myself to a life of being pampered by a nurse and pushed off to the side by my own family. I raised your father, and I made him the man he is today. I don't see you leaning on anyone, and I can assure you, my dear, you are just as fragile as I am right now."

Taryn's phone pinged, and she looked down to see a text from Angelina.

Would you like to come for dessert with the Second Chance Club tonight?

Taryn couldn't help but smile. A dinner club of women who understood… Did they know how priceless they were?

She texted back.

I'd love to. Thanks for the invite.

"Granny," she said, flicking off her phone's screen. "Everyone has to lean on someone. It might not be a husband. It might not be the father of this baby. But even I have to find someone I can count on. We might be strong, but we aren't invincible."

Granny shrugged. "Then tell your parents to be more available. They should be embarrassed suggesting that strangers should take their place in my life."

Would they be? It was hard to tell, but Taryn was a little embarrassed for herself.

"I'll see you later, Granny."

ON TARYN'S RIDE back up the winding road that led to the resort, her own words kept resounding in her mind. She wasn't invincible, and when she had this baby, she was going to need support. There would be sleepless nights, there would be colds and flus, there would be parenting panic... And she'd need a strong support network as she raised this child so that she could build her career, provide for her son and also give him all the love and support that he'd need...that she'd need, too.

And there was a father in the picture who said he wanted to help...

But she'd done this before.

FOR NOAH, THE REST of the day was busy with meetings. He crossed paths with Taryn a couple of times, and they paused to talk. It felt more like chitchat or meaningless banter today. She was holding back, and he could feel it. When he asked what she was doing for dinner, she said she already had plans.

She was maintaining space, and he had to respect that. But he had to wonder if it was because of that kiss on her cheek. It had felt right in the moment, but was it too far?

Maybe that was clear by the way she was acting today. He didn't know how to balance this—a woman who had caught his attention the way Taryn had, carrying his child. He was spinning, trying to catch up with this emotionally, and maybe she was, too.

Noah noticed when Taryn headed out of her office for the evening. She glanced into his office and gave him a smile of farewell, and then was gone. He'd thought the challenge here was going to be getting to know her, to understand her. But the bigger challenge seemed to be keeping himself from tripping past platonic with her. His feelings weren't exactly in line with their goals here, and maybe she could feel it.

But putting Taryn out of mind wasn't that easy.

So when Noah got a text from his friend Gabe, asking him to come by that evening, Noah agreed. Maybe his friend could provide a bit of perspective. And Gabe always had been the levelheaded one of their group.

Gabe didn't go out with buddies like he used to before he was married with three kids, but he was known to invite the guys over for a beer on the porch. It was the half-way point for him and his wife, Cassie—a system that worked for them. So when Noah arrived that evening to the little house at the end of a road, he found Gabe sitting on the porch with his pajama-clad little girl on his lap. The lights were on, illuminating the porch, as well as half the yard.

"Hey," Gabe said as Noah hopped out of his truck. "Good to see you." Then he put his daughter down. "All right, a deal's a deal, kiddo. Time for you to go inside to bed, okay?"

Cassie opened the screen door, and the little girl went scampering inside. Cassie cast Noah a tired smile.

"Hi, Noah," she said.

"Hi, Cassie," he replied.

She let the door swing shut behind her, and Noah could hear her calling the other two kids up to bed as he settled into the Adirondack chair next to his friend. He felt his pocket for his phone out of habit and didn't feel it. He frowned, checked his other pockets.

"What's wrong?" Gabe asked.

"I think I left my phone at the office," he replied.

"You need to go back now?" Gabe asked. Gabe passed Noah a beer and a bottle opener, and Noah declined. "I'm driving."

"Have a Coke, then." Gabe grabbed a bottle of cola and passed it over. "It's been a while since I've seen you."

"Yeah…" Noah opened the bottle and took a swig, then put the Coke on the floor next to his chair. "How are you doing?"

For a few minutes they discussed unions and layoffs, and the uncertainty for the guys working at the mill these days. Gabe was hoping layoffs would come mostly from middle management, not the union guys. As they talked, joked a bit and then fell silent, Noah felt some of his tension seeping away. He'd miss nights like this if he moved to Seattle—companionable evenings spent with guys who'd known him since before he'd even hit puberty. Inside the house, Noah heard a child start to cry…

"So…have you talked to Brody lately?" Gabe asked.

They were getting to the reason Gabe had invited him over; Noah could feel it.

"Yup. I talked to him."

The child's crying from inside the house stopped.

"And?" Gabe prodded.

Noah turned to look at his friend. Gabe regarded him evenly. Was this an intervention or something?

"Why, did Brody ask you to talk to me?" Noah asked.

"Nope," Gabe said, and he took another sip of beer. "Just wondering if he'd managed to track you down."

"It's fine," Noah said. "I know he's planning on proposing to Nevaeh."

"He did propose. She accepted," Gabe replied.

"Oh…" So maybe he didn't have all the current information there. Nevaeh had accepted… Brody and Nevaeh were getting married. He searched inside of himself, but didn't feel the stab of betrayal he expected. He felt sad, and a little adrift. But it wasn't like he wanted to be the one in Brody's place—not anymore, at least. Too much had changed in the past few months. Maybe it was just a sign that he was making the right decision by looking for a career elsewhere.

"When did that happen?" Noah asked.

"He had a big barbecue at his place and invited a lot of us," Gabe replied. "He surprised her with the proposal—he had it all rigged so that during a game of charades, he acted it out."

"Clever," Noah said woodenly.

"Yeah, it was quite the event," Gabe replied. "Made Cassie ask me why I hadn't planned a bigger thing when I proposed to her. I guess a KFC parking lot feels a lot less impressive next to that."

Noah smiled ruefully. "I guess so."

His proposal over a nice dinner felt less impressive, too. But whatever. It wasn't like he and Nevaeh were meant for each other.

"Are you going to talk to him?" Gabe asked.

"Probably not."

"Man, we've all been friends since elementary school," Gabe said. "You're going to have to talk to him at some point."

As far as Noah was concerned, he'd done all the talking he wanted to do.

"He did track me down at work the other day," Noah said. "If that counts."

"No, I mean actually talk it out," Gabe said.

"Wait, so you're siding with him?" Noah asked incredulously. "Nevaeh broke off our engagement, and Brody literally dashed to her side and never left it again."

"I'm not saying that was right," Gabe said. "I'm saying…" Gabe took another sip from his bottle. "Noah, we've all been friends for decades. That's got to count for something. These friendships have lasted longer than some marriages."

"Friendships end," Noah said.

"So do marriages," Gabe shot back. "Still hurts like hell, and you're smart to avoid it."

Gabe pursed his lips, and they sat in silence for a minute or two. Gabe was right that their friendships had probably weathered more storms than some marriages had, but every relationship had a line people shouldn't cross. If their friendship had mattered so much to Brody, he would have considered that seven months ago.

"Were you softening on having kids or something?" Gabe asked, looking over at him.

"No, why?" Noah said.

"Because Cassie and I have talked it over every which way, and that's the conclusion we came to. That you were softening to the idea of a family. And that's why you're so hurt—"

"No, I wasn't," Noah replied. They were theorizing about him behind his back? Maybe he shouldn't be surprised. People were curious, and he couldn't blame them. "If you must know, Nevaeh said she was okay with not having kids. She could be happy without children and just have a nice lifestyle."

"And you believed that?" Gabe asked, squinting at him.

"I should expect the woman I'm engaged to to lie to me?" he demanded. "Yes, I believed it!"

Granted, he was a little more skeptical now...

"But obviously, she's *not* okay with not having kids," Gabe pressed. "You see that, right?"

"Gabe, I'm not pining for her," Noah said, leaning his head back. "She wasn't honest with me, but that's not even the part that upsets me the most. I'm mad at my best friend for betraying me. That's what I'm upset about."

"They want the same things out of life, man," Gabe said. "They both want kids and Little League baseball and birthday parties..."

And Noah wasn't arguing that. They did want the same thing, and if Nevaeh had cried on literally any other shoulder but Brody's, he could have made his peace with it. It wasn't just the kids that were coming between him and Nevaeh. They had more differences than that.

"It's true, though," Gabe replied. "Look—
if I had told Cassie I didn't want kids, she
would have dumped me, too. She wanted a
family—a big one. I'm the one who's begging her to stop at three kids. She still wants
another baby, and you know what? We'll
have another one. Because a happy wife is
a happy life. That's how it works."

"Are you trying to talk me into having
kids?" Noah asked with a low laugh.

"Nope," Gabe replied. "You know what
you want. But I'm pointing out that this isn't
all on Brody. Nevaeh wanted kids, and while
she loved you, I highly doubt she'd have been
blissfully happy with just you. I'm sorry. You
weren't enough for her, and much as that
hurts, this isn't just about Brody doing you
wrong."

"I know that…" Noah leaned his head
back.

"And you aren't mad at Nevaeh at all for
lying to you about that?" Gabe asked. "I
would be."

He sighed. "Maybe I am, a little bit. She
could have told me the truth instead of hint-
ing about engagement rings. You know what
I think? She figured she'd change my mind
on it."

"Yeah, of course."

"What do you mean, of course?" Noah demanded, twisting to look at his friend.

"I mean, of course! She figured you'd change your mind and she'd talk you into it," Gabe replied. "We all knew that."

Always the last to know… Noah heaved a sigh.

"At first, she liked the idea of not having kids, you know," Noah said. "In my own defense. She liked the quiet evenings, and money spent on the finer things in life. For a while there, she agreed that being two working adults with no kids would be a really nice lifestyle."

And then she'd changed her mind… Would Taryn do the same thing? Would she decide that she didn't want him in their son's life anymore? Or would she suddenly want more than he could give? Was he stupid to believe that Taryn was being one hundred percent honest with both him and her herself right now?

"So you're single, you don't want a family of your own and you're cutting off friends," Gabe said, tugging his attention back to the conversation. "The way I see it, Brody saved you from a divorce. Plain and simple. And you're going to need your friends in your life. Brody's been there for you for decades.

You two were joined at the hip all through high school. Brody fell in love with Nevaeh, and I get that was crossing a line, but dude, Nevaeh fell in love with Brody, too."

Noah was silent.

"You never noticed that, either?" Gabe asked. "I mean, you must have seen how Brody fawned over her…"

"Yeah, I noticed *that*," Noah said curtly.

"And that she really depended on him," Gabe added.

"They were *friends*," Noah said.

"It started out that way," Gabe agreed. "And I don't think there was any cheating, but she really relied on him. He…he might have been friend-zoned while she was with you, but they'd developed a real relationship. Everyone could see it. I mean, *I* did, and Cassie always tells me I'm dense about these things."

Noah rubbed his hands over his face. "I really don't want to talk about this."

"She could have married you and 'accidentally' gotten pregnant," Gabe said.

"That would have been underhanded." That would have been a betrayal, too.

"Still—that does happen," Gabe said. "So maybe realize that things might be complicated, but not quite so complicated as a baby arriving that you'd never planned on!"

Noah felt the bitterness of that irony, because a baby was arriving...just not with Nevaeh. And he was going to be a father whether he'd planned for it or not. The only difference was, he hadn't been duped in the process of this child's conception. What would Nevaeh think when she found out that he was going to be a father?

"So how do you figure we all move forward, then?" Gabe asked when they'd been silent for a couple of beats. "Are you just going to avoid anything that includes Brody and Nevaeh from now on? Dinners, barbecues, birthday parties, graduations? Like— how do you figure we do this? Because we're all friends with both of you."

That group of friends had been part of what had drawn Noah back to life in Mountain Springs when he'd moved here five years ago, and it was the reason that he was hoping to get out of here and start fresh in Seattle. But Gabe was right. There would be a wedding for Brody and Nevaeh. There would be baby showers for them, and baby showers for other friends, too. There would be all the parties that Brody and Nevaeh would be invited to. And if Noah shut himself off from anything that included Brody, he'd end up alone. This was Noah's problem—no one else felt it deeply enough to pick a side. They were adults, and life was messy—they'd made their peace with that.

"I figure I'll move," Noah said quietly.

"Funny." Gabe took a swig of his beer, then eyed him uncertainly.

"I'm serious," Noah said. "I'm applying to a job in Seattle."

"Really?" Gabe looked over at him incredulously. "You'd leave the sweet gig you have at the resort?"

"There are other sweet gigs," Noah said.

"There are other women, too!" Gabe said. "Look, if you leave your home, your sister, her kids, your friends, your job—if you leave all of us because of Brody and Nevaeh, I think you'll regret it. Because life *will* go on—our lives will all go on. And there will be no turning back that clock. Life here in Mountain Springs is bigger than the two of them."

"Life changes sometimes," Noah said. His own life was even more upended than Gabe knew.

"Look, if you have to leave, then leave. But don't do it before you look Brody in the face and talk to him. Even if it's just to say your piece. You owe yourself that much."

He might have a point—he might move across the country, but if he didn't sort out his issues here at home, it would still hold him back emotionally.

"You might have a point, Gabe," Noah said. "Seeing Brody once more might be a good idea."

"Yeah?" Gabe sounded hopeful.

"I just can't promise that I'll be all sensitive and talk it out," Noah said.

"You know, or hit him," Gabe said with a grin. "Whatever it takes to clear the air."

CHAPTER NINE

THAT EVENING, TARYN stayed in her sleeveless black dress—it wasn't formal, but it was suitable for a dessert invite with the Second Chance Dinner Club, and she'd added a sparkly floral-patterned rhinestone necklace to dress it up. It would do.

As she headed into the dining room, she spotted the women in a far corner, tucked away from most of the other diners. Outside, the sun had already set, and the moon hung low over the mountains and shimmered on the rippling surface of the lake. Problems seemed smaller with this kind of scenery outside.

She'd read that in the International Space Station, astronauts looked down on earth from above, and when they returned to the earth's surface, they just never saw things the same way again. There was something about the beauty of the planet and the massiveness of space that put things into perspective. The mountain lake did something similar for her—at least for the span of one evening.

The sampler platter of desserts sitting in the center of the table drew Taryn's attention, and she smiled at the women who were already there. There was Jen and Gayle, the aunt and niece who had sat together last time, too. There was Belle and Renata, who seemed to share a special bond. Melanie looked effortlessly beautiful tonight in a crimson off-the-shoulder dress. The only one who was missing was Angelina.

"Thanks for inviting me tonight," Taryn said, and slid into a chair next to Gayle.

"So we're getting together to talk weddings tomorrow, right?" Gayle said.

Taryn had called both Gayle and Melanie that day to make plans.

"Yes, absolutely," Taryn said. "I'm looking forward to it."

"Me, too," Gayle said. "Any excuse to pull out the wedding album."

"You are just so cute, Gayle," Melanie said with a grin. "I remember when you wanted some understated wedding behind a barn or something."

"It wasn't *behind* a barn," Gayle said with a laugh. "It was going to be outdoors in blue jeans."

"It didn't end up being a blue jean wedding," Renata said for Taryn's benefit. "It was stunning—the event of the season. You should have seen Gayle. She was very old-Hollywood. She oozed glamour."

"Oh, go on," Gayle said, but her cheeks pinked. "I didn't think I needed a big, fancy wedding this time around, but you all were right. I loved it."

"I've seen a couple of pictures," Taryn said. "It looked gorgeous."

"I was a nervous wreck," Gayle said. "If it weren't for these women here, I don't know how I would have pulled it all off."

"Well, if it weren't for us and *Matthew*," Belle said.

"Oh, right, the groom," Gayle joked, and they all laughed.

Taryn watched Gayle's face as she turned to laugh with Belle, and she was happy. That happiness made her glow—she was deeply satisfied. Had Gayle always looked this fresh? She doubted it. A woman stuck in a marriage that didn't fulfil her seemed to age ten years. Taryn had certainly felt that way with Glen, but it wasn't just an unfulfilling marriage; it was the infertility. She'd gotten pregnant before they ever took those vows, so why couldn't she do it again? Why had her body betrayed her? That had drained her energy away, too.

Her baby moved inside of her, and Taryn rubbed the side of her belly where his foot was pushing.

"How did you do it, Gayle?" Taryn asked quietly.

All eyes turned toward her, and she smiled uncomfortably.

"I mean, I'm pretty newly divorced, and you're just so…beautifully happy," Taryn said. "I suppose I want that, too."

"It was this group," Gayle said, and the other women nodded knowingly. "We got together for a meal one day, and we were talking about how a lot of us had been Mom for so long, that we wanted to be more than that. We wanted to be women. And for me, my first husband was gay, so I missed out on the kind of romance the rest of you might take for granted… I went home that night, and I decided that I didn't know what would happen. I didn't know if I'd find love again at my age, but I decided I wanted to try. So when I met Matthew at the gym, I…flirted back."

"You never told us that!" Melanie said, leaning forward. "I do remember that dinner, though. It was one my first dinners with all of you. We toasted to being more than mothers."

"I wanted to have what everyone else had," Gayle said quietly. "I wanted it so badly…"

Taryn nodded. "You were ready."

"I was *so* ready," Gayle said, and her eyes sparkled as a smile spread over her face.

These women wanted to be more than mothers, but Taryn had longed to be a mother, period. She'd wanted a child of her own, a baby in her arms. More than a mother? No, *finally* a mother! And yet, she understood that longing for love and passion, too. Taryn just wasn't ready to try for it. She was still cherishing the victory of her pregnancy.

Angelina arrived at the table then, and when she slid into the seat next to Taryn, she shot them a smile.

"You made it," Jen said.

"Sorry I'm late," Angelina said. "I got some emails I had to respond to right away, or I'd just think about them all evening. You know how it is."

"You work too hard," Renata said.

"I love it, though," Angelina said with a shrug. "The dessert is on the house tonight. Albert made up some samples for a photo shoot with Taryn, which left us with all of this left over."

"Lucky us," Belle said with a grin in Taryn's direction. "I think tonight could use a large dose of chocolate."

"Any night, really," Renata said.

They all chose a dessert and they chatted while they ate. Taryn chose a raspberry chocolate mousse served in a little chocolate cup, and it was just as delicious as it looked in the photos she'd taken. She listened while the women chatted. Belle, who sat next to her, took a small bite of her cheesecake, then put down her fork. Taryn looked over at her.

"You okay?" she asked quietly.

"Hmm?" Belle looked over, then shrugged. "Oh, um, I'm a little down tonight. Philip and I broke up."

"What?" Renata said from the other side of Belle, and the table silenced.

All the women were focused on Belle now.

Belle's eyes misted and she blinked back the tears. "Sorry, I'm still a little moody about it."

"What happened?" Taryn asked softly.

"He came to my place for dinner," Belle said. "And everything was fine at first. The last time I was at his place, I was looking through some of his old yearbooks and stuff, so he wanted to see mine. Anyway, I have some albums from my modeling years, and from my marriage to Curtis, and I…hid them."

"So he wouldn't be insecure about it," Renata said.

"Exactly." Belle sucked in a breath and shot Renata a grateful look. "When I was married to Curtis, I hid so many things from him. And I was doing things to please him. Like, he'd complain about models who didn't get enough sleep, so I'd be careful to go to bed early even when I wasn't tired so I wouldn't be 'one of those girls.' And then I'd hide eating a cheeseburger because he'd go on and on about trans fats and eating garbage. It was constant! So I was standing in my own living room distracting Philip from the albums I didn't want him to look at, and I realized I was doing the same thing! I was hiding parts of myself from a man who I wanted to love me."

"Oh, sweetie…" Gayle breathed.

"And I was sick of it!" Belle said. "With Curtis, I was trying to be thin enough, and beautiful enough, and keep looking young enough… With Philip, I'm trying to be ordinary enough so that he stops worrying that I'll cheat on him. I'm sick of trying to be someone different than who I am. I'm forty-two years old, and I'm sick to death of pleasing men!"

"Did you tell him that?" Taryn asked.

"No. I told him it wasn't working and asked him to leave," Belle said. "Some explanations aren't worth it. He wasn't going to get it, anyway. You want to know the worst part?"

The women were silent, waiting.

"When he left, he asked me if there was someone else, if that was why I was breaking up with him," Belle said. "I almost punched him."

"Maybe you should have," Renata muttered, and Taryn smiled at the other woman's bitter humor.

"I'm sorry," Jen said. "I know you really cared for him."

"I did. I do," Belle said.

"So what do you need to get over him?" Angelina asked.

"This—" Belle looked around. "And you know what? I love you girls! You don't know how much I cherish what we have here. I have other friends who are less supportive. They figure I don't deserve any sympathy with my modeling past, and...you all make a world of difference in my life. You know that?"

"You do the same for us, Belle," Melanie said.

"And we'll always be on your side," Renata said.

"I needed this evening out with all of you." Belle sighed. "And some gossip. I realized that we never found out how Taryn caught her husband's affair. I've been curious…"

"So have I." Renata leaned forward to get a better look at Taryn.

"Well, I found some texts he'd sent to this other woman, and—" Taryn's mind went back to that painful day "—he'd never spoken to me like that. I mean, ever. He told her how when he looked at her, he felt like he was coming home. How her eyes intoxicated him, how her lips—" She shook her head. "You get the idea."

"Ouch…" Jen said softly.

"Yeah," Taryn agreed. "And when I told my mother about it, she thought I should fight for my man, but there was no point."

"Because you couldn't trust him?" Melanie asked.

"Well, that," Taryn said, "But it wasn't just about the lies he must have told. I realized in that moment that he'd never lit up for me like that. I'd never inspired him to that kind of poetry. All I'd inspired was some noble obligation. And I didn't want to fight to be Glen's obligation any longer. There was no glorious history to fight for."

"Gayle wanted to be more than a mother," Belle said quietly. "Taryn wants to be more than an obligation. And I want to be more than a body—more than a face."

"I just want to be loved," Renata murmured.

The table fell silent. Wasn't that what it came down to? The women looked around the table at each other, and Angelina lifted her glass.

"To being loved," she said, and there were tears in Angelina's eyes.

They lifted their glasses in quiet solidarity. It was all any of them wanted.

As NOAH DROVE away from Gabe's house and back toward the office to grab his phone, his mind was on Brody. Gabe might have a point, he had to grudgingly agree. Even if Noah left for Seattle, he couldn't cut off his entire history in this town. There was no such thing as a completely fresh start. He had a history, and even if he got the job, he'd come back and visit his sister, at the very least. Life in Mountain Springs would go on. People would keep getting married, having kids, reaching milestones and celebrating all of it together. Unless he wanted to lose his connection to all of his friends and family, he had to make some sort of peace with Brody.

The drive up to the resort was a quiet one. The moon was high and full, and he needed the time alone to think, anyway. When he parked and got out, he could hear the soft sound of a late dining party on the patio— the murmur of voices, some laughter, the clink of glasses.

He headed inside and nodded at the young man working the late shift at the front desk as he made his way to his office. Phone retrieved, he typed out a text to Brody.

Brody, you're right. We need to talk man-to-man. There are things that need saying.

He sent the message, and sighed. He doubted that Brody was going to jump at the chance to be told off, but before Noah could pocket his phone, he'd received a reply:

I'm free tomorrow night.

So Brody was actually game for this... Noah rubbed a hand through his hair.

Alpine Pub. 8:00.

It was neutral territory—a place where they always used to meet up.

See you then was Brody's reply, and Noah didn't bother answering that text, but he did feel a strange sense of relief to be finally facing this. Maybe a friendship like this one needed a proper goodbye.

Noah locked his office door behind him and headed to the main doors. He pushed out into the fresh night air, the voices on the patio murmuring pleasantly in the background. As he made his way toward his truck, he heard the women on the patio calling farewell.

"See you next time, Taryn!"

His heart sped up a little at the sound of her name, and Noah turned to see Taryn ambling around the building in his direction. Her hair was swept up in a twist at the back of her head, and a floral necklace sparkled in the low light. She seemed to spot him at the same time, and they stared at each other for a moment before he waved and smiled. She smiled back, and he felt a flood of relief. Things had become awkward between them, and maybe it was time to straighten that out, too.

When he reached her, she rested her hands on the top of her belly. Her cheeks were pink, and a tendril of hair fell down along her creamy neck.

Noah nodded in the direction of the patio. "I didn't realize that was you."

"We started out inside, but we moved outside when the patio became available," she said.

"It's a nice evening for it," he said. "I sat on a porch tonight with a friend."

"Brody?" she asked. "Did you talk things out?"

Why was everyone so concerned about the status of his relationship with Brody these days?

"No, I have more than one friend," he said, and he smiled faintly to show he was teasing her. "This was a guy named Gabe. But we ended up talking about Brody a lot, though. What about you?"

"We talked about our exes, but that's about all I can say," she replied with a small smile. "We're sworn to secrecy."

"Right." He paused and the warm night breeze whisked past them. "Are you in a hurry? You want to take a walk? The pathway around the side of the building leads to a really beautiful spot by the water."

Taryn smiled. "Sure."

She fell into step next to him, and they wandered down the walkway. There were a few people out tonight—a couple was down by the water, a blanket thrown around their shoulders together. A bonfire farther down the shore glowed against the night sky, and the sound of a guitar playing softly surfed the breeze.

"I thought you were avoiding me today," he said.

"I was," she replied.

He looked down at her. "I'm sorry."

"For what?" she asked.

"Kissing your cheek. Making this weird."

"You didn't make it weird," she said. "This *is* a weird situation."

"Yeah," he agreed. "But we'll sort it out."

They meandered down the walkway next to the lodge. The windows here were in the employee break room, and the blinds were all shut.

She sighed. "If only you were more of a jerk, I could have lied to you. And if only I was okay with keeping a few more secrets, because then I could have lied to my son about knowing who his father was. That would have kept things simple."

"Would you have lied to me?" he asked. Did she really want to—now, after getting to know him?

Taryn shook her head. "No. That isn't me. I can't raise my son on lies, either. It isn't who I am, and it isn't how I want my son to turn out, either."

"But you'd rather I went away?" he asked, his voice low.

Taryn glanced up at him, and for a moment, he thought she'd say yes, but then she shook her head. "No. Not anymore. Unfortunately, I like you."

He felt an unexpected rush of satisfaction at those words. She liked him... He smiled ruefully. "That's too bad."

"It is," she said, but he saw the joking sparkle in her eyes.

There were lights that illuminated the path as they moved past the lodge, and he put a hand on the small of her back to nudge her in the right direction. The breeze was cooler the closer they got to the water. The rocks along this part of the pebbly beach were sharper, making it less appealing to guests, but Noah had always liked this spot. It was secluded with a surrounding of bushes, but the view was the same stunning panorama of jagged mountains and pristine lake.

When they emerged onto the sliver of beach, he heard Taryn's soft intake of breath. Silver moonlight reflected on the surface of the lake, the water beneath glowing dark turquoise. Where the moonlight ended, the lake turned murky black.

"Wow..." she breathed.

He bent down and picked up a flat pebble, then threw it across the water, watching as it skipped along the surface before disappearing into the deep.

"After that night together, I thought about you," he said, straightening. "A lot. I don't mean that in a crude way..." He paused, searching for the words to explain what it had been like for him. "I kept thinking about how easy it was to talk to you, and how funny you were, even when you were having an incredibly tough night. I'd never felt that way just talking to a woman before. Not with Nevaeh, or with anyone else. I opened up with you—and I know how crazy that sounds because it was a one-night stand that wasn't supposed to mean anything—"

He looked over at her and shrugged helplessly. "But to me, it did."

Her cheeks pinked, and she hitched her shoulders up. "I was a stranger—"

"You were, but that wasn't it," he said. "I've found in life that there are a handful of people that you really connect with on a deep level—and there is no faking it, or forcing it. I think you're one of those people for me."

Taryn looked up, and this time she met his gaze. "I know you probably won't believe me, but I'm cautious normally. I do things in a particular order, and that doesn't involve falling into bed with a stranger. That was risky, and while I kicked myself for taking that kind of risk, I couldn't ever quite regret it, either. You made me remember that I was a woman still… and talking like we did was healing for me, too."

"We had something," he said softly.

She turned back to the water. "Yeah, we did."

That felt like a victory for her to admit to it, because he'd spent the past seven months remembering the intoxicating woman from a night that felt almost like a dream. Her hand hung at her side, and he brushed her fingers with his own. She didn't move, and he could feel her holding her breath.

"For what it's worth," he murmured. "I was really glad to see you again…"

He closed his hand over hers, and she twined their fingers together. She squeezed his hand tightly, and his breath caught.

"If things were less complicated, I'd be making a move right now…" he whispered.

"But things are very complicated," she whispered back, meeting his gaze.

"Yup…" He pushed a stray tendril of hair away from her cheek. He knew he shouldn't even be thinking about it right now, but his gaze moved down to her lips.

"Besides," she said. "We were just two heartbroken people back then. It was different."

She was still gorgeous, and smart and insightful… And he was still drawn to her.

"It doesn't feel any different," he murmured.

This time, she didn't protest, and he stepped a little closer. He leaned closer still until his lips hovered over hers, and then he tugged her against him and ran a hand down the soft swell of her belly.

"Now's the time to stop me," he whispered.

But instead of pushing him away, she lifted her mouth to his, and he felt a crashing wave of relief as their lips met. He kissed her tenderly at first, then he slipped his hand into the back of her hair and pulled her closer against him. She tasted of chocolate, and even though she was seven months pregnant, he found a way to hold her that made her form fit against him.

The kiss was everything he'd remembered, and when she finally pulled back, his breath was ragged. She shut her eyes and licked her lips. Her hair had come loose, tumbled down around her shoulders. Her lips were plump from his kiss, and he couldn't drag his gaze away from them.

When he leaned in again, she put a hand against his chest, and he stopped.

"You can't tell me there's nothing there," he said softly.

"I know…" She swallowed. "But you can't tell me there's a future for us, either."

Her words slammed against him like a shutting door. She was right. He needed to rein this in. He felt out of control in his own life, and this powerful draw toward Taryn… She wasn't just a woman he was deeply attracted to; she was the mother of his son.

Noah moved back, putting a couple of inches between them, but he caught her hand in his, and she didn't tug it free.

"If things were less complicated, would you be tempted?" he asked softly.

A smile flickered at her lips. "Oh, definitely."

He chuckled at that, but then Taryn pulled her hand free and moved toward the path.

"It's late," she said over her shoulder.

"Yeah…" It was late. "Taryn?"

She paused and looked back at him, her dark gaze shining like the depth of the lake behind him.

"Your hair," he said. She put her hands up, and then rolled her eyes as she felt the disarray.

"Thanks," she whispered, and he watched her expertly twist her hair back up as she made her way up the path once more.

There was definitely something between them…and the bitterly ironic part was that the thing holding them back was the baby they'd made together.

He wasn't thinking straight tonight. He needed to catch his breath and remind himself why this was a bad idea. Because for the life of him, tonight under a full summer moon, it almost made sense.

CHAPTER TEN

THE NEXT DAY was another busy one for Taryn. She went to Melanie McTavish's lake house, where Melanie and Gayle were waiting. They sat outside on the wharf, their feet trailing in the cool water as they talked about the women's divorces and subsequent remarriages.

They'd both gotten married at the resort, and they'd both emailed her photos that could be used for the campaign—stunning shots that showed shared jokes, relieved kisses and family celebrating with the newly married couples. The lodge, the lake and mountain scenery only intensified the sense of happiness and love in those photos.

"I like this one," Taryn said, holding up her phone to display a photo of Matthew looking adoringly at Gayle.

Gayle smiled. "Me, too."

"What's it like?" Taryn asked. "Being married to a man who feels like that about you?"

"It's…" Gayle was silent for a moment. "It's like coming home after a long trip, when you're out of clean clothes, and you're tired and cranky, and you finally drop your suitcase by your front door and you smell that scent of your home, and you feel this overwhelming sense of…at last. You know what I mean?"

"I think I do," Taryn said.

She'd felt a bit of that in Noah's arms last night. That strange relief of being pulled back into his muscular embrace…

"Well, that's what it's like," Gayle replied. "You don't have to change yourself or be anything else for that man to think you're amazing. For the first year I was with him, I was waiting for it to wear off. It never did."

Taryn nodded. "Can I quote you?"

"Feel free." Gayle smiled.

Taryn wrote with her stylus on her tablet for a moment, and then she let her gaze move across the water toward the lodge. It was in full view from the creaking wharf, and the sunlight shone like silver off the windows.

"I think I saw this house last night from the shore," Taryn said. "All the lights were on, and it was glowing."

"You probably did," Melanie agreed. "We were home."

And last night while those lights were glowing, Taryn had been kissing Noah. She felt some heat in her cheeks.

"Melanie and Logan were high school sweethearts," Gayle said.

"A very, very long time ago," Melanie said, and she lifted her feet from the water, then dropped them back in. "We were different people then. We were young and dumb and…it just didn't work. We met up again after my divorce and after his wife had died, and we started over." She was silent for a beat. "It was the scariest thing of my life."

Taryn chuckled. "I didn't expect that!"

"It was just terrifying!" Melanie said. "He wasn't exactly husband material back in the day. He was a bad boy. A rebel…and as much as we grow up, there are some parts of our personalities that just don't change that much. I was afraid that Logan would be the same guy at heart—sweet, but impenetrable, you know?"

"Obviously, you warmed up to the idea," Taryn said with a low laugh.

"Yes, I did," she said. "Basically, we realized what we had to lose, and we took the leap."

"And it was worth it?" Taryn asked.

"Oh, yes. To be with him. I don't think

it would have been for anyone else, but for him…"

But how did a woman know when a man would be worth the terrifying leap? Right now, the only person Taryn was willing to take any risk for was her son. He was her miracle, and for him, she'd be willing to do just about anything.

After some lunch, Taryn headed back to the lodge with her newest batch of content to work with. The day had gotten steadily hotter, and the air-conditioning in Taryn's car couldn't keep up. She unrolled her window, and it didn't seem to help.

When she got back to the lodge, she meant to go inside and cool off, but the light was just perfect and the lake was still and clear. When Taryn went down to the water, she could see straight down to the fish darting about, and the photo opportunity was just too amazing to miss.

By the time she finished, she stood back up with some difficulty, and her head swam. She was thirsty, and she rubbed a hand over her eyes, trying to get her brain to refocus.

"Ma'am, are you okay?"

Taryn glanced over to see a teenage girl looking at her uncertainly. "You okay?" the girl repeated.

"Yes, I'm fine, I'm just—" Taryn shut her eyes against a headache that had suddenly sprung to life. She was definitely overheated, and probably dehydrated. "I'd better get back inside."

"Why don't I walk with you?" the girl said.

Taryn had overdone it—she could feel it, and she allowed the girl to guide her back up the walk toward the lodge. As they got closer to the building, she could see straight into Noah's office. He was standing by the window, and when he saw her, he shaded his eyes to get a clearer look. Then turned around and disappeared. Taryn wanted water—and some cool darkness. That would help…

The heavy wooden front doors swung open to reveal Noah standing there, a worried look on his face.

"I think she's sick," the girl said.

"What happened, Taryn?" Noah asked.

"Just a little overheated," she said.

"Thanks for helping her back," Noah said to the teenage girl. "I appreciate it. I'll take it from here."

The girl left, and Noah put an arm around her and brought her into the air-conditioned interior.

"You want to rest here, or go up to your suite?" he asked.

"Um—" Taryn licked her lips "—I'd really like some water, and I want to lie down upstairs."

"Tell you what," Noah said. "I'll help you get upstairs, and I'll get you everything you need."

His voice was authoritative, and he released her and grabbed a water bottle from behind the front desk, and then headed over to the service elevator and hit the call button. Then he came back to her side, cracked the bottle open and handed it to her. She took a welcome swig and allowed him to lead her to the elevator. She felt weak and light-headed, and when the elevator door closed behind them, Noah moved in closer.

"Noah—"

"Lean on me," he said, his voice low.

She leaned her head against his shoulder, and it felt good.

"I shouldn't have stayed out as long as I did," she said. "It's a hot day."

"Yeah, no kidding," he said. The elevator door pinged and opened, and Taryn felt some relief at the dimmer light in the upstairs hallway.

"Thanks," she said as she pulled out her

key card, but she fumbled with it, and Noah slipped it out of her fingers and opened the door for her. He followed her inside.

"Go lie down," he said. "I'll bring you a cool cloth."

Taryn was too tired to argue, and she went over to the bed and eased herself up onto it. Her head was pounding, and she shut her eyes, listening to the sound of running water. Then Noah's voice…

"I need a lemon water up in suite 210, please. Also some orange slices… Thanks."

A cool cloth descended over her forehead, covering her eyes, and she let out a sigh.

"Thank you…" She lifted the corner of the cloth to look at Noah standing next to her. "You don't have to do this, you know."

"Do what?" he said, and his dark gaze met hers.

"Don't tell me you escort every guest back to her room and order her lemon water."

"No, I don't," he replied, and he pulled up a chair next to her bed, and sat down.

"I'm fine," she said.

"You're overheated, probably dehydrated, and you're seven months pregnant," he said. "If one person in this lodge has the right to help you, I think it's me."

"Noah…"

"Should I get someone from housekeeping to look in on you instead?" he asked. "Because I'm not comfortable just leaving you on your own right now."

She peeked at him again from under the cloth, and he was eyeing her with a stubborn look on his face.

"You're preferable to housekeeping," she murmured with a rueful smile.

"I figured I might be," he said with a low chuckle.

There was a knock on the door, and Noah went to open it. He returned a moment later with a plate of orange slices and a tall glass of water with a lemon slice floating on top.

"Drink this," he said.

She pushed herself up onto her elbows and took a few sips. When she handed it back, Noah put the glass on the table next to the bed.

"What would you have done if I weren't here?" Noah asked.

"I don't know," she said. "Probably asked Janelle for some water."

"Janelle would have called an ambulance," he said. "That's what would have happened."

She sighed. "I don't need a hospital."

"I know, but that's the protocol here. If a guest can't get upstairs under their own volition and they're obviously in some distress, it's an immediate call to 911."

His gaze was locked on her now, and she sucked in a wavering breath.

"What are you trying to tell me?" she asked.

"I'm just pointing out that you might need... I don't know...a backup plan, just while you're pregnant, or when the baby is small," he said.

"I've got a plan," she said, and closed her eyes again.

"I know," he said. "But while you are here, maybe you could just consider me your backup plan. If you need a hand, you let me know." He stood up and eased the cloth off her eyes. "Let me cool that cloth off again."

Noah disappeared into the bathroom, and she listened to the water running.

The baby stretched and squirmed, and Taryn rubbed her hand over the spot. He was active in there, so he was fine. That was a relief.

Was she as ready to be a single mother as she thought she was? Or was she going to need more support than she'd ever imagined?

Noah came back out with the cloth, and he handed it back over. Taryn used it to wipe her arms and face, the coolness feeling good against her skin.

"I'm serious about you calling me," Noah said. "You have my number, and I don't want you to hesitate to use it. I know we have an unorthodox arrangement, but I *am* the father. At the very least, I can step in and do a few of those things a partner would do for you."

"Like foot rubs?" she joked.

Noah shot her a grin. "You want a foot rub? Because I will."

"No," she smiled. "Not just now. I think I'm feeling a bit better."

She pushed herself up to a seated position and took the cloth off her head.

"Are you sure?" he asked.

"I'll probably stay up here for a bit to cool off in the air-conditioning," she admitted. "But yes, I'm feeling better."

"Then I'll head out," he said, and he glanced around, spotted her phone next to the TV and brought it over to her bed and put it next to her. "Anything, Taryn. Okay?"

He caught her gaze and held it.

"Okay," she said.

Noah headed for the door and let himself out. She lay back down in the semi-darkness, feeling her son's small movements inside of her. She put the cloth back onto her forehead, and then her phone blipped. She looked down at it, and then laughed softly. It was Noah.

Drink more water.

She reached for the glass of lemon water and took another sip, then she ate an orange slice. It was cold and sweet and made her feel better still. She closed her eyes. Today, she'd needed a little bit of help—she'd admit to that. But it would be easier if the man she was forced to rely on weren't Noah. She needed a buddy right now, not potential heartbreak.

NOAH SAT AT HIS DESK, a report open on his computer in front of him, but he couldn't seem to focus on it. His mind was on Taryn. When he'd seen her staggering toward the building, the teenage girl she was leaning on looking downright panicked, his heart had just about stopped in his chest.

But she's fine, he reminded himself. She was upstairs and resting…and every instinct inside of him was pushing him to go up and check on her.

This wasn't really his place, though… He'd given himself the job of protector, but disturbing her when she was resting might be over the line. It had been two hours. She might be asleep.

He turned back to his computer and put his glasses on. He'd been kicking himself for that kiss last night. It had been honest, but it hadn't made things any easier.

His phone pinged, and he looked down to see a text from Taryn.

I'm feeling better. I'm just taking a shower, and then I'll be down to work.

He felt more relieved than he probably had a right to.

Glad to hear it, he texted back.

The orange slices hit the spot, Taryn texted back. Thanks for that.

He texted back a wink, and smiled to himself. Good. He wasn't willing to examine how he was feeling right now. Seeing Taryn again, and knowing that baby was his, had stabbed under all his defenses. He'd never wanted to be a father, but he could see now why other men did. Maybe he could even see why Brody wanted that family...

Taryn was going to need help, and while he might never be the kind of man who made a good dad in the home, he would definitely be the kind of parenting partner who provided what he could.

He'd support his child financially, and the more he made, the better he could provide. Hey—sometimes his instincts weren't terrible.

A few minutes later, Taryn passed his office and poked her head inside.

"Feeling better?" he asked.

"A lot better," she said. "I'm going to edit some video in my office."

"Okay."

She smiled, then disappeared again. She *was* fine. The color had evened out in her face, and she didn't look sweaty anymore. No need to worry. So why was he feeling this protective urge toward her? His feelings for Taryn had gotten complicated, and kissing her hadn't helped. If anything, he'd made things worse. And being able to help her out when she was vulnerable?

Noah wondered if they'd only met under normal circumstances, there might have been a chance for them. Except she wanted a baby… So no matter how great she was, he'd never have been her answer. He would have been a disappointment.

He sighed and turned back to his work.

There was a resort to run, and he had meetings to attend. Angelina still needed his best.

THAT EVENING, NOAH headed off to the Alpine Pub. For the last few hours of the day, he'd dreaded this meeting with Brody. Gabe would say it was a good idea, but Noah really didn't feel like opening up with Brody. This wasn't going to be polite... Twice, he almost texted to cancel, but maybe it was better to just get this out of the way.

The Alpine Pub was a rustic little place off the beaten path so that not too many tourists had discovered it. There were always a few chalk clapboard signs set up to lure passersby down the unassuming lane toward the pub, but they weren't terribly successful. That was why the locals liked the place.

When Noah arrived at about five past eight, Brody was already there. He'd staked out a booth in the back, and he didn't wave or stand. He just stared straight at Noah, looking like he was dreading this, too—that would be small solace.

Noah ordered a beer and headed over to the booth. Brody looked up at him uneasily, and Noah slid in opposite him.

"Hi," Brody said. "I almost called this off, but Nevaeh said I had to do it."

So it was Nevaeh's influence. Noah smiled faintly. "She wants me around? I thought she'd be glad to keep me at a distance."

"She says she wants *me* to be happy," Brody said.

"And I'm the source of your unhappiness?" Noah said.

Brody rolled his eyes. "She cares."

About Brody, at least. Noah took a sip and eyed the other man uncomfortably.

"She feels guilty," Brody added. "She knows that me and her getting together was…kind of close for comfort. I mean, you and I being best friends, and going from being engaged to you to dating me…"

Noah eyed Brody irritably. "I don't think it is her fault. She broke up with me for good reason—she wanted kids after all. That was fair. What wasn't fair was my best friend dashing to her side. That's what I've been wondering all this time. The very weekend she broke it off with me, you rushed to her side. Could that not have waited a few weeks?"

Brody leaned back. "No." There was no apology in his voice.

"No?" Noah couldn't help the way his tone dropped.

"No, I couldn't wait," Brody replied.

"Were you already hooking up?" Noah cast about, looking for the explanation. "I honestly thought there was no cheating—"

"There *was* no cheating," Brody retorted. "Look, I told you before how I felt about her. I told you that if you ever let her go—"

"You were seriously just waiting for your chance with my fiancée?" Noah shot back. "You don't hear how base that is?"

"Look, feeling about her the way I did, I wasn't going to let some other guy swoop in there when she was finally available. The thing with Nevaeh is that she *is* faithful. If she started up with some other guy, even if he was a rebound, I'd be stuck in the wings. I knew her well enough to know I had to get in there. So I did."

"The way you felt about her—" Noah leaned forward. "Gabe seems to think you were in love with her for quite a while."

"I was. I am." Brody's voice shook. "I fell in love with her the first time I met her."

"You met her when I introduced you to my girlfriend," Noah said flatly.

"I'm not saying it was great timing," Brody replied. "And I'm not proud of it. But I thought our friendship could tough it out."

"And you didn't worry that you might be a rebound for her?" Noah asked.

"I have considered the fact that she probably still has a few unresolved feelings for you," Brody said.

"Yet you figure marrying her right away is a good idea?" Noah said. "Yeah, Gabe filled me in. Are you trying to rush this so she won't change her mind about you, too?"

He saw the flicker of anger in Brody's gaze, and for a moment, he felt satisfaction at having hit a nerve. What made Brody think he was so special?

"Yeah, I do think it's a good idea," Brody replied. "You know why? Because I'm willing to give her everything she wants, everything she's longed for. I'm ready to start that family with her."

That was what it had come down to—children.

Noah felt a wave of guilt. He was on the road to fatherhood. Was that going to feel like a betrayal to Nevaeh later? Maybe. Should it even matter to him? It did a little, because he'd loved Nevaeh, too, and he didn't want to hurt her. She didn't deserve that. His son might be an irritation between Nevaeh and Brody later on, too, if Nevaeh ever thought that she might have changed Noah's mind after all… But he couldn't worry about all of those what-ifs. Life was messy and complicated. The fight seeped out of him. Had Brody been the friend he'd needed? No. But maybe he wasn't quite the villain Noah had been picturing him as, either.

"Are you ready to be a father?" Noah asked, softening his tone.

"I think so," Brody replied, and something in his gaze softened, too. They were backing away from their battle lines.

"It doesn't scare you—the thought of fatherhood and all that?" Noah asked. Because it sure scared him...

"Nevaeh and I are solid. We built a really strong friendship over the last couple of years. And I know the same people you do, Noah. Dennis and Audrey broke up when the twins turned two. And then there was Ben and Allison, Tony and Vanessa—"

All divorced couples who'd split up after the kids arrived. The men had all complained about how things changed once kids were in the picture. The women changed— they were mothers now, and there were certainly more demands on them. The relationship changed—it wasn't just about the two of them anymore. Even extended-family dynamics changed... Even for Noah's mother and Tom, it was parenting that was the problem between them. Kids didn't make relationships any easier, if other people's relationships were any indication.

"They all seemed to split up after the kids came," Noah said.

"Yeah, I know."

"You aren't daunted?" Noah asked.

That sounded like he was trying to freak Brody out, but he wasn't. He was looking for wisdom here—something he could use for his own situation.

"No, I'm not daunted," Brody replied. "What about Gabe and Cassie? They're completely in love and have three kids. Your sister and Henry are doing just fine, too. So I'm not scared. Nevaeh and I can talk about anything. And I think that's what makes us different. We don't shy away from the tough stuff. I think we'll do just fine."

Noah eyed Brody for a moment, the pieces falling into place in his mind. Brody and Nevaeh had been friends first… And Brody was probably right that the strength of their friendship would make the difference. Noah and Nevaeh had had a passionate relationship, but they'd never really been friends. What had meant the most to him when he'd met Taryn in that pub? A conversation—

being able to finally fully open up, even if it was with a stranger.

"Look, here's the way I see it," Brody said. "Romance—that comes down to sparks and passion and connection. And we have plenty of that. But raising kids—that's built on the friendship. You don't have a strong united front because of a romantic spark. Parenting is more like being soldiers in the trenches together. And it's based on a different connection. It's less about candlelight and more about high fives."

A memory popped into Noah's mind of Laura and Henry miming a high five across the kitchen. Noah had to grudgingly agree. When it came to pulling together to raise a child, that friendship just might be the difference between success and failure.

"Is that just a theory based on zero actual parenting experience, or did you hear this from someone reputable?" Noah asked.

"I read a parenting article," Brody said with a smirk.

Noah didn't answer, his mind was skipping ahead. Noah was going to be a father, like it or not, and he'd have to maintain some sort of relationship with Taryn. Maybe that was the secret—build a friendship. If parenting was more about the high fives, then maybe he and Taryn could develop that kind of connection for the sake of this little boy. They had limited time, though. Their passionate connection wasn't going to get them anywhere—not as co-parents. It would only get in their way.

"So anyway, I think we're going to be okay," Brody said, pulling Noah's attention back.

Noah was silent. Brody and Nevaeh would be fine—great. But how was Noah going to navigate being a father? He wasn't equipped for the job.

Brody eyed him. "Is this it? Our friendship is over?"

"What do you want me to do?" Noah asked, trying to keep his voice low, but not sure he was managing it.

"I know this wasn't…ideal, but I want you to recognize that we didn't try to hurt you," Brody said.

"You act like you tripped over a rock in the street," Noah said. "You *chose* this."

"No, I chose *her*." Brody's eyes glittered, daring Noah to counter that. And he couldn't. He couldn't fight whatever had tugged Brody and Nevaeh together. It was bigger than him.

"Acknowledged." Noah slid out of the

booth and stood up. He didn't want this fight after all. "I'm not holding a grudge. I'm not wishing you ill. I'm just—" Noah's voice caught with an expected swell of emotion. Everything had changed… Everything. "You two have moved on. You have to let me do the same."

Because while Noah and Nevaeh had broken up, in a way, so had Noah and Brody. That friendship, the camaraderie, the loyalty and trust—it was broken. Things weren't going back to what they used to be for any of them.

CHAPTER ELEVEN

THAT EVENING, TARYN turned off the TV and picked up a bottle of lotion to smooth into her hands before bed. Noah had surprised her today. Not only had he taken care of her when she was overheated, but he had a protective, sensitive side. She almost wished she hadn't seen it.

It would be easier to move forward with their co-parenting arrangement if he wasn't so sweet. What she needed was practicality and respect, not tenderness…not this strong, testosterone-filled attentiveness…because that was making her long for things she wasn't going to get. Not with Noah, at least.

Taryn kept remembering the rumble of his bass voice as he'd gone about her suite, getting her a cool cloth, ordering up some lemon water… She'd been somewhat judgmental of his fiancée before—a woman who didn't know what she wanted, and left pain in her wake because of it. But now Taryn felt more sympathetic to Nevaeh's plight. Noah was a very tempting man—more so than he even seemed to realize.

He'd be easy to fall for...and perhaps it'd be rather easy to tell herself lies in order to keep him.

Her phone blipped, and she glanced down, expecting a text from her mother or one of her friends.

But the text was from Noah.

You up still?

She could ignore it...go to bed and do her best to not make the same mistake Nevaeh had made with this man. That might even be smart. She paused for a moment, considering. But if she did that, she'd only be thinking about him.

I'm not a pumpkin yet, she texted back.

How are you feeling? he asked.

She smiled at that. I'm fine. I was just overheated. No need to worry.

Good. There was a pause, then, Just checking.

He wanted to talk—she could sense it. What had happened with his friend? For all of Noah's anger over that betrayal, he wasn't over it.

Did you see Brody tonight? she asked.

I did. Another long pause, and she almost put her phone down when he added, Am I crazy to think the friendship should be over after what happened?

He wants to stay friends? she typed.

He seems to, he replied. I think he wants me to forgive him.

Taryn pursed her lips in thought. She'd never seen men's friendships close up before. Glen had a few buddies, but nowhere near as close as Noah and Brody seemed to have been. And yet friendships mattered…friendships could be healing, as she was discovering with the Second Chance Dinner Club.

What did you say? she asked.

Nothing much. I said they're moving on, and I need to do the same.

She couldn't blame Noah for that response, and it seemed mature and measured. Still, she noticed something.

You're staying up thinking about it… Was it cruel to point that out?

He didn't answer at first, and she looked down at the screen, wondering if she'd overstepped. Then he called her.

"Hi," she said, picking up. "I don't know if that came off as a little mean—"

"No." He laughed softly. "It didn't. This is just easier than typing."

"So what happened?" she asked.

"He wants to make peace. He says they didn't mean to hurt me, and I believe that. I guess I hadn't realized my best friend was in love with my girlfriend. Am I completely unobservant?"

"Maybe," she chuckled. "Maybe not. You trusted them both. That isn't a bad thing."

"I suppose," he said. "I feel like an idiot, though."

Taryn sat on the edge of the bed. "You miss Brody, don't you?"

"No, I—" He stopped.

"You can admit it," she said.

He let out an audible breath.

"Of the two of them, I feel like losing my friendship with him hurt more," he said. "And I don't know what that says about Nevaeh and me—she probably made the right choice in breaking things off. But Brody and I were friends since we were kids. We backed each other up in scuffles, and we confided in each other when we had crushes on girls… He was my best friend, and we never did drift apart like normally happens over the years. We stayed tight. Until now."

"Until Nevaeh," she said softly.

"I guess so…" He sounded sad.

"I think friendships matter," she said. "For what it's worth."

"Speaking of friendships, Brody said something tonight," Noah said. "He was talking about some parenting article he read. Apparently, if the mom and dad have a solid friendship, the parenting is easier. It's not based on the romance," Noah said. "He told me parenting is less about candlelight and more about high fives. I think that's how he said it."

Not based on the romance... Something inside her wanted to argue that just a little bit. Their situation—raising a child outside of a committed romantic relationship— wasn't exactly the ideal...not for her, at least.

"But kids don't have to kill romance," she said. "I get what you're saying, that we have hope of raising our son well and still liking each other in the process. And I appreciate that. But for the record, I know plenty of happily married couples with children. You notice them more when you want a baby and can't seem to have one..."

"I'm not saying you won't...have that."

A husband... Did she dare hope for some romance of her own? The universe had handed her the desire of her heart in the form of this baby. She hadn't expected romance, too.

"It's okay," she said, and she forced a laugh. "You don't have to worry about my romantic life. I'll sort it out."

Noah was silent for a beat, then he said, "Well, Brody's point was about his compatibility for a lifetime of happiness with Nevaeh, so... He has no idea about our son. He was saying that because Nevaeh was with me, they developed a friendship. And because of that friendship, he figures they'll have the parenting down pat." He was silent for a moment. "It got me to thinking about us. I know you a little, but not well enough. And vice versa. I was thinking it might be good for us to get to know each other better...as friends."

Having known his kisses and his strong embraces, a simple friendship felt anticlimactic. But he was right—they needed to think ahead.

"I can see the wisdom there," she admitted.

"Right?" He sounded more enthusiastic now. "I watched my sister and her husband dealing with my nephew the other day, and they have this great united front. They back each other up, and they get results. You and

I could definitely have each other's backs—right?"

"Definitely," she replied. He was offering emotional support—and now she knew that she wouldn't turn that down.

"You sound…sad about that?" he said.

"No, no…" She let out a breath. "I'm adjusting. I think it's good that there is some science to back up our plan."

"Well, in the spirit of getting to know each other better," Noah said, "how would you feel about coming to my place for dinner tomorrow night?"

Dinner at his home… Noah had no idea how tempting he was, did he? But she'd have to adjust to that fact, too.

"You can taste my cooking, you can see how I live, look at a few photo albums…" He paused, and she could feel the hope in his voice.

Hadn't Belle's romance faded over the sharing of photo albums? But this wasn't a romance—that was their current strength.

"Sure," she said. "That sounds nice."

"Great. So tomorrow after work, I'll bring you to my apartment and you can silently judge me," he said, his tone teasing.

She laughed softly. 'It's a date."

"It's late, I should let you go," he said.

"All right," she agreed, glancing at the clock. "I'll see you in the morning."

"See you." His voice was low and warm, and she tried not to enjoy it. Did he have to be so attractive?

She ended the call and plugged her phone into its charger. Having this baby would have all been so much simpler if she hadn't found Noah again, but he'd offered something she'd never have expected.

Maybe it was that lonely, moody time of night, or maybe it was pregnancy hormones, but his offer of friendship, while pragmatic, felt just a little bit heartbreaking. It was so much less than she'd dreamed for herself at this stage of life.

Being a single mom wouldn't be easy, and she'd heard of enough women fighting with the fathers of their children after a nasty breakup... If she and Noah could avoid all that, they might have the kind of friendship that would carry them through all the ups and downs awaiting them.

She pulled back the covers and slid into the crisp, cool sheets. She'd have to think it over in the light of day. Because despite her attempt to be logical, her heart was still just a little bit heavy.

THE NEXT MORNING, Taryn ordered up a simple breakfast of oatmeal and some sliced fruit to her room. And after a good sleep, Noah's offer of getting to know each other seemed less heartbreaking. She'd heard enough complaints from women who were constantly frustrated with their kids' fathers. A respectful relationship with her baby's father would be incredibly helpful. But Taryn and Noah could be a step ahead of them—no romantic hopes or disappointments between them, and mutual respect, too.

Because Taryn honestly liked Noah. If they'd met some other way...if he'd been a guy who was open to having kids...she could have fallen for him in a heartbeat. In fact, she had on that night in Denver—it was why she ran away. She'd seen just how dangerous he was to her peace of mind.

When Taryn had finished eating, she got dressed into a pink business-style dress, and she did her makeup and pulled her hair back into her usual twist. Then she headed downstairs to start her day.

The campaign was coming together nicely. She already had a selection of shareable content—photos with some quotes, and brief stories from guests and employees alike talking about what the resort meant to them. She'd written a couple of articles about what Mountain Springs Resort had to offer, and she had a whole array of photographs that showed different rooms in the lodge, close-ups of details like the sparkling crystals of a chandelier and the deep plush of the carpet that went up the center of the massive staircase.

And then there were the pictures of the lake…those felt more personal now. Maybe Lisa, the writer, was right about the soul-deep draw of the lake and mountains. For Taryn, they were now connected to Noah. Whenever she looked at them, she remembered what it felt like to be pulled into that man's arms, his lips coming down over hers, the warmth of breath against her face, the strength in his hands as they ran down her arms…

"Taryn?"

She startled, pulling out of her thoughts. Belle stood in the foyer. She wore a long, rust-colored ombré dress that hung beautifully off her lithe figure. An oversize pair of sunglasses sat on her hair, and she smiled at Taryn.

"Hi, Belle," Taryn said, and she headed across the foyer toward her. "What brings you by?"

They met in the center of the foyer, and Taryn noticed that Belle's usually impeccable makeup looked mussed. Had she been crying?

"Are you okay?" Taryn asked.

"Oh—" Belle ran a finger under her eyeliner "—I'm fine. Philip wanted to talk, and I thought it would be easier for me to do it here. It reminds me of our dinner club, and keeps my feet on the ground."

"You're broken up, though?" Taryn asked delicately.

"We are," Belle replied. "This is just part of the unraveling, and I suppose I owe him that much."

"I don't think you owe him anything," Taryn replied.

Belle licked her lips. "I do want to explain why I'm breaking up with him. That's for me."

"And that's fair," Taryn agreed.

The front door opened, and a lanky man came inside. He had receding blond hair and a pair of dark rimmed glasses. He looked gentle, cerebral, maybe even a little bit shy in the way he held himself. He wore jeans and a button-up shirt, and when he looked at Belle, Taryn saw him freeze, his eyes filled with emotion.

"That's him," Belle said softly.

"He's not what I expected," Taryn admitted. Although she wasn't sure what she'd expected with Philip. No man really seemed to be a natural match for Belle's beauty.

"Well… I'd better—" Belle looked toward Philip again, and she straightened her shoulders.

"Yes, of course," Taryn said. "Good luck…"

Belle crossed the foyer toward Philip, and they moved toward the dining room. Philip's hand hovered over Belle's back for a moment, and then he let it drop.

Taryn felt a wave of sympathy for both of them. Breakups were never easy, and no matter how well-thought-out and logical the reasons a couple had for calling it quits, it hurt.

As Taryn reached her temporary office, she let out a slow breath. This was why it was best to keep things strictly platonic between her and Noah. Whatever she'd felt when Noah kissed her, when he stood protectively over her, when he smiled and caught her eye… Whatever that man could make her feel, she needed to keep her heart protected.

Belle and Philip could choose to never see

each other again if they wanted to—Taryn and Noah weren't going to get that luxury.

WHEN ANGELINA POKED her head into Noah's office that evening, he gave his boss a tired smile.

"Hi," he said. "Heading out?"

"I have a vendor coming by, and I was wondering if you wanted to sit in on this meeting," Angelina replied.

Noah was usually available for impromptu meetings like this, but not tonight.

He glanced down at his watch. "Actually, I've got plans tonight, so I can't stick around."

"Oh!" Angelina nodded. "No problem. I knew it was short notice. I'll take care of this one myself."

"Thanks," he said.

Angelina turned as Taryn came up behind her.

"Hi, Taryn," Noah said. "I'm just done here."

"Perfect," Taryn replied, and she cast a smile at Angelina.

Angelina's eyebrows went up. "You two have a good night."

She disappeared down the hall, Taryn watching her.

"It looks like a date," he said, keeping his voice low. It looked like a blossoming romance—maybe even slightly inappropriate considering that they were professionally connected.

Taryn smiled wanly. "A little difficult to explain, isn't it?"

"A little," he agreed. "Don't worry. Angelina is a big respecter of boundaries. I doubt she'd even ask me about it."

But she'd wonder. How long was he going to be able to go before he told people the truth about Taryn and the baby—that he was going to be a father? His friends here in Mountain Springs would all be pretty shocked, and it would be weird with Nevaeh and Brody… It would be easier to navigate from Seattle—a little more distance, and less chance of bumping into people every other day.

He turned off his computer and stood up. "All right, let's head out."

Noah lived in an apartment on the far end of town. As they drove around the lake toward town, Noah couldn't help but notice the way Taryn ran her hand over her belly in slow circles. Was he kicking in there?

"So, how many other jobs do you have

scheduled before the baby comes?" Noah asked.

"I have two more," she said. "I've worked for both places before, and they're okay with remote work, so I won't have to travel."

"That's good," he said.

She cast him a sidelong look.

"I just meant—" He laughed uncomfortably. "I'm not supposed to have an opinion on that, am I?"

"I'll forgive it," she said with a small smile. "But I'm fine. I'm a planner. I always make sure I know where my income is coming from—it's under control."

He believed in her competence. It was one of the things he'd liked from the start—even at her lowest, she'd been in control.

"I'm curious to see where you live," she added.

"Yeah?" He signaled a turn.

"It's the best way to get to know someone," she said.

She'd see it all—his too-tidy ways, his music collection, his library… The books on a man's shelf spoke more than anything else.

"But we're going to really do this, right? Get to know each other—open up?" he asked.

"We'll try." She shot him a smile, and he couldn't help but return it.

This was backward—all of it. But he was looking forward to an evening with her all the same.

Noah's apartment was in a new building with all the modern conveniences. There was an indoor pool, a gym and, from his suite, a stunning view of the mountains. After parking underground, he led the way to the elevator, and they headed up to the eighth floor.

"Here we are," he said as he led the way in, flicking on lights as he went. The air-conditioning kept the apartment comfortably cool, and he watched her as she surveyed the apartment.

His living room sported low leather couches, some prints of famous paintings on his walls and a few framed black-and-white photos of his ancestors. The room was lit by standing lamps, and a couple of sheepskin throws warmed up the couches. Taryn glanced back at him.

"This is beautiful."

"Thanks." He'd worked hard to create this space for himself, and it had taken a couple of years to get everything to his liking. Would it all transplant to Seattle and end up being this comfortable and cozy? And even though Seattle would be easier in some ways, it would be farther away from Taryn and the baby, and that didn't sit comfortably.

Taryn crossed the room to the family photos, and he left her looking at them while he washed his hands and started pulling ingredients out of the fridge.

"Who are they?" Taryn asked.

"My grandparents on my mother's side," he said. "Dad left and we never did have much from his side of the family." He turned on the gas stove and put a pot of water over the heat.

Taryn was silent again for a couple of minutes while he worked.

"This man looks like you," she said. He knew the picture she was talking about. It was a portrait of a man in his forties with a full beard and an intense stare. "Well...you when you had the beard, at least."

"My great-grandfather," he said. "Yeah, there's a family resemblance."

She looked at him over her shoulder. "Do you look alike without the beard?"

"No idea," he said with a chuckle. "We have no photos of my great-grandfather without it."

She turned to face him, one hand resting on her belly. "Do you mind if I use your washroom? This little guy is standing on my bladder."

"Yeah, sure—" He pointed down the hallway. "Feel free."

Dinner wasn't going to take much preparation. He had some chicken already cooked and sliced, and there was a jar of Alfredo sauce that was pretty good. With some freshly grated parmesan, the meal would be downright acceptable.

He heard the bathroom door open again as he was setting the table, but Taryn didn't appear. He put the utensils down by the plates, and then ambled in the direction of his library.

It was actually the second bedroom of this apartment that he'd turned into a library. He liked the coziness of the room, and the walls lined with mahogany bookshelves, packed with hardcover copies of his favorite books. He stopped in the open doorway and surveyed the room. There was a Persian-styled rug that covered the hardwood floor, a leather wingback chair in one corner, and the rest of the room was encircled by shelves, the space between the shelves and the ceiling filled with gilt-framed pencil drawings of castle ruins. Taryn stood near the gas fireplace he'd had installed.

"Wow…" she murmured.

"Thanks."

Taryn turned. "You aren't what I expected."

"What did you expect?" he asked.

"I don't know…more sports memorabilia, maybe?"

He chuckled. "Have I once mentioned sports?"

"No, I just thought it might fit in there," she replied.

"I have a few baseball cards somewhere if you wanted me to dig them out."

"That's okay." She cast him a sparkling smile and moved closer to a bookshelf, touching the spines of the books with one finger. "You like the classics."

"Yeah, I always did."

"*Frankenstein*, *Dracula*, *The Three Musketeers*…" She turned toward him with a twinkle in her eye. "You do have a bit of the noble knight in you, don't you? You have a sense of right and wrong, and you have a tendency to rescue people."

"You got that from my taste in literature?" he asked.

"That, and the fact that you don't blame your ex for calling off the wedding," she said. "That's noble of you."

"It wasn't her fault."

"A lot of guys might have blamed her if she was hoping to change your mind about having a family," she said.

Noah wasn't sure what to say. "I *do* believe in right and wrong."

"You should be careful with that," she said quietly, turning away from him again.

"What—be careful with moral fiber?" he said.

"It can lead you in very noble directions that you ultimately don't want to go in," she said.

Did she really think that she was such a poor catch—that ending up with her would be such a disappointment for a man? Her divorce had chipped away at her confidence—he could see that plainly. Did she not look in the mirror and see the stunning beauty that she was? Hell, he'd looked at her across a bar and felt drawn to her as a perfect stranger, and now that he knew her better, seeing her ensconced in all the trappings of his home that made him feel safe and secure, he couldn't take his eyes off of her.

"Did it ever occur to you that your ex-husband might have *wanted* to marry you?" he asked. "Maybe he took one look at you and thought he'd never find another woman quite as wonderful as you—and the baby had less to do with it than you thought."

Taryn didn't turn, but her whole body stilled.

"Sometimes people change," he went on. "Maybe both of you did. I don't know. I'm only guessing. All I'm saying is, from where I'm standing, it's pretty easy for me to believe that a guy took one look at you and fell hard."

She turned at last, and when she met his gaze, her gaze shone like burnished leather in the low light of the library. She took a wavering breath.

"Then why leave me for another woman?" she asked.

"That's a man who didn't have *enough* nobility in him," he replied. "The problem there isn't having too much." He took a step closer, and he reached out and touched her arm. "I hate to make it so annoyingly simple, but some men are just stupid."

She smiled at that, then rolled her eyes and shook her head. "So how do you know when a man isn't one of the stupid ones?"

"Find a guy who reads," he said, a slow, flirtatious smile tugging at his lips. She gave him a hesitant look, and he felt a pang of guilt for his flirting, so he added, "Just not me. That would complicate matters."

She laughed softly. "That's a given."

Even though he agreed, and even though he knew all the reasons they didn't match, her words stung just a little.

Noah nodded toward the door. "You hungry? Dinner's ready."

"I'm starving," she said, and her relaxed smile warmed something inside him.

This was the mother of his child, and while they both knew he couldn't offer more, he'd feed her. It was the most basic thing he could offer... They'd find their balance here, eventually.

CHAPTER TWELVE

NOAH HAD MADE a simple, delicious dinner of fettuccine Alfredo, and they'd chatted as they ate. Taryn had started to relax more in this calm, orderly space. This was his safe place—she could feel it. But there wasn't room here for more than Noah—there wasn't any clutter, any opportunity for another person to add their touch to the decor. There certainly wasn't space for children.

"You're very clean," Taryn said as she took her last bite of pasta.

"People say that," he said with a low laugh.

"Do they?" she joked. "Who else has told you that?"

"Every woman in my life," he said. "My sister finds it annoying." He eyed her for a moment. "Can I guess? I think you're my opposite. I bet you love some cozy clutter."

"Why would you assume that?" she asked with mock defensiveness.

"Because opposites attract," he said with a wink. "And I know that you and I are keeping this strictly platonic, but you have to admit that we do…attract."

They did, and she felt her face warm. "I'm not messy," she said. "But I'm probably less organized at home. I haven't figured out where I'm putting all the baby stuff yet, although I do have the nursery set up. The one place that is meticulously organized is my office, and that's because I don't mess with the success of my business."

"Hmm." He looked at her thoughtfully. "That's interesting."

"Is it?" she asked.

Noah shrugged. "It's just good to know. I mean…to understand you better."

"How were you raised?" she asked. "Was your mom strict?"

"That's a good question," he said. "Do you want to come sit in the living room, get more comfortable?"

"Sure." She carried her glass of apple juice to the couch and got settled, tucking one leg up underneath herself.

Noah opened a cabinet and pulled out a photo album, then brought it over to the couch. He sat down next to her. She couldn't fit the album on her lap because of her belly, so he held it on his, and she opened it.

"My mom was pretty strict," he confirmed. "She was really honest with us. She told us that life wasn't going to give us unlimited chances, so we had to make good choices and make the most of our opportunities."

Taryn glanced up at him. "That's wise."

"Yeah. She was practical that way. I remember her telling me more than once that I wasn't any more special than anyone else's child on this planet, and that I needed to remember that. I might be her favorite boy in the world, but I wasn't going to be anyone else's." He was silent for a moment. "When she died, I couldn't help but remember those words... I'd lost the one person who loved me unconditionally."

Taryn felt her eyes mist. "She was a good mom."

"A good mom makes all the difference," he murmured.

Taryn flipped through the first few pages of the album. There were baby pictures of Noah, and Taryn looked a little closer at those. They were quickly followed by toddler photos, and then his sister was born, and there were photos with a toddler and infant together... Their mother beamed proudly in the background of the photos, her hair permed.

"You haven't changed much," she said, looking down at a toddler photo of Noah grinning into the camera with spaghetti on his face. He had the kind of grin that aged but stayed fundamentally the same, and she touched the photo with a fingertip.

"Yeah, you can tell it's me, can't you?" he agreed.

"The lack of beard did throw me when I saw you again," Taryn said, and she looked up at him. "I can't believe I didn't recognize your eyes, though…"

Noah stroked a hand down his stubbled chin, and his warm gaze met hers. "I recognized you immediately."

"Did you panic?" she asked with a teasing smile.

"Uh—" He shrugged. "A bit. Yeah."

"You're staying honest," she said.

"Yup." He flipped a page and pointed to a picture of a shirtless man in denim shorts, sitting on a step with a toddler Noah leaning against his leg. "That's the only picture I have of my dad and I together."

Taryn looked closer. The man appeared distracted, but the toddler was looking straight into the camera.

"Your mom must have been crushed when he left…" she murmured.

"Yeah. I think so. I mean, I don't remember it, but she said she never saw it coming."

And that would be the hardest part—the shock of realizing that her husband had been planning this exit, and she hadn't known. Taryn had felt something similar when she found out about Glen's affair. Two years of lies, of hiding this relationship, and she'd never once suspected.

"And that's Tom," he said, flipping another page.

The photo was a wedding picture showing Noah's mother with a bearded man dressed in a black suit. She glanced toward Noah— the beard he'd had was similar to his stepfather's. The man's influence on Noah's life had been strong. It was interesting to think what kind of relationship the two men might have had if Tom and Noah's mother had stayed together.

Taryn flipped through a few more pages— this was where the family photos really seemed to start. There were smiles and laughter, playing and birthday cakes.

"Those were good years," Noah murmured. He slid an arm behind her back— more a movement to get more comfortable, but she could feel the warmth of his arm behind her and it felt safe. The baby shifted, and she adjusted her position, too, leaning toward Noah ever so slightly. She put her hand over the spot where the baby was stretching.

"He's waking up in there," she said.

"Yeah?" Noah looked down at her belly, and she could see the sudden wash of tenderness over his features. She took his hand and pressed it against the spot, and Noah was motionless for a moment. The baby stretched again.

"Wow," he murmured. "He's really moving."

"He does that…" She smiled.

"Feeling him move makes it feel more real, somehow," he said.

"For you?" she asked. "I could see that. For me, he's with me all the same—standing on my bladder, poking me in the ribs, rolling around in there…"

Noah smiled, and he didn't pull his hand away. He moved it to the top of her belly, and the baby seemed to want to push at him again, so she felt him roll inside of her.

"So how were you raised?" he asked softly.

"Well…" Taryn watched his hand as he moved it gently in a little circle. "My parents were both college educated, so school was really important in our home. I have three sisters—all married. Only one has kids, though, and she lives in Brazil right now."

"Wow."

Taryn nodded. "My mom homeschooled us for the first few years, and the first year I went to public school was grade five."

"Is that something you'd want to do?" he asked.

Taryn shook her head. "No, not me. I have to keep working."

"Yeah. Of course." He stopped moving his hand, and he looked up at her. "What's the important stuff for raising this little guy? What's the nonnegotiable stuff?"

"I want him to be raised with books and reading," she said.

"I like that."

"And I want him to experience as much as possible. I want to take him to art galleries and museums, take him camping and show him wildlife..."

"Do you think you'd ever let me take him camping?" Noah asked.

She froze. "Um..."

"When he's older, of course," he said.

She felt a rush of anxiety at that thought. They'd agreed to complete honesty, hadn't they?

"I can't even imagine letting him out of my

arms right now," she said. "And one of the things that I liked about not knowing who you were was that I wouldn't have to share custody. I don't want to give him up for a few days, or a few weeks, even. I—" She felt tears mist her eyes. She didn't want to cry about it, but she did need him to understand.

"Hey…" His voice was low. "It's okay. Maybe that's too far in the future to even talk about yet. I think for now, we can plan to keep this baby in your arms."

She felt a wave of relief at that. "Are you just saying that?"

"Taryn—" He reached out and moved her hair away from her face. His warm touch lingered against her temple. "I'm not trying to overstep. You're calling all the shots, okay?"

She leaned her cheek into his touch, and let out a slow breath. "It must be the hormones. I'm not normally this emotional. For the record."

He leaned in and pressed a kiss against her forehead, his five-o'clock shadow tickling her skin. He smelled musky and good, and he didn't pull back all the way. He looked down at her, his dark gaze softening as his eyes moved over her face.

"Are we going to be any good at parenting together?" she whispered.

"Yup," he murmured. "We are."

"What makes you so sure?"

"I know who the boss is." A smile flickered at the corners of his lips.

She chuckled, and before she could think better of it, she reached up and touched his stubbly chin. He was different than he'd been seven months ago. He'd been intoxicating back then, but now he was alluring in a new way. Perhaps that just came with knowing him better...

Noah leaned in toward her, and she could feel his strong torso press against the side of her belly. His hand moved gently over the top of her bump, and he paused a couple of inches before his lips touched hers.

It would be so easy to lean into him, to let him kiss her, to shut her eyes and forget about all the very good reasons not to do this...

"I told myself I'd open up with you tonight," he murmured.

"I should take advantage of that," she said, and she pulled back.

Kissing him would be the easy way out. She wasn't here for that.

"What do you want to know?" he asked softly.

She was silent for a moment, and her gaze

moved down to the photo album. The photo of his stepfather was still front and center. That relationship had formed him...she could feel it.

"All right, then..." She hesitated, and then licked her lips. "Why haven't you contacted Tom before this?"

THAT WASN'T QUITE the kind of question Noah expected, and he paused. What was worrying her? Was there something about Tom she didn't like? Funny how even opening up with her made him realize how little he knew her. He could forget that detail when looking down at her plump lips.

"Tom isn't going to be a part of this baby's life," he said.

"I know," she said. "I'm just wondering."

She tapped a picture of Tom and Noah sitting side by side on the couch, a bowl of chips between them. He remembered that day—it was the middle of summer, and they'd both been hot. There had been some oscillating fans running, and Tom and Noah were watching TV together. Laura had been annoyed because it wasn't a show she liked.

"You might look like your mother's side of the family," Taryn said. "There's no denying that. But you've patterned yourself after your stepdad."

Noah looked down at the photo.

"You grew your beard the same," she clarified. "You even sit like him."

Noah looked at the photo—Tom's arm was over the back of the couch, just like Noah was sitting next to Taryn right now. He frowned. He'd figured he'd turned out a bit like Tom by happenstance, not that he'd mimicked the guy.

"I never noticed that," he admitted.

"He meant a lot to you," she said.

"Yeah, he did," he agreed. "But he wasn't worthy of being copied, either. My biological father left us and never looked back. My stepdad was booted out, but he didn't fight for a relationship with us."

"It might have been complicated," she murmured.

"It was definitely complicated," he agreed. "But..." He swallowed. "He might have been a fun stepdad, but he made my mom cry a lot. I remember lying in bed at night listening to them argue. Mom would point out how he was being immature and not manning up to the job, and he'd come back with some comment I wouldn't quite understand, but then I'd hear her cry. It would rip my heart out to hear her weep. He made her cry a lot."

"And you still liked him?" Taryn asked.

His relationship with his stepfather was hard to explain—even to family. He felt like he betrayed his mother by loving Tom like he had...

"I—" He felt that old wave of guilt. "I did. He was fun. And he was a guy. He understood me in a way my mom and sister didn't. I felt terrible about it, because I loved my mom, obviously, but I loved Tom too. And I *knew* he was mean to her."

Noah leaned forward, resting his elbows on his knees. He'd just been a kid... He hadn't known how to navigate any of it. Maybe he still didn't.

"Is that why you never did contact him?" Taryn asked. "Loyalty to your mom?"

"Loyalty, guilt," he said. "Take your pick. We were the guys in the family, and I don't think we took very good care of my mom."

"You were pretty small to be able to take care of an adult woman," she said softly.

Noah looked down at that picture of himself. He was maybe six or seven, and he'd been small for his age.

"That doesn't matter in the heart of a boy," he said, meeting her gaze. "There's something hardwired into us to want to protect, and slay some dragons. Call it nobility or whatever you like, but even as little boys we want to be the hero who makes things better."

"Did you ever say anything to him about how he treated your mother?" she asked.

"No." Another regret. He'd hidden those angry feelings away, because if he said anything, he'd been afraid that Tom would stop taking him out, stop calling him "buddy," stop loving him...

"I didn't know how to discuss things that big, and he left when I was ten. I used to beat myself up about it until some of my friends had kids who hit the age of ten and I realized how young it really is. You look back on your childhood and imbue your memories with adult ability. But I was just a kid."

"Ten is very young," Taryn said softly.

"I didn't talk to him again after he left, so there was no chance to bring it up later. And now, he's moved on with his life, and Mom is gone. There's nothing left to say, really."

He'd been telling himself, at least. Did he have anything left to say to the only father he'd ever known about how he'd made his mother cry those bitter, heartbroken tears?

"I wonder if Tom regrets any of it," she said.

"I don't know. He said he regretted not getting in touch with me and my sister again. That's something. But he didn't mention Mom."

Noah sucked in a breath. He'd been putting off getting into any discussions with his ex-stepfather. But maybe there was something to discuss with Tom after all... Maybe it would do Noah good—some redemption for the boy who couldn't be man enough to protect his mom from cruel words, or man enough to choose *her*.

"Tom isn't a part of my life anymore," Noah said. "But my sister is. And my niece and nephews. They're great kids, and Laura is an excellent mom. Maybe...you'd want to meet them sometime. Meeting people's families tends to give you a wide-open window into why they are the way they are. It might be more educational than Tom."

And he'd rather introduce her to the people who'd stayed in his life than focus on the ones who hadn't.

"I think I'd like that," she said, and she shot him a smile.

An idea had occurred to him...one that was less about showing Taryn who he was than it was about getting a little more time with her, but still—

"My sister asked me to babysit this weekend," Noah said. "I don't normally babysit, but she wanted a date night with Henry, and I agreed. Do you feel like seeing my family and finding out what I'm actually like around kids? It's not going to instill any confidence in you, but I could use a hand."

"Sure." She nodded. "I'd like to see you in action." Then she paused and shot him an uncertain look.

"What?" he said.

"I'm going to see my grandmother tomorrow," she said. "In the spirit of getting to know each other's families a little bit, would you like to meet her?"

Noah couldn't help the smile that tugged at his lips. He'd heard enough about this old lady to be intrigued.

"She has no idea that you're the father," Taryn added. "And she'll probably say all sorts of dated, old-fashioned and possibly offensive things. Heads up."

"I'm not easily shocked," he replied. "Should I drive?"

He wanted to lock this down before either of them backed out. This was also why they needed a solid friendship. Their son was going to have more family than just a mom and a dad.

"I can't talk you back out of it?" she asked with a nervous laugh.

"Hey, you'll see me with kids, so it's only fair that I see you with your grandmother. I think it will be good for us in the long run. Besides, you act like I've never met a stubborn old lady before."

"All right," she said, and he shot her a grin.

He wasn't going to be the only one showing his weaknesses, and the chance to see her family before she saw his felt good. Besides, he was looking forward to getting a glimpse at the family behind this woman—the people who formed her and raised her. Appreciating how a woman fit into his arms was only one kind of knowledge. Understanding how she fit into a family—now, that was intimacy.

CHAPTER THIRTEEN

As Taryn headed upstairs, her mind kept going back to that moment on his couch when she'd thought he'd kiss her. Why was this man so attractive to her? That was what she wanted to know. Of all the potential men to get romantically involved with, Noah was the worst choice. Whatever they were feeling for each other was strictly chemical. She was pregnant with his child—that was bound to cause some confusing feelings between them… She liked the sensation of his strong arms around her. It made her feel safe and cared for in the moment. But this searing attraction was like the honeymoon phase of a marriage. The novelty wore off—it always did. That simmering, slow smile of his would change over time, and when it did, she didn't want it to hurt.

Noah was going to be in her life, so she needed to keep things respectful and simple between them.

But now, she was nervous that she wasn't

making these decisions as a woman building a parenting relationship with this man. Instead, she was reacting on an emotional level...maybe even a chemical one. And she couldn't do that. Her child deserved better than inheriting an emotional mess his mother had created when she could have set up a truly balanced and happy relationship with his biological father.

She dug her key card out of her purse and let herself into the room. She kicked off her heels and dropped her purse onto the dresser with a sigh.

Her phone rang and she looked down at it, half expecting, maybe even hoping, to see Noah's number. The name that popped up was Belle Villeneuve.

"Belle?" she said, picking up the call.

"Hi," Belle said. "Are you still up?"

"Yeah, I'm just relaxing. What's going on? How did that lunch go with Philip?"

"It went...well, not great," Belle said. "I explained why I broke it off with him, and he understood. He has his own stuff he's been dealing with, too, and it just seemed like it wasn't going to work with us. We were both really sad. But that isn't why I called."

"Oh?" Taryn said.

"I'm pregnant."

"What?" Taryn couldn't help but smile. "That's wonderful…isn't it?"

"The timing is miserable," Belle said. "I only just found out. I was late—like a month and a half late—and I had myself convinced it was early menopause."

"Oh, Belle," Taryn laughed.

"Yeah, well, it wasn't," Belle said with a chuckle. "I'm two months' pregnant. I haven't even told Philip yet."

"When will you tell him?" Taryn asked.

"I don't know… I'm scared of what he'll say, honestly. We've only been dating for six months, and we just broke up and got back together… This wasn't planned."

"Wait, you're back together?" Taryn asked.

"Yeah…and it wasn't because of the pregnancy, either. We talked about a lot of his insecurities. Basically, his ex cheated on him, so he's gun-shy."

"Understandable," Taryn murmured.

"I told him that I'm sick of being treated like I'm either stupid, or untrustworthy because of my face," she said. "Just because men want me doesn't mean I'm available. I'm tired of being chosen, and with Philip, I chose the man I wanted. And if that doesn't give him any sense of security, then I was done."

"And he said?" Taryn prompted.

"He said I was right," she said. "He apologized. He asked if he could have another chance and take me to the wedding to meet his family. Family is going to mean even more going forward."

"And you haven't told him about the baby yet?" Taryn asked.

"No. I was thinking about what you said about your ex-husband, how he wanted to be with you because of a pregnancy, and how that didn't make up for anything else in your relationship."

"But Philip isn't Glen," she said.

"Maybe not," Belle said softly. "But as much as I want a regular guy, I also want him to be with me because he loves me, not because he feels like he owes me."

"I think he'll be happy about the baby," Taryn said. "For what it's worth."

"I think so, too," Belle said. "It's just all happening really quickly, and a baby changes things. A baby *complicates* things."

Taryn let out a slow breath. "Yeah. It does."

A baby took a relationship and changed it into a family—vows or not. And that family could be in one home or spread over two, but they'd never stop belonging to each other once that child arrived.

"Do we even have what it takes to last?" Belle asked. "Philip has a lot of great characteristics, but he's not terribly secure in our relationship."

"I don't know…" Taryn said softly.

They were both silent for a couple of beats, and Taryn's heart squeezed in sympathy. Belle might be stunningly beautiful, but she had all the same problems the rest of them had.

"Have you told Renata yet?" Taryn asked.

"Oh, yes," Belle said. "She's very supportive. I suppose I came to you because you're going to raise your child alone, and… Well, it doesn't matter. I just thought you might understand."

"I do," Taryn assured her. "Of anyone, I understand how complicated this is. And no one can tell you what's right for you and your baby. I'm happy for you, though. A baby is good news—always."

"Thank you," Belle said softly. "I needed to hear that."

After they'd said their goodbyes, Taryn sank onto the edge of the bed.

Was Belle going to regret choosing Philip? Would they have what it took to make a marriage work…to make a *family* work?

If Taryn had learned one thing, it was that

when adults struggled through a breakup, it wasn't just the grownup hearts that got mangled. The kids were dragged through it, too.

She thought of the photo of Noah as a little boy sitting next to his stepfather. Just one little boy who loved his stepdad and his mother, and felt responsible for the ugliness of a relationship breaking down. One little boy whose heart had never recovered.

Taryn couldn't knowingly put her son through that... Belle might take a chance on Philip, and she'd wish them well. But the risk was no longer about two hearts; it was now about that third little heartbeat that she listened to every time she went to see her obstetrician.

Belle would have to make her own decisions, but that third heartbeat had to be Taryn's priority.

NOAH SAT IN the leather chair in his library, a book open on his lap, but he'd stopped trying to read. He was thinking about Taryn. He'd almost kissed her tonight...again. And he knew all the reasons to keep his emotional distance here, so why was that proving so difficult?

He pushed his glasses up on his face and stared at a bookshelf, his mind chewing over the problem. Maybe it would help to see each other's families—pop this bubble that surrounded just the two of them with their secret. Maybe seeing her grandmother and watching Taryn interact with her would help him to see her as any other woman and put the brakes on his snowballing feelings here.

That was the hope.

And letting her see his family—see him for who he really was, not for who he might pretend to be—that was important, too. Parenting with her, visiting her, talking with her on the phone, was all going to feel a lot more intimate than they were aiming at, and he had to get his balance now.

His cell phone rang, pulling him out of his thoughts. He looked down at the number. The area code was from Seattle. Was this about the interview?

He picked up the call. "Hello, Noah Brooks here."

"Noah, hi, this is Ellen from Oceanside Hotel. How are you tonight?"

He glanced at his watch. It was pretty late to be calling for professional purposes.

"I'm doing alright," he replied. "How are you?"

"I'm doing well. I'm glad I caught you tonight because I have to head out on business early tomorrow morning."

"It's no problem," he said. "It's not too late at all."

"I also wish I had better news for you," she said.

"Oh…" So this wasn't good news.

"It was a tight race," Ellen said. "In the end we chose a different candidate, but there was a lot of debate before the decision was made. I want you to know how much we appreciated meeting you, and how impressed we were with your résumé and all of your experience. This is a pretty small industry, so maybe we'll be able to work together in the future sometime."

"That would be great," he said. "It was a pleasure to meet you, too. Thanks for the personal call. I appreciate it."

"Not a problem. You have a good night, Noah."

As he hung up, Noah pursed his lips and sat motionless for a few beats. Then he tossed his phone onto the shelf next to him.

His escape from Mountain Springs wasn't going to be quite so easy now, and he searched for an emotional reaction to this news. Seattle was supposed to be his fresh start away from all the drama of Mountain

Springs, yet he didn't feel a wave of disappointment at this news.

Instead, he felt relief.

Taryn was in Colorado, and if he stayed here, he'd be that much closer to her if she needed help. If she needed...*him.*

He wasn't reining in his emotions surrounding Taryn very well, was he? But this baby was arriving in two months, and his life was about to change. So was Taryn's. But more than that, he realized in a rush that when Taryn had the baby, he wanted to be there...

If she'd let him.

He'd never thought about anything like this before—being present for his child's delivery. Holding his son in his arms, making sure that the mother of his child had everything she might need... That was something he'd written off for other people to experience.

When Taryn needed help with something, he wanted to be her first call. And when that little boy thought about his dad, Noah didn't want him to face all the uncertainty that Noah had faced as a boy. He never wanted his son to wonder if his dad loved him, or to feel guilty or confused for loving a father who wasn't good for his mom. Noah was going to be good to Taryn, respect her, and never make her cry. He'd seen a little too much of that in his life already.

And the best way to ensure that security for his son was to stay the course with their plans to be good friends who raised this boy together—even without the thirteen-hundred-mile buffer zone between them.

He had to deal with whatever he was feeling, and not make it a burden for Taryn. She'd already been married to a guy who made his guilt and need to be the good guy into her problem. He couldn't make her go through that again.

Damn it. He had to stop thinking about kissing this woman! He had to find some way to open up with her, be there for her and not start feeling more for her than he should. Because when he opened up with her, his emotions seemed to follow.

How exactly was he going to pull this off?

THE NEXT AFTERNOON, Noah and Taryn drove down the winding road around the lake toward the town. Noah always had liked this drive. Some parts of the road were closed in by dense trees, the sunlight all but blocked out. And then there would be a flicker of light through the trunks, the sun reflecting off the lake just beyond. There were a few clear areas where the view suddenly erupted from the trees, and the turquoise lake spread out beside them, the water sparkling in the summer sunlight.

"You're quiet today," Taryn said.

"Am I?" He glanced toward her. "I have a lot on my mind."

Last night, he hadn't slept well. He'd been thinking about Taryn, but also about Seattle. The disappointment had finally hit him. He'd mentally tallied up a life for himself there, and he'd been looking forward to a step in a new direction. In a lot of ways, staying in Mountain Springs felt like his life was grinding to a stop. Seattle had represented forward momentum, and it also offered an escape from his personal troubles here.

What was he supposed to do—stay in Mountain Springs and deal with all these conflicting, confusing relationships?

"You don't have to do this with me," Taryn said. "You don't owe me anything—"

"I'm not bent out of shape because of this visit to your grandmother," he said, and he softened his tone. "I...heard back about the Seattle job. I didn't get it."

"Oh... I'm sorry. I know how much you wanted that."

He allowed himself a glance at her, and she shot him a sympathetic look. It helped, actually. Not many people knew he'd applied, so the disappointment would be his alone to bear.

"They said it was really close," he said. "And the woman I spoke to—the president of the hotel chain—said that they debated long and hard about it. So there's that."

"That must be a bit of a consolation, at least," Taryn said.

"Yeah…"

"It's not?" she asked.

He looked over at her and found Taryn's dark gaze locked on him. He didn't want sympathy right now. He wanted to shove this down and deal with it another time, but he was the one who'd brought it up, wasn't he?

"It'll be nice to be closer to Denver," he said. "But Seattle would have paid better, and I might have been able to do a bit more financially to help you out."

"You know I don't need financial support," Taryn said.

"I know. I'm just saying, it was something I was considering. And I liked the idea of being able to pitch in more that way." Instead of in person—a way to make his son's life better without too much of a chance Noah would mess things up.

"Your sister will probably be happy to have you stay," Taryn said.

"Probably," he agreed. He wondered if Taryn would be happy to have him closer by.

"A friend of mine just found out that she's pregnant," Taryn said.

"Oh, yeah?" The trees closed in around them again.

"It wasn't planned," Taryn said. "And the relationship isn't the most solid… He's a bit insecure, and she really wants a certain type of guy, but they aren't in a really good place right now…"

"Okay," he said. He wasn't sure what she was getting at.

"She's worried," Taryn said. "It's one thing to see where a relationship goes. It's quite another to be forced together for the rest of their lives because they have a baby."

"Like us," he said.

"Actually, *not* like us," she said. "This friend and her boyfriend really do love each other—which isn't always enough to make a relationship work, and I think they're both old enough to know that. Anyway, I realized last night how fortunate we are that we didn't start out with romantic hopes or tender promises. We aren't in love with each other. I know that no one else but you might understand that, but I think we actually have a chance at making this work—co-parenting and being friends."

Was it going to be easy for her? Because that line wasn't going to be an easy one for him to walk. Maybe when she went back to Denver and they were safely ensconced in their own cities, it would be easier.

"I was thinking about how my son will see me," he said quietly. "Watching a man make my mother cry was hard. Seeing her so disappointed, so heartbroken. I never want my son to see me hurt you. You know what I mean?"

"I think I do," she said, and she smiled. "And I agree. We're luckier than I realized."

"So what is your friend going to do?" he asked.

"I don't know," Taryn said. "She's still in shock, I think. She's happy about the baby, but I think the pregnancy has made her think twice about their relationship."

"Did you give her advice?" he asked.

"No, I can't. That decision is too personal," Taryn replied. "She just wanted someone to understand how complicated it was."

"And you did," he said.

"Do I ever..."

They were coming around the side of the lake, and there was a sign announcing the Mountain Springs town limits.

"What's the plan with your grandmother today?" he asked.

Taryn adjusted her position in the seat. "She's almost ninety. And she's determined to stay on her own in her house, but we were all scared that something would happen and we'd only find out after it was too late. But you know, she seems like she's doing just fine. She's rather annoyed with us for being such worrywarts when none of us were close enough to actually see how she's doing."

"How is she with your pregnancy?" he asked.

"She's worried about me doing this on my own," she replied. "She thought I should have held on to Glen, even with the cheating, so I'd have a man to take care of me."

"Knowing you, I don't imagine you took that well," he said, unable to help the smile that tickled his lips.

"I didn't," Taryn confirmed with a short laugh, and then she sobered. "We do have a decision to make, though. Eventually, you and I will have to tell our families about our...unique relationship. I'm just wondering if we tell my grandmother who you are today."

Noah tightened his grip on the steering wheel. How exactly would the old woman react to that kind of news?

"Do *you* want to?" he asked.

"It would skip over the whole 'why didn't you tell me that was who he was?' conversation later," she said. "And while I know she doesn't approve of my choices, it might give her a little bit of relief. You'd be the—" Taryn looked over at him. "I don't mean this as pressure, but she'd see you as the man who would take care of me."

Noah smiled faintly. "I'm going to pay child support—no question about that. I know you're not asking for it, and I know you don't trust nobility in a guy, but you aren't going to have to take care of this little boy on your own. Not with me in the picture."

"I know, I know..."

Taryn was silent for a moment, and Noah ran the idea through his mind. All of this had come up so quickly—from seeing Taryn again to realizing he was going to be a father... They were both going to have to navigate this with the people in their lives, and Noah would rather have it known up front that he was going to meet his responsibilities. He didn't want her family thinking he was some kind of deadbeat.

"Sure," he said after a moment of silence. "If you want to tell her, tell her. And I'll do my best to reassure her that you'll be taken care of."

"Okay," she said. But somehow, Taryn didn't seem reassured.

They arrived on an older street, but the houses and lawns were all well kept up. Noah parked in front of the house Taryn indicated, and circled around the truck to help Taryn out.

The front door opened, and an elderly woman pushed open the screen. She wore a pair of polyester pink pants and a matching pink blouse.

"Hello, dear," she called.

They headed up the walkway together, and the old woman eyed Noah speculatively.

"Hi," he said, and he offered his hand.

"Granny, this is Noah Brooks," Taryn said. "We're working together up at the resort."

"Nice to meet you," the old woman said. "I'm Mrs. Cook."

"Pleasure," he said, and he shook her frail hand in a gentle handshake.

They all went inside, and Taryn nodded toward the couch.

"Why don't I help you get the tea, Granny?" Taryn said.

Noah sat down on the plastic-covered couch and looked around the small sitting room. There were a lot of pictures of children at various ages—school pictures, group shots, family photos. From the kitchen, he could hear the low murmur of voices. A cat appeared out of nowhere and wound around Noah's legs, and he reached down and petted it.

From deeper in the house, there was the tinkle of china. This home was so…grandmotherly, and he realized that this old woman would be a part of his son's life. His son would have a great-grandmother that he might very well remember. Noah hadn't had a lot of extended family, and he was glad that his son would.

Taryn appeared in the sitting room again first. She carried a platter with a teapot, several delicate cups and saucers, and a sugar bowl. They were going to drink tea, apparently. And talk about difficult things.

Mrs. Cook came into the room behind her granddaughter, and she looked at Noah again, this time with a different understanding in that clear gaze. She folded her hands in front of her.

"So, you're the father," Mrs. Cook said, and then pressed her lips together.

"Yes," Noah said with a more confidence than he felt. "I'm the father."

CHAPTER FOURTEEN

TARYN'S GRANDMOTHER HAD taken the news with remarkable composure. She'd simply nodded a couple of times, reached out and patted Taryn's belly tenderly, and then went to find her sugar bowl. And now that they were in the living room with Noah, Taryn cast her grandmother a nervous look.

"I think we should discuss this," Granny said, and she went to the platter, bent down and poured three cups of tea. "Noah Brooks, is it?"

"Yes, that's me," Noah said.

"Do you like sugar in your tea?" Granny asked.

"Yes, please."

"Hmm," she replied, as if that little fact told her something, but she put a trembling spoonful of sugar into one cup and handed it over to Noah.

"Granny, there isn't anything to discuss," Taryn said. "Like I told you, we had…an encounter…and we've decided to stay good friends and raise our son with the benefit of parents who are respectful and supportive of each other."

Granny passed Taryn a cup of tea in her shaky grip, and then turned to her own cup. She moved slowly, settling herself into her old rocking chair and taking a sip of tea before she spoke.

"You sound like those divorce announcements the people in Hollywood put out," Granny said. "The gossip magazines are my guilty pleasure," she said to Noah with a small smile. "They say things like 'We remain best friends, and love each other dearly, but have decided to part ways. We remain dedicated to raising our children in love and harmony...'" She shook her head. "I don't believe a word of it. If they felt half as tenderly toward each other as they claimed, they'd try to make a marriage work. The truth of the matter is, they can't stand each other and they want to move on. All pretty words—that's it."

Taryn glanced over at Noah. "It's different for us, though."

"Because you weren't married, and you weren't dating," Granny concluded.

"Exactly," she replied. "There are no dashed romantic hopes here."

"Are you so sure?" Granny asked, raising her eyebrows. "You shared an…encounter… that produced a child. Most people would call that some kind of romance. Human emotions aren't so easy to categorize, are they? Noah, look at her."

Noah looked over at Taryn, and his gaze rested on her easily. He smiled, a slow upturn of his lips.

"Are you telling me," Granny went on, "that when you look at Taryn—this beautiful woman who is carrying your child—that you feel nothing?"

Noah's gaze flickered between Taryn and her grandmother, and Taryn's stomach dropped. She didn't want to hear this. They'd already been tumbling past all sorts of lines, and she was half-afraid that Noah would admit to it.

"Granny…" Taryn said.

"Nothing?" Granny prodded. "No protectiveness? No tenderness? No desire to keep her safe?"

"Of course I do," Noah said, and his voice was deep and strong. "I'll be making sure she's okay, and we're going to talk about how I can get to know my son. I'll damn well be paying child support, and if she needs anything at all—"

"All very proper," Granny said softly. "But there's a baby on the way. And the two of you seem to think you can avoid all the difficult emotions. And I think you're both idiots."

Taryn rolled her eyes. "Granny, Noah doesn't know you yet. You can't just call him an idiot."

"I called you *both* idiots, and he's the father of my great-grandchild, so I suggest he get to know me," Granny replied curtly. "I have another solution that could solve your problems. But it's an old-fashioned one, and you probably won't like it."

"Get married," Taryn said.

"So it occurred to you!" Granny said brightly, and she smiled.

"It's more complicated than that," Taryn said.

"Is it?" Granny asked, turning to Noah. "Is it really that complicated?"

"It is…" he confirmed.

Thank goodness he was keeping his cool. Taryn cast him a grateful look.

Granny sighed. "I'm glad to know that you are taking responsibility for your son, at the very least. It's not anything to congratulate you for, but it's something."

"Thank you." Noah glanced toward Taryn,

and she shrugged weakly. He couldn't say she hadn't warned him.

"Now, I do see something very promising in this relationship," the old woman went on. "The two of you are in each other's corner. You're on the same page, so to speak. You're both determined to hold your ground with me and prove that your way—the one you've agreed upon together—is the best. And you don't care what an old woman thinks about it." She waggled a finger at Taryn. "And that is actually a relationship trait of a successful couple."

"Granny, we're very different people," Taryn said. "I'm just about forty. I've been married before. Noah is no spring chicken, either."

"I'm forty-two," Noah said, and they shared an amused smile.

"The fact that we've both agreed that the nonromantic way is the best way says something. We've both been through a lot, and so have the people close to us. We're not naïve."

"I agree," Granny replied. "But I'm going to point something out—neither of you are *young*. You're both single and middle-aged. By the time I was your age, I'd been married and given birth to eight children already. How much time are you going to give the universe to deposit the perfect spouse in your lap? Marriage is a commitment, and it's hard work. But if you're willing to be kind and faithful, you could have the family that I know Taryn, at the very least, has dreamed of all her life."

When Granny stopped speaking, they were all silent for a few beats. Taryn watched a robin flit by the window, and she felt a wave of wistfulness. Was it as simple as that? Or was that the kind of story people told in her grandmother's day to get couples married who'd conceived a child?

"Now," Granny went on, "I've talked enough. But it might be nice for you to see a few photos of Taryn when she was young, Noah." She rose to her feet, put her tea cup back on the tray and went over to her piano and picked up a framed photo. "Come here, Noah."

Noah put down his tea, as well, and shot Taryn a rueful smile before he joined Granny by the piano.

"Is that her?" he asked, pointing.

"No, that's her cousin Bridget. This is Taryn—the little one with the Popsicle."

Noah chuckled softly.

"That was one summer when I had four of my grandchildren here all at once. It was hectic and wonderful. There is no better way to get to know a child than to be with them for twenty-four hours a day—now, you remember that, Noah."

Taryn felt a rush of annoyance as her grandmother's glittering gaze flicked in her direction. Granny was making a point Taryn didn't want made. The last thing she wanted was Noah going for joint custody! But Noah didn't seem to be taking the bait. He picked up another photo.

"That's Taryn for sure."

"Her high school graduation," Granny agreed. "She always was a beautiful girl, wasn't she?"

"Yeah…" Noah looked over at Taryn with a smile.

"She's also very stubborn," Granny added, lowering her voice as if it kept her words private. "You should know that about her up front. But under that stubborn streak of hers is a very loyal heart. She's kind—and that's not something that comes easily these days."

"Thanks, Granny," Taryn said dryly.

"She's also a bit of a workaholic," Granny said with a faint wince.

"Granny, you are not helping!" Taryn said.

"My dear, I thought you two were going to have a—how did you call it?—a respectful and supportive relationship." Granny said. "I dare you to try that without knowing each other inside and out. And knowing you, my dear girl, means knowing your family, too. Because we can offer insights."

"What was she like when she was a kid?" Noah asked before Taryn could interject.

"Oh, our Taryn was a spitfire!" Granny chuckled. "We all thought she'd end up being a lawyer. But a woman running her own business needs a spine of steel, too."

"So she argues well, does she?" Noah asked, and Taryn could make out the mildly amused tug at the corners of his lips.

"Oh, yes. She's most eloquent when she's furious, too," Granny said. "Have you not seen that yet? Well, since you're both so keen on knowing each other well, I suggest you see her angry."

"You're about to," Taryn said, shooting her grandmother a warning look.

"You don't scare me, missy," Granny said with a low laugh. "But I will tell you both something. In my day, lasting marriages started on less than what you've got here."

"Like you and Grandpa?" Taryn asked meaningfully.

Granny looked at Taryn, and her eyes

misted. "Fine. You don't want my input? I can see that."

Taryn's heart gave a squeeze. "Granny, I—"

"No, no," Granny said. "We weren't a perfect couple by any stretch. Therefore, any advice I have after nearly ninety years on this planet must be garbage."

"That isn't what I'm saying," Taryn said. "But these days people don't just stick with it when their hearts are broken, Granny. Women don't put up with husbands treating them like Grandpa treated you. Men don't stay in marriages after they've fallen out of love… We don't have a society insisting that we endure. So we have to be more careful. We *have* to. I've been through a painful divorce, and Noah has had his own share of heartache. We know what heartbreak feels like, and we don't want to put this little boy through any more than he needs to go through." She rubbed a hand over her belly. "Don't you see that?"

Granny looked between them, then nodded. "Yes, I see it."

They were all silent for a moment, and then Noah leaned forward and put his cup of tea back down on the platter.

"Did you talk to your parents yet about

leaving me alone about moving?" Granny asked.

"Not yet."

"I have a more thought-out response now. Tell your father that if he wants to discuss downsizing me, that he come and face his mother himself," Granny said curtly. "In person, where he can look me in my eyes and tell me that I'm too feeble and scattered to care for myself. You go ahead and pass that along. I'll be waiting to hear what he says."

Her father wouldn't do it—there was a reason why Taryn had felt responsible for this mission. He'd coordinate with his brothers, and they'd try to force Granny into that retirement home. And Granny would hate it.

"Granny, I'll back you up," Taryn said. "I will."

Granny pursed her lips.

"We should get back," Taryn said to Noah.

"Time is money," Granny said, and she gave them a nod. "Thank you for coming by, all the same."

This was the problem with Granny. She was full of opinions, convinced she was right and willing to use manipulation to make things happen her way. But she was also old, and one of these days, the world would stop bending to her will.

Noah stayed silent while Taryn said her goodbyes to her grandmother. When they stepped outside, the screen door propped open, Granny said, "Can I say just one more thing, Taryn?"

Taryn paused, waiting.

"As far as men go, I've experienced a lot myself. And this one here—" Granny put a hand on Noah's arm. "He's got kind eyes. I know it's no guarantee, but Glen didn't have kind eyes. And your grandfather had laughing eyes…but not kind ones. I just thought it was worth mentioning."

Taryn looked down at her weathered old grandmother, at the lines in her face framed by wispy white hair, and felt a wave a protectiveness. Granny did want to help…

"I love you, Granny," Taryn said, and she leaned down and kissed her grandmother's cheek.

"All right," Granny said. "I love you, too. Go back to work now."

She gave her grandmother's hand a squeeze.

Taryn followed Noah back to his truck, and when he opened the door for her, she took his hand as she hoisted herself into the passenger's side seat. He held her hand just a moment longer than necessary.

"You okay?" he asked softly.

"Yeah… I'm fine."

Noah slammed the door after her, and as he headed around to the driver's side, Taryn looked out the window toward her grandmother, still standing on the step.

If only marrying a handsome guy and having his baby was the easy solution that Granny made it seem. But life wasn't that simple, and she had a feeling that it never had been, not even for Granny.

Noah got into the driver's side and put the key in the ignition.

"She's a real force of nature, isn't she?" Noah asked. He put on his seat belt, and they pulled away from the curb.

"She is," Taryn agreed.

"For the record," he said, "I'm not scared off by your ability to argue well. I think it's kind of attractive."

Taryn laughed softly, and Noah reached over and took her hand in his. He twined his fingers through hers, and she looked over at this strong man sitting next to her, one hand on the steering wheel, the other holding hers…

"Don't let Granny get in your head," she said.

"Because I'm holding your hand?" he

asked, and he didn't take his eyes off the road. "Don't worry—I think there will be times that a high five isn't enough. And this is one of them."

She should pull back, get things onto a logical, even keel, but she couldn't bring herself to do it.

Did Granny have a point? Or was Taryn toying with unnecessary heartbreak by making the same mistake all over again and letting a pregnancy dictate her romantic future?

She'd been down this road before...and it was painful. But Granny made things seem not only possible, but reasonable.

She stole a glance at Noah, and while he didn't look toward her, his grip did tighten on her hand just a little bit.

He was tempting...oh, so tempting. But kind eyes and physical chemistry just weren't enough.

NOAH HAD TO release Taryn's hand in order to signal, and once they were on the road that curved around the lake and led up toward the resort, he glanced over at her.

"I'm being selfish, aren't I?"

"Hmm?" She looked up.

"Tom told me once that when he married my mother, he closed his eyes and jumped and just hoped for the best," he said. "And I remember thinking how selfish that sounded."

"Don't let my grandmother get to you," she said. "She has these ideas of the order things should happen, and for her, babies belong in wedlock. Period."

"Yeah, I got that," he said.

"And while she and my grandfather stayed together, my grandpa was cheating on her for a lot of their marriage," she said. "She loved him, and she probably hated him in equal measure, but they needed each other. They had eight boys to raise, and they weren't going to manage that in separate households. So…they stuck together."

They were both silent for a couple of beats.

"We have a good plan," Taryn added.

"I think so, too," he agreed. "I just… I like your grandmother. She's spunky."

"Just wait until she turns that attitude your way," Taryn chuckled.

"I think I understand you a little bit better," he said.

"Oh?" He saw the wariness in her eye.

"You've got a big, connected family," he said. "And I always imagined that kind of upbringing would be soft and supportive. I think you've had to dig your heels in and get tough, though. You needed to stay true to yourself in the face of all these people who love you and figure they know you better than you know yourself."

Taryn shot him a surprised look.

"That's kind of true," she agreed. "Big families are wonderful, but you have to step carefully with them, too."

"I only have my sister," he said. "There are fewer expectations there."

"Fewer *clashing* expectations," she countered. "But family always expects something."

That was true, but his relationship with his sister kept him grounded, too. Birthdays, Christmas, Easter—he had somewhere to go, somewhere he was needed, or else the day wouldn't be the same. Family gave structure, and you either used that to form yourself, or you kicked against it.

"So are you ready to see the family I come from?" he asked. "Tomorrow night, we're watching my sister's kids."

"I'm curious to see you with kids," Taryn said, and she shot him a grin. "And four of them sounds like it'll drive you to the edge. That'll be interesting to see."

"You think?" he asked with a short laugh. "My oldest nephew is getting an attitude.

So this might be more daunting than you imagine."

"We can handle one evening," she said. "Besides, I'm giving my presentation to Angelina on Monday, and then I head home."

"So soon?"

Taryn didn't answer, and Noah sighed. Their time here had flown by, and he didn't feel ready to say goodbye to her yet. Despite all they'd shared, he felt like a lot would change when she left. While she was here, she needed him here—on some level. She might not need as much from him at home, where she had her own supports...

"I...look, I was wanting to talk to you about something," he said slowly. "When the baby is born, are you... I mean, who's going to be with you?"

"My mother," she said.

"Yeah, that makes sense." He nodded. "And I'm sure you have friends."

"I do," she said.

"It's just—" He swallowed. "I know my place, okay? I'm not pushing. I'm not asking for any kind of custody arrangement. But I'd really like to see him when he's born. I'd like to see—" He swallowed. "I'd like to see you."

He wanted to make sure Taryn was doing

well, was cared for, was healthy. He'd feel better seeing her with their son in her arms, knowing they were both okay, *seeing* that they were okay.

"You want to be at the birth?" she asked, her voice low, and he couldn't read what she was feeling.

"That's too much, isn't it?" he asked, but he reached out and took her hand again. This time she squeezed his fingers hard.

"It'll be sweaty, and ugly and I'll be screaming, no doubt," she said. "There's nothing easy about delivery."

"I'm his father," Noah said quietly. "And I want to… I don't know. I want to see you through it, in whatever way would actually help you. I'm not foolish enough to push myself on you, but if I might be…comforting—"

What was he doing? He was asking for far too much.

"The thing is," Noah said, sucking in a breath, "I'm just going to tell you what I'm thinking, okay? So there's no misunderstanding here. I want to know that you're safe—both of you. And I have this image in my head of you holding our boy, and that would be comforting for *me*. I want to know that he's in your arms, and that you're well cared for. And if you need anything, I want to be there to make sure you get it. That's all. I'm not asking to get between you and the baby, or…anything like that. If that makes sense."

"You want to be there…"

"Yeah."

"It might be nice," she said. "Just…a bit more support."

"I'd be there for you—and you can send me on errands, or break my hand during contractions, or curse me for doing this to you—"

"We'll see what I need," she said, and he noticed that she hadn't released his hand. Maybe she'd want this—him at her side, letting her crush his hand as hard as she needed to.

"When I go into labor," she said, "I could let you know."

"That would be really nice," he said.

For the first time in his life, he was thinking about holding a woman's hand while she delivered their child…about giving her his strength.

It was a good thing to be staying in Mountain Springs—in Colorado. He might not have much of an instinct toward parenting this child, but he did feel deep inside of him that closer was better. For whatever that was worth.

When they arrived at the lodge again, Taryn had more work to do, and she headed into her office. He went to his, and for a moment, he just sat at his desk, his mind spinning.

So much was changing so quickly. He'd gone from being a bitter guy who'd lost his fiancée and his best friend to being the father of an unborn baby. And he was thinking about what it would mean for his life, for that child's life…for Taryn.

Noah turned on his computer, and while he flicked through a few work emails, his cell phone rang. He looked down at the number—it wasn't one he recognized, but it had a Denver area code.

"Hello. Noah Brooks," he said.

"Noah? Hi, it's Tom."

Noah's heartbeat sped up, and he turned away from the computer. "Tom? Hi…how did you get my number?"

"Your sister passed it along," he said. "I'm sorry if this is too much—"

"No, it's fine," Noah said. "How are you?"

"I'm not too bad," Tom replied. "I've been thinking about you kids lately, and when you found me on Facebook, I guess it brought back a lot of memories."

Noah was silent for a moment. "Good memories?"

"Yeah, of course!" Tom said. "Very good memories. I missed you kids a lot when your mom and I split up. It's nice to see you all grown-up now—looks like you turned out okay."

"Yeah, we did," he said. "I was actually hoping to see you at Mom's funeral."

"It didn't feel right to go," Tom said. "I mean, your mother wasn't crazy about me at the end, and showing up with my new wife—that felt disrespectful. I did send a flower arrangement, though."

"Actually, that was probably a good call," Noah admitted. He was silent for a moment. "Tom, you weren't good to my mother. You know that, right?"

"I'm—" Tom cleared his throat. "I'm really sorry, Noah. You're right. We didn't bring out the best in each other."

"That's not an excuse, though," Noah said. "At some point, a man has to take responsibility for how he behaves. I remember listening to you two fight. You'd always find a way to get that last word in, and my mom would be in tears. Do you have any idea what that did to me?"

"I didn't know you heard any of that," Tom said. "I'm sorry about that."

"Over the years, I tried to make sense of your relationship with my mom," Noah said. "For a long while, I blamed myself for the breakup. I mean, Mom was mostly upset because you weren't very good at making responsible choices for my sister and me—" Now that he'd started talking, Noah could feel the floodgates opening. "But all the same, you're the one who actually understood me. You were another guy—you were my dad. Maybe it was different for you—I wasn't actually yours."

"I didn't have any legal right to you, Noah," Tom said.

What did that mean? Had he not felt the same connection?

"I get it," Noah said quickly. "I do. We were her kids from a previous marriage. But to me—a six-year-old boy—you were the dad I'd prayed for. And when you and Mom split up, I kept praying every night that you'd remember me and come back—"

Noah's voice broke and he stopped talking. This was a bad idea… What was he even doing?

"I was a kid who took it hard," Noah said. "That's all I'm trying to say."

"I wasn't any good with kids," Tom said quietly. "I guess I messed you up more than I thought... I didn't know that you...loved me."

"Yeah, well—" Noah cleared his throat. "It was a long time ago. Forget it. I'm sorry to lay all that on you."

"Hey, it's fine," Tom said. "I really loved you kids, but I wasn't your real dad, and your mom wanted to move on. We were really different, your mom and me. Now that you're a grown man, I'm sure you get that. We had this chemistry between us, but I wasn't what she needed on a deeper level."

"Why did you marry her, then?" Noah asked.

"I guess I was just hoping for the best," Tom replied. "I always said I just closed my eyes and jumped, and for a while I thought it was the right thing. I had your mom and you kids, and my life felt complete. But it didn't change that we were fundamentally different. I didn't make her as happy as you all made me."

Noah was silent.

"We weren't bringing out the best in each other," Tom repeated. "That happens at the end of a marriage—you don't break up because you can't stand the other person. You break up because you don't like who you've become. I was willing to go because I didn't want to be like that anymore. I honestly thought you kids would be glad to see the back of me."

"Maybe I should have been," Noah said. "But I wasn't. I missed you a lot."

"Maybe you want to come out and visit my rescue operation here," Tom said. "It would be nice to see you again, and spend a bit of time with you. If you wanted…"

Did he want to take this, or did he want to push all those childhood memories down and move on? He'd thought about Tom far too often to be able to brush him aside with one conversation.

"That would be nice," Noah said.

"And for what it's worth now," Tom said quietly, "I did call your mom after the divorce and apologize for the stuff I said, for the times I hurt her. I did say I was sorry—"

"I didn't know that," Noah replied.

"You were a kid," Tom said gently. "You weren't supposed to know. We were supposed to be making things better for you, not dumping you in the middle. We did try to protect you from it all, you know."

Except, kids were smarter and more perceptive than adults ever realized... And then they carried that trauma around with them for the rest of their lives. If there was one thing Noah could learn from Tom, it was that closing his eyes and leaping in wasn't the answer. And fulfilling a woman's emotional needs for the long run didn't happen with a few good intentions.

There was a ping from his computer, and Noah looked over to see a new email. This one was from Seattle, and the subject line read Job Offer.

"Hey, I've got to take care of a few things here," Noah said. "Do you think we could talk again later?"

"Of course!" Tom said. "Call me anytime."

After he'd hung up, Noah clicked on the email. It was from Ellen at the Seattle hotel. She'd emailed to say the successful candidate had had to turn down the position for personal reasons. And they were circling back to him...

As you know, we were incredibly impressed with you, and if you'd like the job, it's yours.

Noah swallowed. Seattle. A better-paying job—a better opportunity to provide for his son…and halfway across the country from Taryn and the baby.

It wasn't the direction his heart was tugging him anymore, but maybe it would be better for all of them. Who was he kidding? The best of intentions were seldom enough. Maybe he should simply provide what he could—a comfortable life that kept his son safely in his mother's arms and away from any drama that might arise between himself and Taryn.

CHAPTER FIFTEEN

TARYN'S BELLY HAD grown since she'd arrived at the resort—she noticed it in how her clothes were fitting.

Maybe it was all that delicious food she'd been having from the mountain resort kitchen, but the baby was getting stronger, too, and she noticed it in his kicks and jabs. She adjusted herself in the seat as Noah drove, rubbing her hand over a place where the baby's foot was pressing.

"When I get back to Denver, I have a checkup with my doctor," Taryn said. "And every time I sit in that waiting room with all the other pregnant women, I see the life that's waiting for me. Most come with their other kids in tow, so I see all the different ages. One woman I see pretty often has an infant that she carries in a baby car seat. She got pregnant the second time like…weeks after delivering her first baby. Not recommended, by the way."

"Yeah, I imagine."

She wasn't sure why she was talking about this stuff with Noah. Maybe it was that she was going to miss him. She'd be back in Denver in a matter of days, and her time in Mountain Springs was coming to an end. Taryn glanced at Noah, at his faint shadow of whiskers, and the strong hand resting on the steering wheel. His warm gaze flicked in her direction.

She *was* going to miss him…

"I think you'll like my sister," Noah said. "She's less scrappy than your grandmother, but they have a similar no-nonsense vibe."

Taryn chuckled. "Granny is a handful, but you can count on her—always. I don't think she's quite as frail as my parents were afraid she was, either. And she wants to help—she just tends to offend you first, and help you second."

"She means well… deep down," he said.

"That sums it up."

"Laura, too," he said. "You'll see. Except Laura won't offend you first. And, um, I should probably mention that I told my sister about our situation."

"Oh!" She looked over at him. "Okay. That was the plan, right?"

"Yeah," he agreed. "At least we don't have to explain all over again."

The house was a broad, low ranch-styled house with bushes out front and a tangle of bikes leaning up against the garage. They parked in the driveway next to a minivan, and when they got out, two preschoolers came running outside—a boy and girl.

"That would be the twins, Micah and Libby," Noah said.

They were also eating Fudgsicles that dripped onto the ground in the summer heat.

"Uncle Noah!" Micah said, bouncing up and down.

"Wait…have you grown?" Noah asked, and he measured the boy's head against his thigh. "I think you grew! You're bigger!"

"Yeah, I'm bigger!" Micah said proudly.

"This is my…my friend, Taryn," Noah said.

Friend. It would do. Although it felt like they were something deeper and more complicated than friends. Micah looked at her shyly. He had big brown eyes and a hand that was sticky from his frozen treat. Libby, his sister, was a little smaller, and she hung back, her eyes fixed on Noah in adoration.

"Uncle Noah," Libby whispered, and Noah bent down and picked her up.

"Hi, Libby," he said.

She put a sticky hand on his shoulder, and Taryn chuckled as Noah visibly winced.

"It's okay," he said over his shoulder. "After an evening with these guys, you just hose off. You're going to be sticky—guaranteed."

Inside, there were two other children—boys. One looked to be about five or six, and the other was tall and sullen and looked like a preteen.

"Thanks so much for doing this!" Noah's sister came bustling out of the kitchen, obviously dressed up for their date night. Her husband was a slim man, and he smiled good-naturedly at them.

"It's so nice to meet you!" Laura said, and she put her arms around Taryn and gave her a squeeze. "Don't hate Noah, but he told me. And we're thrilled! We really are."

"Thanks. And it's fine that he told you—really."

"I don't have time to have the whole baby gab right now," Laura said, scooping up her purse, "but if we don't leave now, something is going to stop us, and I've been counting on this night out just a little too much." Laura laughed, and shot her husband a grin. "You ready to show me a good time, Henry?"

"Always," Henry said.

"Okay, Aaron, you know your chores, and I want them done by the time we get home," Laura said, addressing the older boy. "And Nicholas, if I hear that you pinched Micah again, there will be trouble, capital *T!* You hear me?" Laura glanced at Taryn and Noah. "There's been a tiny bit of pinching…"

"I didn't do it!" Nicholas said.

"And a tiny bit of fibbing…" Laura added, then she rolled her eyes.

"Okay, okay," Henry said. "Be good, kids. Love you. If Uncle Noah has to call us because you're acting up, we're going to buy ice cream and then eat it all in front of you. Come on, beautiful. It's you and me tonight." Henry held out his hand for his wife, and they beamed at each other.

They looked happy, Taryn realized. All these kids, and Laura and Henry still had eyes for each other. The parents headed out the door, and Noah shut it firmly behind them.

"Hi," Libby whispered, and Noah passed the girl over to Taryn. Her little arm twined around Taryn's neck. Her heart melted.

"Baby?" Libby asked.

"Yes, there's a baby in there," Taryn said.

Libby smiled and squirmed against Taryn's belly. Taryn followed Noah into the house. Toys were spread all over the living room floor, but the kitchen looked relatively tidy. Libby hummed happily to herself, seeming quite pleased to have landed with Taryn.

"How old are you?" Taryn asked.

"Three!" Libby held up two fingers, and Taryn laughed.

"Three? Wow. That's a very big girl!"

"Do you want to see my dollies?"

"I do!" Taryn bent down to put the little girl on the floor, and she dashed off toward the living room to find her dolls. Taryn straightened just as Micah howled.

"Nicholas pinched me!" he hollered, pointing at a telltale red mark on his arm.

Nicholas stood next to him, his face arranged in exaggerated innocence, and Noah looked over at Taryn. Before Noah could do anything, however, Aaron marched over to Nicholas and punched him solidly in the shoulder.

"That's for pinching!" Aaron said. "Cut it out, you little twerp!"

Nicholas started to cry, and he flung himself at his older brother. They went down in a tangle of fists and sneakers. Micah stood there watching them in mild amusement, and just then Libby came back into the room with an armload of Barbie dolls. She looked at her brothers for a moment and then headed for Taryn.

"Come play dollies," Libby said. "Come? Come play?"

Taryn stared at Noah, and he stood there, frozen.

"Do something!" Taryn said.

"Um—" Noah reached into the fray, receiving a kick to his face for his efforts, and he grabbed an arm and pulled on it. Aaron seemed to be owner, because he was the one Noah hauled out.

"Aaron, what are you doing?" Noah said. "Now you beat up your little brother?"

"He hit me first!" Nicholas complained from the ground.

"After you pinched Micah!" Aaron shot back, his face red.

"Well, one of you kicked me in the face," Noah said, rubbing a hand over his jaw. "So cut it out! I don't want any more of that. Aaron, tell your brother you're sorry."

"No!" Aaron retorted. "I'm not sorry! He's spoiled and he's stupid!"

Nicholas then started crying again. "I'm not spoiled!" he wailed.

"But you're okay with being stupid?"

Aaron yelled. "See? And he's always doing stuff and pretending he didn't!"

"I did not!" Nicholas wiped his nose on the back of his hand, and there was a smear of blood. The boy paled. "You made me bleed! I'm telling Mom!"

"You can't tell Mom," Aaron snapped. "They're gone! Tell Uncle Noah!"

Taryn could hear the victory in those words. None of the kids expected their uncle to do anything, and Noah stood there, looking down at the boys with a frown.

"Aaron, go to your room for a few minutes," Noah said.

"Or what?" Aaron retorted.

"Or I make you!" Noah said, raising his voice, and Aaron jumped at the suddenly loud bass. Taryn had startled, too. Aaron went stomping off, and hollered something over his shoulder about the unfairness of it all and how his siblings were brats.

Nicholas and Micah stared up at Noah, openmouthed, and Noah shot Taryn a panicked look.

"What now?" he said.

"Why don't we put the TV on?" Taryn suggested.

"Yes!" Noah looked relieved. "TV!"

After a small tussle over which show to

watch, Noah flicked on some old-school *Tom and Jerry,* and the kids all settled in. All except Aaron, of course.

"Maybe you should talk to your nephew," Taryn said quietly.

"He's fine," Noah said. "His parents just send him to his room."

"But he seems really frustrated with his brothers," Taryn said. "And I think he was actually trying to help there."

Noah looked in the direction of the bedrooms, and Taryn could feel his reluctance.

"I'm not good at this," Noah said.

"Talk to him!" she said. "Or we will have mutiny on our hands. If you hadn't noticed, we're seriously outnumbered here."

"A solid point," he said, and Noah pushed himself to his feet and headed out of the living room, stepping over toys as he went.

These kids were more than Noah could handle. Would he be better with their son? She could see how frustrated he was, definitely not a man who was naturally inclined toward children...

"Play dollies!" Libby said, pushing a Barbie into Taryn's hand.

Taryn made the Barbie talk to Libby's doll, and Libby beamed up at her. Taryn looked over at Nicholas and Micah just as

Nicholas pushed a foot into Micah's back. Taryn sighed. She was tired already. The baby was standing on her bladder, and she adjusted her position.

"Nicholas, I saw that," she said, just loud enough for the boy to hear. He looked back at her innocently. So this was how it was going to go. "But I have a special job for you."

The boy didn't look impressed.

"Are you hungry?" she asked.

"Yeah!"

All three children turned at that, and she laughed. "Okay, let's go find a snack for everyone, but you have to put the exact same amount on every plate…"

The promise of food brought all three kids into the kitchen, and she directed Nicholas in the making of peanut butter crackers for all of them.

"And a plate for Aaron," she said.

"He's in time-out," Nicholas said with a firm shake of his head. "No food in time-out. Those are the rules."

"You're about to join him," she replied curtly.

Nicholas eyed her for a moment. "Okay, a plate for Aaron."

There would be peanut butter just about

everywhere, but maybe a snack could unify these kids. It was worth a try.

Taryn stopped to look at a few pictures stuck to the side of the fridge with magnets. Laura and Henry looked happy together— more than happy; they looked in love, even when they had kids between them and around them, and climbing them like trees. It looked hectic, but this was what Taryn wanted—the kind of relationship that could weather the kids at any phase, and come out stronger in the end.

How many people got that these days? How many people found it after forty?

NOAH SAT ON the side of Aaron's bed, while Aaron stood across the room, his face red.

"Aaron, look—" Noah sighed. "I'm here for one evening. Do you miss your parents, or something?"

"No!" Aaron scowled.

"Okay, so not that." He glanced around the room, his gaze passing over a desk that was covered in drawings of trucks. They weren't half-bad. The kid had some talent. "Here's the deal. I've got to make sure you all get along well enough that your parents can have dinner out. It's a rare luxury for them, and I'm not letting any of you call them to tattle."

Aaron was silent, chewing the side of his cheek. This wasn't going to be an easy night, and he wasn't sure whether he was happy Taryn was here. Was it a good idea to show her the very real limits of his abilities with kids? But that was why they needed to be friends above all—because they couldn't be lying to each other to impress them. They had to be real and honest. She had to know just how much she could realistically expect from him.

"What's it going to take to get you to help me out?" Noah asked.

"I don't know…" Aaron picked at a fingernail.

"How about ten bucks?" Noah asked.

Aaron was silent for a moment. "I need fifteen."

"Seriously? You're negotiating with me?" Noah said. "Your mother would already kill me if she knew I was paying you!"

"I'm saving up for a LEGO set, and I need fifteen more dollars to get it," Aaron replied.

"What set?" Noah asked with a frown.

"It's a semitruck, with a trailer and there's a cop on a motorbike that chases it down," Aaron replied. "And I've been saving for it."

The boy had a goal. That seemed valuable in itself.

"Can you break a twenty?" Noah asked.

"What?"

"If I give you twenty bucks, can you give me five back?" Noah asked.

"I don't want to give you money!"

"It's giving me *change*. You're still fifteen dollars ahead—" Noah let his head sink into his hands. He was exhausted already. "Okay." He looked up. "Twenty bucks. I will give a crisp twenty-dollar bill if you help me keep everything going smoothly tonight."

Aaron brightened. "Okay!"

"Wait—" Noah put up a hand. "But you can't do anything I can't do. No punching. No kicking. No brawling. No pinching. No verbal threats. None of it. And everyone is in bed by eight, on the dot. Including you."

"Libby and Micah go to bed at seven-thirty," the boy replied.

"Even better," he said. "You help me make that happen."

"Okay. Can I read in bed?"

"Yes, but if you beat on any of your siblings, the deal is off," Noah said. "And I duct-tape you to a wall until your parents come home."

"What happened to verbal threats?" Aaron said, narrowing his eyes.

"I was *joking*!" Noah said. "A joke. I wouldn't actually duct-tape you to anything. I'll just call your mother and let her do it."

Aaron smiled. "Twenty bucks?"

"Twenty bucks." Noah sighed. "Okay, let's go back out there."

Noah followed Aaron out of the room, and they found everyone else in the kitchen. Taryn picked up a plastic plate off the counter with four peanut butter cracker sandwiches in the center of it, and held it toward Aaron with a smile.

"That's for you," she said.

"Oh...thanks." Aaron took the plate and picked up a cracker sandwich with peanut butter oozing out the sides.

"How did it go?" Taryn asked quietly when Noah joined her at the sink.

"I bribed him."

"What?" She shot him a look of surprise.

Noah shrugged. "I'm not even going to apologize. I'm giving him twenty bucks toward his LEGO set to help us get the kids all in bed by eight. And you tell me that's not worth the expense."

Taryn laughed softly. "It might be worth it."

"I told you I'm not good at this," he said.

"And I told you we're outnumbered," she said.

Noah looked at his watch. "We have an hour and a half."

AARON WAS TRUE to his word, and after his young siblings were all bathed, in their pajamas and in bed, he came out and eyed Noah hopefully.

"You wanting to get paid?" Noah asked.

"Yeah. I did it. They're all in bed now."

"Are you going to help keep them there?" Noah asked, pulling out his wallet.

"Yeah, of course," Aaron said.

Noah considered his nephew for a moment. It would be smarter to pay the kid later, but he didn't plan on telling his sister about this, so he pulled out a twenty and handed it over. Aaron accepted the money with a grin.

"Thanks, Uncle Noah!" he said, and he dashed back down the hallway. Noah heard the sound of a piggy bank emptying out. He'd ignore that. Let the kid count his money. He'd earned it.

Taryn shot him an amused smile. "I'll give you this—you got Aaron on your team."

"That isn't a long-term solution," he said.

"No," she agreed. "But we aren't their parents."

"Laura and Henry run this zoo pretty well," Noah said. "The kids listen to *them*."

Noah sank onto the sofa next to Taryn, and he reached out and took her hand. He wasn't sure why he did it—the physical contact between them felt natural. An old movie musical was on the TV, and Noah let out a long sigh.

She felt good next to him. Her hand was cool in his palm, and when she adjusted her position, her belly touched his arm and he felt movement within. He put a hand on her belly and felt the sensation of the baby moving.

"I...heard from the Seattle hotel chain," he said, his voice low.

"Again?"

He pulled his hand away from Taryn's belly. "They offered me the job, after all. Their first choice turned them down."

Taryn's gaze clouded, then she nodded. "Okay. What did you tell them?"

"That I need a couple of days to think it over." He licked his lips. "I should feel happier than I do."

"Congratulations," she said belatedly with a weak smile.

"You don't have to pretend to like it," he said.

"This was your goal. It's a step up," she said. "You *wanted* this."

"It's a plan I made before you appeared

in my life," he said. "It was the plan before I knew about our baby."

Taryn was silent, and her gaze moved toward the window.

"If I'm in Seattle, it'll be a whole lot harder to jump in the car and come to the hospital when he's born, won't it?" he went on.

"You could come afterward," she said, but her voice had lost the animation.

"I wasn't planning on being a father," he said. "You know that. But now that I'm getting used to the idea, I want to be a good one."

"I think you'll be just fine, no matter where you are," she said with a quick nod, but she sounded distant.

"Say what you mean," he said. "We said we'd be honest, right?"

"What am I supposed to say?" Taryn said. "We have a plan, Noah! We're sticking to it. We'll be friends, we'll do well by our son and that's that. If you have a job that takes you to Seattle, well, I was planning on doing this alone. I'm fine—" tears misted her eyes "—I don't know why I'm going getting emotional. I'm sorry." She dashed at an errant tear on her cheek. "I'm blaming pregnancy hormones."

"What if I turned it down?"

"What?" She shook her head. "You worked for this! You have every reason to leave this town!"

And he did. He had every reason to leave, and just one to stick around.

"I know. I just— Things are different now. I can't explain it, but the thought of being farther away from you and baby than I already will be is…it doesn't feel right. If you need me for something—"

"I have a support system in place," she said. "I'll be okay."

His heart sank. It hadn't occurred to him until just now that she might not feel the same way he did about those miles between them.

"And you'd rather I stuck to it and took the job," he concluded woodenly.

"No! I—" Taryn looked at him helplessly. "We said we'd be good friends and we'd respect each other and back each other up. We said we'd put our son's needs first and we'd never put him in the middle of some bitter breakup. That's what we said."

"We did," he said. "And we can do that—"

"So you'd be putting this big step up in your career aside for a good friend?" she said, shaking her head. "You'd give up career advancement, a wage hike, a new start in the city of your choice, away from all the drama here that's been driving you crazy, all for a *friend*?"

Her gaze caught his, and maybe it was the tears sparkling in her eyes or the emotion he saw swimming there, but he slipped his hand behind her neck and tugged her closer. She smelled sweet, like vanilla and strawberry, and all he could think about was closing the distance between them.

"I'd do it for *you*," he murmured, and he covered her lips with his.

She leaned into him, and for a moment, it was only them—the scent of her perfume, the warmth of her hair against his hand, her lips pressed against his... She pulled back, and he rested his forehead against hers.

"Are you going for force me to say it?" he asked miserably.

"Say what?" she breathed.

"I'm in love with you... No, we didn't plan that. We said we'd keep it platonic. We said we wouldn't get any romantic hopes involved. But Taryn, you had me seven months ago on that one night together. I knew you were incredible then, and you're incredible now..." It was a shock to him, too, and it was only in this moment that he could put a word to all the tangled emotions that had been growing inside of him. "I don't know how else to explain what I'm feeling for you. I know it's fast—in a way. I know it's crazy—I see that pretty plainly. But it is what it is. The thought of going to Seattle, that far away from—from the both of you—is…" He shrugged, looking for a word that could properly describe the pull in his heart at the thought, but he couldn't find one. "It's…awful."

CHAPTER SIXTEEN

TARYN'S HEART HAMMERED to a stop. She could see the misery in Noah's dark gaze. How had this happened? How had they gone from reasonable adults who knew where they stood to two people who were feeling too much?

"Is this just me?" Noah asked softly. "Am I just a guy who got caught up in you while you…kept your feet on the ground?"

"No, it's not just you," she breathed. "I've been feeling it, too. I've been trying not to—"

"You love me," he said, his breath coming out in a rush.

"Yeah…" Tears misted her eyes. He'd somehow become entangled in her heart, along with this miracle baby.

He pulled her in again, and this time, he deepened his kiss. His arms felt strong and secure around her, and as he ran his hand over the top of her belly, she felt the baby move in response. Did he know that this was his daddy? Could he sense it from within?

Taryn pulled back. "Noah, wait—"

He brushed her hair away from her cheek, his fingers lingering against her skin. He felt so good this close—too good. She could get used to this, start depending on it...

"This is because of the baby..." she said.

"No, I fell for you sitting in that pub and listening to you talk," Noah said with a small smile.

She had to smile at that, too, but she knew what she was getting at. This baby had turned her entire world on its head, and he was doing the same thing for his father. But the difference between them was that Taryn *wanted* her life to be tipped upside down. She was grateful for it, ridiculously thankful for this chance at filling her arms with a baby at long last. But Noah...his life was just tipping, and he hadn't longed for the plunge...

"If I weren't pregnant and we met, we wouldn't have gotten even this far," Taryn said, begging him to understand. "I want children. And you don't. We want different lives, even if this baby shocked us both."

"He's on his way now—" Noah said. "There's no undoing that."

Taryn looked around the living room. There were several tubs of toys the kids had picked up before bed, but there were still a few lying around—a Barbie lay in the middle of the carpet, inexplicably missed. The TV screen was covered in fingerprints. The couch they sat on had LEGO blocks between the cushions.

"This baby doesn't change who we both are fundamentally," Taryn said, and her voice shook. "I want to be a mom, to have a garden, to run my business and focus on my family. I might even want another baby if I'm able to conceive again… This pile of kids—I love this. You want your career, your comfort, your beautifully streamlined life, and there is nothing wrong with that! I'm not criticizing, I promise. But a baby doesn't fit into that gorgeous apartment you live in, Noah. There's no space there for gardening gloves and muddy boots. You've built your ideal life for yourself, and it's truly lovely. But there isn't room in it for children. Kids are messy! They're loud. They're demanding… You've seen your niece and nephews…"

"Yeah, they're pretty wild…" he said.

"They're pretty *normal*," she replied. "They're kids! They're complicated little people that keep every single adult in their lives hopping. That's how they grow up. That's how they figure out who they are…"

"You might be right," he said quietly. "I'm not saying I don't love those kids—"

"I know," she said softly. "But loving them and visiting them is different than embracing life as a dad and husband all in one place—" She looked around the room. "And our son is going to be no different. He'll be just as demanding, just as full of personality, just as...sticky. I'm okay with that. I'm expecting that. I'm looking forward to it!"

"I know the life I wanted," he said. "But sometimes life changes, and you've got to roll with it. Yes, I love a quiet library, a tidy home, a well-made meal and a cozy evening. But that doesn't mean I want to give *you* up!"

Her heart lurched, and she longed to latch on to those words and let them be enough. She didn't want to give him up, either, but what if it was inevitable? What if they were exchanging a truly warm friendship for a messy breakup and broken hearts? What if they were taking away the united, supportive environment their son was going to need? Because his needs had to come first. Trying this out, seeing where it went, giving a shot—that was selfish.

"Your deepest desires aren't going to change..." She shook her head. "You were willing to let your fiancée go, to let your wedding go, to face that heartbreak rather than agree to a family life. And I respect that! But what makes *me* different?"

"I don't know," he said. "But you are."

"This baby...that's who's changed things," she said. "This little boy is *yours*, and you're feeling that," she said. "But look around you—this is what's waiting after the romance of a newborn wears off!"

"I'm not going to stop loving you," he murmured. "Either of you."

"Me, neither," she said. "But I've done this before, Noah. You know that. Glen and I got married because of a pregnancy, and it didn't stop any of the issues that came up for us."

Noah leaned back, and he let his hand drop from her belly back into his lap.

"I don't want to be the guy who left," he said, his voice a low rumble. "Or was asked to leave... My son would always see me as the one who abandoned him."

He didn't want to be the guy who left, and she didn't want to be the woman who had to put her life together again when he did. They had a solution—the one they'd come up with in the beginning.

"Then be the guy who shows up," Taryn whispered. "Be the one who's there for him no matter what, who's only a phone call away."

"You mean go back to our original plan," he said. "Be friends. Be supportive. Put our son first, and keep whatever we're feeling for each other out of it."

"I think it's the only way to guarantee that we can give our boy what he needs," she said, her voice shaking. "Don't you?"

"I can be the guy who shows up for you, too," he said. "Anything you need—you tell me. I'll be here."

Taryn was silent because her heart was so full that she didn't trust herself to speak.

"Okay?" he murmured, and he bent and kissed her forehead. "I mean it. This isn't goodbye. We have a son to raise together."

Taryn nodded. "It's not goodbye," she whispered.

Outside the window, headlights swung up the drive, and they both looked out toward the returning minivan. Laura and Henry were home.

Somehow, those two had managed to build a loving life with a houseful of kids—but that didn't happen unless both parents loved that life. With one resentful parent, one giving up all their interests and joys, there couldn't be a harmonious and happy home. It wasn't possible.

Love wasn't always enough.

"Let me drive you home," Noah said, and he rose to his feet and held out a hand to her.

The front door opened, and Laura and Henry came inside. Henry gave his wife a peck on the cheek, and Laura unwound a shawl from around her shoulders and tossed it over the back of the couch.

"Thanks for watching the kids," Henry said. "How were they?"

"Great," Noah said. "No problems at all."

"You sure?" Laura asked suspiciously. "You look like you've been through the wringer tonight, and I know my children."

"No, it was fine," Noah said. "We sorted it out."

"How are you feeling these days?" Laura asked Taryn. "Can I get you some tea, or—"

"No, but thank you," Taryn said. "I'm pretty tired. I should probably get back to the resort."

Laura looked between Noah and Taryn, and Taryn could see the other woman coming to a few conclusions, but Taryn didn't have the strength to hold everything together tonight.

"Of course," Laura said softly. "No problem. Thanks for helping out. I'll return the favor in a heartbeat when your little guy arrives."

Taryn smiled weakly.

"I'll call you later, Laura," Noah said.

"See you…" Laura exchanged a look with her husband, and when Noah and Taryn went out the front door, they closed it behind them.

"Was that rude?" Taryn asked, her voice choked.

"Don't worry about it," Noah said. "They're family. I'll explain later."

It was time to get back to her room, to her solitude, so she could let her tears fall. Taryn wasn't going to be able to cut Noah off to get over this… Noah was now a part of her life, and she'd just have to find a way to pull her emotions back from the edge.

NOAH DROPPED TARYN off at the resort, and he felt like his heart stretched out after her as she went inside. He wanted to call her back, to make this right, to find some way to bridge this gap between them. But she was right—they were the same people they were two weeks ago, before he knew about his son, and before he'd laid eyes on Taryn again.

His emotions were sitting so close to the surface that he could feel them on his skin, between his ribs, blocking his throat. But he didn't cry. That would have been a relief, and he didn't want one. He let the ache settle into his chest as he rode up the elevator and headed down the hallway to his apartment. He let himself in and tossed his keys into a dish by the door.

Home sweet home. But it didn't feel the same. It was clean and warm—the welcoming sight of soft light, and the faint scent of cinnamon coming from an air freshener on the dining room table.

That weekend was a quiet one. Noah spent it alone with a few good books, and with his memories and heartbreak. Somehow, his home wasn't quite so soothing. Funny—a few messes around here, some crumbs, another voice or two, would have felt good... He texted Taryn once on Sunday morning, but she texted back that she needed a couple of days to regain her balance.

He'd ruined things. He shouldn't have told her how he felt. She was right—he'd already seen how much of his orderly life a woman could handle with Nevaeh. She'd liked his apartment, too. She'd loved the quiet and comfort, but he'd driven her a little crazy with his clean ways...

But that wasn't why Nevaeh had left him. She'd wanted the same things that Taryn did—the sticky fingers, the life full of children. It was going to take some time for his heart to catch up.

On Monday morning, Noah sat in his office, the job-offer email open in front of him. He should take it. It made sense—it was a step up, it came with a hefty raise and that signing bonus. He'd been working for this, and he deserved to grow his career. All the same, he didn't feel the excitement that should accompany a chance this big.

If he took the job, he could support his son…and Taryn. He wasn't supposed to be thinking about her that way. She could support herself just fine—she was a successful businesswoman, and she already had plans in place for raising her child. She was competent, smart and self-sufficient, so why did Noah want her to need him?

He wanted to be her protector, her provider, her hero. And she wanted him to let her heal…

His fingers hovered over the keyboard to type his reply when there was a knock on his door.

"Come in," he said.

Brody stood in the doorway.

"What now?" Noah said. He was too tired to do this—too exhausted from all he'd been through the past couple of weeks. Besides, he had an email to write.

Brody came inside and shut the door behind him.

"We need to talk more," Brody said. Noah didn't answer, but Brody came into the office and sat down in a visitor's chair. "You're my best friend."

"Still?" Noah said.

"Look, I've been thinking about some of the stuff you said," Brody said. "And I need to know—do you love her?"

"Nevaeh?" Noah asked.

"Yes, Nevaeh! Who else?" Brody scraped a hand through his hair. "Are you still in love with her?"

Brody's expression was agonized, and he leaned forward, waiting for Noah's answer.

"No," Noah said. "Not anymore."

"Okay," Brody said with a nod. "Okay. You don't love her. That's a good thing. I needed to hear it. So I get how this is complicated. I can understand that having your best friend move on with your ex is not ideal. But she's the one for me, Noah. You don't love her, but I do. She lands right here—" Brody thumped his chest. "I can't explain how it feels, but she's not just another girlfriend. She completes me."

"I know how that feels…" Noah admitted.

"You loved her like that?" Brody asked feebly.

"No, not Nevaeh. Someone else," Noah said. It was Taryn lodged in his chest, and the thought of moving to Seattle was feeling as impossible as leaving a piece of his body behind.

"Wait, so this—" Brody swallowed. "The last couple of weeks, I've been thinking maybe I was wrong. Maybe you were still in love with Nevaeh, and—"

"Oh, you were wrong in moving on as fast as you did," Noah replied. "But…" He looked up at Brody, and for the first time in seven months, he saw the best friend he'd missed so much. Just a guy—a buddy who understood him, and up until the end of his engagement, had had his back.

"I'm going to be a father, Brody," Noah said, and his voice shook.

"What?" Brody blinked. "Wait—"

"I met someone," Noah said. "And we had a connection right away. We spent one night together, and she got pregnant. I only just found out a couple of weeks ago. I'm going be a dad…"

"You aren't joking," Brody said.

"Who jokes about that?" Noah demanded.

"To make it worse, it can't work between us, but I'm in love with her."

They stared at each other for a few beats, and Noah felt his reserves crumbling. This was his oldest friend, and through all of this upheaval, he'd missed having Brody in his life to talk thing out with.

"So who is she?" Brody asked. "And when is the baby due?"

"Can I trust you with this?" Noah asked.

"Yeah, you can trust me," Brody said earnestly.

And somehow, Noah knew that he could.

"Her name is Taryn Cook—she's in town doing a marketing thing for Angelina." He quickly told the broad strokes about what had happened. "And she's due in a matter of weeks. It's a boy. I'm going to have a son…"

"And you're in love with her," Brody said. "That's pretty important."

"It won't work," Noah repeated. "We love each other, but we're very different. Our son needs invested parents who respect each other, not two people bitter from some awful breakup."

"Who says you'll break up?" Brody asked.

"Look, she's been through this with her ex-husband. And you know how I watched Tom and my mother split. Kids complicate things, and we all know that I'm not exactly a great father type."

"You're the only one convinced of that," Brody replied. "You're such a typical child of divorce, man."

"What?" Noah said.

"I'm serious," Brody said. "You've created this perfect child-free life for yourself, and you're so certain you can't grow enough for your own child. I don't believe it. With the right person, you can grow! For a child of your own—" Brody's voice broke off. "Can I just be honest here?"

"Might as well," Noah replied.

"I need my best friend in my life," Brody said. "And you need me. Okay? You're talking about moving on with your life, but you can't do that without cutting out every person who ever let you down. And I'm sorry, okay? I'm sorry I fell in love with her! I'm sorry I can't turn it off. But you need me in your life, too! There's more to life than one or two relationships, and I'm going to tell you something from my parents' long marriage."

"To this child of divorce," Noah said ruefully.

"Exactly." Brody leaned back. "They've been married for forty-six years. And that doesn't mean my dad was the perfect husband or father. He was faithful, but he was a workaholic and emotionally distant. But over the years, he softened. He grew. He got better at relationships. Today? He's remarkably wise. He was the one who told me that I couldn't just give up on you. He said we men tend to be all strong and self-sufficient, and then we unload our garbage on our women."

"And the answer is to keep your friends," Noah said.

"Simple, but effective," Brody said quietly. "We'll be better dads as a result, Noah. And if you truly don't love Nevaeh anymore—"

"I'm in love with Taryn," Noah said. "You and Nevaeh have my blessing."

"You mean that?" Brody asked.

"Yeah. But tell me one thing. What made your parents' marriage last when I haven't seen anyone last yet?"

Brody shrugged. "Family is family. That's always been my parents' motto. When you messed up, you might have to deal with an upset spouse, but as long as they were both faithful and honest, they could get through whatever bumps came at them. They stuck it out. They got over anger and resentment because they knew that our family was worth fighting for. It isn't about being perfect—it's about commitment."

Noah was silent. His heart sped up in his chest, and he looked toward his computer screen. He wasn't perfect, but he did love Taryn and their baby. And he and Taryn had the faithful-and-honest part down pat…

"I don't think my orderly life is quite so satisfying as it used to be," Noah said quietly.

"You want kids now?" Brody asked.

"I want my son," Noah said. "And I want Taryn in my life as more than just his mother. I might still be kind of backward in a lot of my instincts with kids, but for *them*, I want to learn."

Brody smiled. "So what are you going to do about it?"

"It's not so simple," Noah said. "She doesn't think we'd last."

"Hmm." Brody shrugged. "So prove her wrong."

It hadn't been long, but Noah had one choice ahead of him that looked a whole lot different in light of his son's arrival. So maybe he was growing already. Maybe not every gut instinct he had was going to be wrong…maybe this one was right!

"Alright," Noah said. "I need you to get out so I can turn down a job."

"What?" Brody said.

"It doesn't matter. I was thinking of moving to Seattle, but I'm not going across the country away from them. I have no idea what Taryn will think—if she'll give me a chance yet or not—but I'm following my gut on this one."

Brody stood up and held out his hand. "I'm glad you'll stick around. You'll be a good dad."

"I'll try," Noah replied, and he took Brody's hand in a firm shake.

"We're friends, Noah," Brody said, pointing a finger at him as he headed for the door. "You hear me?"

"Yeah, yeah," Noah chuckled. "You're hard to get rid of."

And maybe that wasn't such a terrible thing, after all.

Brody shot him a grin and opened the door. "Talk to you later. Good luck."

As the door shut after Brody, Noah felt a certainty deep down for the first time. This was no longer a question or an internal debate. Call it a father's instinct—one of his first. But his family needed him closer than Seattle.

His cell phone rang, and he picked it up.

"Noah? We've got a bit of a situation on the Craigsview Trail. There are some teenagers climbing some fragile trees, and they've been asked to clear out, but they aren't doing it…"

Noah heaved a sigh. Work didn't stop, even when his heart longed for a break. But this was the job he'd be keeping. When he got back, he was answering that email, and then he'd go find Taryn.

They needed to talk.

CHAPTER SEVENTEEN

IN ANGELINA'S OFFICE, Taryn had her computer set up so that Angelina could see the screen. She'd been working hard on this marketing campaign, and she was proud of her work. But she still felt that ache of sadness deep inside of her. She was leaving Mountain Springs, and she'd be leaving more than a job, or her grandmother's hometown. She was leaving behind any romantic hopes she'd started to cherish toward Noah Brooks, and that hurt more than she'd ever imagined. She'd weathered a divorce, yet this hurt in a different place in her heart that had never been touched before.

Being a good mother sometimes meant sacrifice, and so did being a mature woman who wasn't going to repeat past mistakes.

"So this is my plan for your campaign," Taryn said. "Mountain Springs Resort is located on the edge of a glacier-fed lake, but deep inside that lake there is a spring of clear, fresh water that pushes up from an underwater geyser—hence the name of Mountain Springs. You know this, but other people don't. This resort is a place of continued renewal, and I want to show people what that looks like in the lives of the people who visit and work here."

She pulled up the next slide.

"As you can see, I've made a broad selection of shareable content, starting with Gayle's and Melanie's weddings." She pulled up a picture from Gayle's wedding showing the bride in her elegant dress down by the lakeshore, the water glimmering with late-afternoon sunlight behind her. "I love how Gayle restarted her life, and how simple and truly gorgeous her wedding was. I want people to see the wedding-venue options that you supply, but also the renewal of spirit that happens here, too."

She flipped to a photo of Melanie's wedding. This one showed Melanie hugging her stepdaughter, their eyes shut, tears on Melanie's lashes. This photo was taken inside the lodge, the wooden walls glowing in the low light.

"These pictures tell a story at a single glance. Mountain Springs Resort offers more than a vacation…" Taryn went on.

As she moved through the slides, flicking through shareable photos, some prewritten articles to be posted on the Mountain Springs website and pitched to magazines and blogs, too, she felt the strange renewal of this place inside of her. She might not have gotten her heart's desire, but she'd learned more about herself, and become more dedicated to being the mother she needed to be. Her growth had been more like that underwater spring—unseen, but powerful, and necessary to all the life it would sustain.

"But this resort is not just a place for guests," Taryn said. "This is a workplace that fuels the hearts and ambitions of the employees who work here. You're known for your fair wages, your compassion to individual situations, and your encouraging culture here. You have an author who works for you in housekeeping—" she pulled up a picture of Lisa Dear "—and she wouldn't be able to focus on her writing if she couldn't depend upon her job here. She told me that this resort seeps into her writing, and you can see why—"

Taryn pulled up photos of the mountains, the lake, the hiking trails, and one shot from the top of those cliffs that Noah had given to her.

"Your employees have had nothing but

praise for you," Taryn went on. "And I want to show a few photos of your workers in action—putting their hearts into creating your vision."

Angelina's eyes were wet with tears as Taryn flipped through the last of the photos, and then she stopped at one final picture—Angelina standing by the lake looking directly into the camera. She looked ageless, like she was somehow a part of the lake and the mountains, the sky...

"Everyone agreed on one thing," Taryn said. "The secret to this resort is you. Because of you, this is a life source for guests and employees alike."

Angelina was silent, and Taryn watched the other woman as her lips wobbled.

"Can I tell you something?" Angelina asked softly. "There was a time when I would have given anything to have the kind of second chance at love that my friends have had. I wanted my own second wedding—my own husband to come home to. But I made my peace with it, and threw all that misplaced love and passion into this resort. Looking at it through your eyes, I can see what I've made here..."

"It's extraordinary," Taryn said.

"It is." Angelina nodded and she blinked

back the emotion. "Thank you. You did an amazing job."

Taryn smiled. "I appreciate that."

"I've been considering hiring another executive to help out with the management of this place," Angelina said. "I could use someone with your creative marketing vision full-time. I don't suppose you'd consider a job change?"

A chance to work at this gorgeous lodge, to watch the seasons change on that pristine mountain lake… It would be paradise, but it would also be hell—she couldn't work next to Noah and not keep falling in love with him over and over again. If she wanted a true renewal of her own, it had to be back in Denver.

Taryn shook her head. "It's incredibly tempting. I mean, look at this place! But I have my own business to run, and I'm all set up in Denver for the baby."

"Understood," Angelina said with a warm smile. "If you ever change your mind, let me know. I'd make room for you."

It was such a kind offer that Taryn felt a wave of unbidden emotion. But no, she had to think of her son, and of her own emotional stability right now. And that involved going home.

They shook hands goodbye.

"You can stay another few days if you like," Angelina said. "Don't feel chased out!"

"No, but thank you," Taryn said. "It's time to get home."

And it was time to visit her grandmother one last time before she left.

As Taryn drove away from the lodge, she glanced in her rearview mirror at the receding log-styled resort. Somehow, she felt like she was leaving a piece of her heart behind. Noah would always be in her life, but going forward, she wouldn't have his strong arms around her, his warm kisses, his low laugh in her ear... He'd be distant—the dad her son needed, but not the husband for her.

Taryn drove the winding road back around to the town. She'd be okay. She'd recover from his heartbreak, too, and she'd be a kinder, deeper, wiser mother to her son as a result.

She parked in front of her grandmother's home, and turned off the car. The thing was, even if she was still quite competent, Granny was alone out here, and Taryn might very well find herself alone when she was Granny's age, too. Not everyone ended up with a spouse who lived as long as they did, or an adult child in the same town to check on them. And truth be told, Taryn recognized her grandmother's stubborn streak all too well. Taryn was just like her. They were the Cook women, and they were determined to take care of themselves.

Taryn got out of the car and headed up the walk. It was a warm morning, and birds twittered from the mature trees that lined the road. When she got to the front door, Taryn knocked and waited.

There was no answer, and she looked through the window, but saw no movement. She sighed and pulled out her phone, dialing her grandmother's number. She could hear the ringing of the phone from indoors, but no one answered. Had Granny gone for one of her walks, maybe?

She was about to head back down the steps when she heard a feeble cry from inside, and Taryn's heart leaped in her chest. She pulled open the screen and tried the door. It was unlocked, and she pushed inside.

"Granny?" she called. "Granny!"

The living room was perfectly clean—nothing out of place. Taryn spun in a full circle, and she heard her grandmother's faint voice coming from the kitchen. Taryn hurried in that direction, and as she came into the bright kitchen, she spotted Granny on the floor next to the fridge. She was wearing a nightgown that was tangled around her legs, and her face was as pale as the spilled sugar on the floor next to her. One bare foot looked bluish, and Taryn felt bile rise in her throat.

"Granny..." she breathed. "What happened?"

"I tripped—" Granny whispered.

"Oh, Granny..." Taryn awkwardly got down onto the floor next to her grandmother and then pulled open her purse, rooting for her cell phone.

"I twisted my ankle," Granny breathed. "And I couldn't get back up again, and—" Tears leaked out of her grandmother's eyes, trickling sideways down her face to follow gravity to the floor.

"Okay..." Taryn dialed 911 on her phone. "I'm getting an ambulance, Granny. I'm here."

The 911 call didn't take long, and an ambulance was dispatched right away. When Taryn hung up, she took her grandmother's trembling hand in hers.

"I'm so glad you came," Granny murmured.

"Me, too," Taryn said, and looking down at her poor, weathered grandmother, tears rose in her eyes. "Granny, you can't stay in this house alone anymore... You know that, right?"

Granny didn't answer, but she did tighten her grip on Taryn's hand.

A COUPLE OF hours later, Noah came back into the resort, hot and tired. He'd dealt with the teenagers—some new guests on the property. The parents were horrified at the destruction their children had caused. One father promised to pay something toward trimming the damaged trees back, and everyone seemed properly apologetic.

Those particular guests weren't going to be using the trails for the rest of their stay. The crisis was dealt with, and Noah was glad to put it behind him. Sometimes a large man in a suit gave exactly the impression needed to get everyone jumping.

But his mind wasn't on the work. He needed to see Taryn, and this had already taken considerably longer than he'd wanted. His chat with Brody had gotten him thinking, and as he made his way back toward the lodge, he felt like he was being pulled in that direction by some invisible force. He'd talk to her… She had to know what had changed for him, at the very least.

As Noah headed back into the lodge, Janelle was at the front desk, and she smiled.

"Good morning, Mr. Brooks," she said.

"Hi, Janelle," he said, shooting her a distracted smile, and headed past her toward the hallway that led past the offices. Was Taryn still in her office?

He poked his head into the office next to his. It was empty—too empty. No purse, no tablet...not even a sweater. The garbage had been recently emptied, too. His heartbeat sped up—she could be anywhere. He pulled out his phone to check for messages, but there weren't any. He headed past his own office and toward Angelina's. He found Angelina at her desk, bent over some papers, her reading glasses on the tip of her nose.

"So what happened with the trail?" Angelina asked.

Noah gave her a quick rundown of the damage and how he'd dealt with it, and she seemed happy with his choices.

"Do you know where Taryn is?" he asked.

"She checked out this morning," Angelina said. "She did fantastic work! I'll have to show you what she put together for us. It's stunning—"

"What do you mean, she checked out?" he said, surprising them both by cutting her off.

"She said she wanted to get back to Denver," Angelina said. "She was ready to get home."

"Right..." His mouth felt dry. She hadn't left any messages, either. No text to say goodbye. Was that how she felt about him now? The thought hurt.

"Noah, is there something going on between you two?" Angelina asked.

Noah looked up to find Angelina's frank gaze locked on him. Fraternizing with the marketing contractor wasn't going to do anything for his professional reputation. Angelina was fair, but she was also a consummate professional.

"It's complicated," he admitted. "I won't lie to you. But I can promise you that I wasn't starting up with a work associate on company time. Taryn and I met a few months ago, so..."

Angelina's eyebrows slowly climbed. "Are you... I mean, feel free to tell me this none of my business, but—"

"I'm the father of Taryn's baby," Noah said, throat tight.

"Oh..." Angelina nodded a couple of times. "Wow... Okay. So you need to talk to her?"

"I really do," he said with a rush of relief. "And the sooner the better."

"Go, go!" Angelina said. "And good luck!"

Noah shot his boss a grateful look as he

pulled out his cell phone and hurried along the hall. He dialed Taryn's number. How far down the highway would she be already? Was he going to be driving to Denver today?

And would she even answer his call?

Taryn picked up on the third ring, and he felt a rush of relief.

"Noah?" she said.

"Hey…" He paused in his office for a little more privacy. "Angelina said you'd checked out. I'd hoped to be able to say goodbye."

"Oh… I just—" She paused. "It was going to be hard to see you and then walk away, and—" Her voice caught.

"I know," he said. "It was going to be misery."

"So I thought I'd just head out, and maybe call you from the road," she said.

"How far did you get?" he asked, his voice low.

"I'm not out of town yet," Taryn said. "I'm actually at the hospital."

"What?" His body went cold. "Is it the baby? Is everything okay?"

"The baby is fine," she said, and he heard her voice soften. "It's Granny. She fell and twisted her ankle last night. I found her this morning on the floor of her kitchen."

"Oh, God—"

"Yeah, but I called an ambulance, and we're at the hospital now," she said. "The doctor has seen us, and they're wrapping up Granny's ankle. No break, thank goodness, but she'll be off her foot for a while."

"What can I do?" he asked.

"We could use a ride back to her place," Taryn said. "I rode in the ambulance with her."

She needed him...

"I'm on my way," he said. Noah headed out into the hallway, pulling the door firmly shut behind him. "And Taryn?"

"Yeah?" He could hear some voices behind her, sounding like they were talking to her grandmother. Her attention was already being pulled away, and he understood. But he had to tell her this much—

"I'm not going to Seattle," he said.

"Noah—"

"I'll explain when I get there," he said. "Just thought you should know."

CHAPTER EIGHTEEN

GRANNY WAS TRANSFERRED to a room where they could wait for their ride home. She was still in her nightgown, but the hospital had lent her a robe, and there was a blanket over her good leg. The doctor had offered to let Granny stay the night so that they could x-ray her foot again in the morning when some of the swelling had gone down, but Granny didn't want to stay any longer than absolutely necessary.

"I'm fine," Granny said. "Or I will be. I hate hospitals. Let me go home."

"She can't be left alone," the doctor told Taryn seriously. "She's much frailer than she seems to think. That foot will need more medical attention, so you should bring her to her family doctor in the morning."

"I will," Taryn said.

"And at her age," the doctor said, lowering his voice, "she really shouldn't be living alone. That fall was a scary one, and she needs to have people checking in on her, at the very least. But like you experienced, even coming by once a day isn't necessarily enough."

"I know," Taryn said. "We're working on that as a family, I can assure you. And I won't be leaving her alone."

After the doctor departed, Taryn pulled a chair up next to her grandmother's bed. Her foot was bandaged, but the toes that peeked out were bruised.

"Granny, your hearing is excellent, so I know you heard what the doctor said," Taryn said quietly. "You need people."

Granny looked away.

"I get it!" Taryn said. "I'm just like you. I'm fiercely independent, and I want to do everything on my own. You know why? I'm afraid of being a burden, and I'm afraid of getting attached to someone and having them stop loving me, or stop wanting me around."

"You have some issues, then," Granny said, but there was a teasing twinkle in her eyes.

"Granny—" Taryn wasn't going to be put off.

"Fine..." Granny sighed. "I might understand those feelings. But dear, I've taken care of an ailing husband alone, and I've lived alone for too many years now. I don't think I'd be good company."

"Then be nicer," Taryn said.

Granny turned down her lips.

"I'm serious," Taryn said. "Granny, you take pride in chasing people off. The only other option here is an old-age home where people are paid to take care of you."

Granny reached out and caught Taryn's sleeve. "Not that!"

Taryn was stunned by her grandmother's fierce clutch.

"I know I can't live alone, Taryn, but I can't go to an old-age home! They'll be strangers, and they won't care what happens to me."

"I don't know what to say, Granny," she said. "I'd love to bring you with me in Denver."

"Not Denver." Tears welled in Granny's eyes. "I have so many memories in this town. Not all of them sweet, but all of them *mine*. And I don't want to leave it. I know I need help, and I might need to hire someone at this point, but I don't want to leave my town."

"Okay," Taryn said softly. "I understand."

"You might want to look at how much you're like me, after all," Granny said. "Being strong is a good thing—you don't bother anyone much. But time sweeps past faster than you realize, and before you know it, you've pushed away anyone who might have been there for you—"

An image of Noah rose in her mind—his kind eyes, his fervent voice as he told her that he'd be willing to make a life with her. Was Taryn doing the same thing?

"Granny," Taryn said slowly. "I have an idea, but I'm not sure how you'll feel about it."

"Oh?" Granny looked up.

"I'm going to have a baby, and I'll need help. You're getting older, and you could use a hand. What if we…banded together? What if I moved in with you? I've been offered a job here in Mountain Springs, and I could take it. I'd be closer to Noah so he could visit his son, and I could be here with you."

Granny's eyes lit up. "You'd do that? I'd dearly love a baby in my house again."

"We'll talk about it," Taryn said. "I don't want to push you when you're fragile."

"Fragile? Hardly," Granny said. "Move in with me, Taryn. I'll be more of a help with that little one than you realize. We'll take care of each other. I have steam left in me, you know. I'm not about to abandon myself to a rocking chair in the corner."

Taryn leaned over and kissed her grandmother's cheek.

"I love you, Granny."

"I love you, too, Taryn," Granny said. "But can I give you a tiny piece of advice?"

"Sure," Taryn said. "I've been dishing out enough of my own, haven't I?"

Granny nodded toward the door. "That man loves you. And that kind of love doesn't come around as often as young people think…"

Taryn glanced in the direction her grandmother was looking, and she stopped short. Noah stood in the doorway. His dress shirt sleeves were rolled up to his elbows, and his shirt was open at the neck. His dark gaze met hers, filled with concern and longing.

"Hey…" he said, and the last of her defenses crumbled. If this was going to be that dreaded goodbye, it was going to tear her heart out.

Taryn got up and went over to Noah. He didn't pause a beat; he just pulled her into his arms and lowered his lips over hers. She leaned into his embrace, and she felt like her heart might break inside her chest.

"I'm staying here," he whispered, pulling back. "I'm following my gut on this—I'm following my heart. I'm not going to Seattle, and I'm going to ask something of you—"

"Noah—" she started to say.

"No, let me finish," he said softly. "I'm in love with you. And you love me, too. I know I wanted this careful, tidy, adult-centered life, but that was before you and the baby. He's changing what I want, the future I want, and that's not a bad thing, Taryn! I want to be a father…with you at my side. I never wanted it with anyone else. But I want it with you."

"Are you sure?"

"I've never been more sure in my life," he said. "So I emailed the hotel people in Seattle and told them that I'm going to be a father, and I can't take the job. I know you might not want to give me a chance yet, but I'm going to be here if you change your mind. And if you need anything—*any*thing—I'm going to be the guy who provides it."

The baby squirmed, and Taryn looked over her shoulder toward her grandmother. Granny wasn't even trying to hide the fact that she was watching them with full attention.

"If it weren't for the baby—" Taryn started her old argument.

"If it weren't for our son, I wouldn't have

realized everything I was missing," he said. "But I'd still be wondering about the incredible woman I met that night. Taryn, I love you. This isn't about being noble—this is a fact. And if you turn me away, I'm not going to stop loving you. I'm not Glen, okay? I'm not trying to be some hero. I'm just trying to be with the woman who fills my heart."

Taryn felt like her head was spinning.

"Noah, what if... I was willing to do this?" she said.

"Wait—" He caught her gaze. "We need to be really clear here. Don't just try to be nice, or I'll just hear what I want to hear."

"What if I wanted to be a family—the three of us, together?" she said.

"Really?" he asked breathlessly.

"Yeah." She nodded.

"I'm all in," he said, and pulled her for another kiss. She leaned against his solid chest, and the baby squirmed again. When she pulled back and looked up into his warm gaze, she felt a wave of happiness.

"I told Granny I'd be taking care of her—" she said.

"She's welcome to live with us," Noah said with a grin. "But Taryn, I'm serious. If we're doing this, I want to do it right. I want to be coming home to my wife—"

"And her grandmother," Granny piped up.

"And her grandmother, and my son," Noah said with a soft laugh. "I want all of it, Taryn. I want you to marry me."

Marriage… This time, it felt right. This wasn't a man trying to do the right thing in the face of an accident. This was the real thing—this was the kind of love she'd been afraid to long for…

"Yes," she whispered.

Noah grinned and kissed her again, then he looked over her head toward her grandmother.

"Mrs. Cook, do I have your blessing?" he asked.

"And then some," Granny replied.

An orderly came into the room with a wheelchair then, and Taryn watched as Noah helped her grandmother into the chair. He was tender and careful, and once the old woman was settled, he looked up at Taryn with such love, her eyes misted.

This was what the rest of her life looked like—a tall, handsome man who'd help her take care of the ones they loved, and year after year to roll out in front of them.

She slipped her hand over his muscular arm, and her heart gave a little leap. There was a wedding to plan, and she knew the perfect place for the vows that would begin their happily-ever-after.

Mountain Springs Resort—there was nowhere better!

EPILOGUE

ON A BRISK morning in early October, Taryn awoke to the sound of her newborn son's whimpers in the bassinet next to the bed. She instinctively tried to sit up, and felt the pain of her C-section incision. She grimaced, then let out a slow breath and pulled herself up a little more slowly.

"Noah…" she murmured.

"Hmm?" Noah sat up, his eyes still shut. "What?"

Taryn couldn't help but smile at her husband's bleary confusion. She'd had their son three days earlier, and Noah had been by her side the entire time. Then he'd brought them home to the house they'd bought together—the one with the generous in-law suite where Granny stayed. She had her own kitchen, but she liked coming in to eat with Taryn and Noah, and they enjoyed her company. Granny had softened considerably over the past two months.

"The baby's awake, Noah," Taryn said.

"Okay…" Noah pushed back the covers and got up. He headed around the bed and leaned over the bassinet, now more awake. He'd started to grow his beard back, and it was short and scruffy looking at this stage—she liked it. What was it about Noah that whatever he did, she seemed to like it?

"Hey, there, Tommy," Noah said softly. "You hungry again?"

Taryn watched as Noah scooped his son out of the tiny bed and softly kissed his downy head before he handed him over to Taryn to nurse. Tommy was a big baby, and he latched on immediately for his breakfast. Noah sank onto the edge of the bed and watched their son drink.

They weren't completely settled in the house yet. There were still boxes stacked in the corners, and it would be a few weeks yet before everything had a place, but their friends and family had all pulled together to help them move. It was amazing how quickly that could happen with many willing hands.

"How are you feeling?" Noah asked.

"Sore," she admitted. "But better than yesterday."

She looked at Tommy—his downy chestnut hair, his plump little cheeks and those big, round eyes that looked up at her as he drank.

Noah leaned over and pecked her lips. "I think I hear Granny in the kitchen. I'm just going to go check on her…"

Taryn shot him a smile. "Sure. You know where to find me."

Noah wrapped a bathrobe around himself, and headed out of the bedroom. Noah and Granny had bonded, and he really seemed to enjoy Granny's blunt, no-nonsense attitude. He'd also gotten rather protective of the old lady, and he'd made sure Granny had what she needed within reach—her tea things, her little stash of canned soup that she liked to make for lunch.

Noah was home on parental leave for four weeks, and Taryn wondered what it would be like when he went back to work—how much he'd miss them.

Tommy gave a squawk of protest, so she changed sides and readjusted her nightgown as he continued to nurse. He was so precious, so perfect, that looking down at him filled her heart to the brim. She ran her hand over his tiny arm, and her wedding band glistened in the low light.

Their wedding had been a small one—just

the two of them in a chapel in town. They had already booked the lodge for a proper reception in the spring, long enough after Tommy's birth for them to be able to celebrate with everyone they loved best. It was a little untraditional, but Taryn didn't mind. Nothing in their love story had been traditional, and it suited them just fine.

Noah poked his head back into the bedroom.

"Granny has decided she's making us breakfast," Noah said. "I'm just going to… I think she might need some help, you know?"

"Go," Taryn chuckled. "But I don't think she'll burn anything down."

"Not today," Noah said.

A couple of minutes later, she could hear Noah and Granny talking to each other, and a minute after that, Noah appeared in the bedroom doorway again.

"I've been sent away," he said.

Taryn chuckled. "She's fine. What's she making, toast? Oatmeal?"

"Oatmeal," he confirmed.

Noah crawled back into bed next to her, and he leaned his cheek on Taryn's shoulder, looking down at their son.

"He's really something, isn't he?" Noah murmured.

"Yeah…" she agreed. "He sure is."

Noah kissed her shoulder, his scruff tickling her skin, and then leaned back against the pillows. Taryn glanced over at him, and they exchanged a smile.

"I love you," she said.

"I love you, too, beautiful."

Tommy finished up, and Noah reached for him.

"Come here, buddy," he said quietly, and pulled the baby onto his chest, and then put an arm around Taryn, too. She closed her eyes, enjoying the musky scent of her husband's chest. She touched Tommy's fingers with the tips of hers.

Through the window, the sun was rising, and a brisk autumn wind whistled around the house. Inside, everything was warm and snug, and from the kitchen, Taryn could smell the scent of coffee brewing.

It was perfect—so perfect, that she'd never been able to imagine it in all of her wildest daydreams. She'd never thought she'd see Noah again, let alone marry him and trust him like she did.

"I never knew I wanted this so badly," Noah murmured.

Taryn knew what he meant. She felt the same way. Neither of them could have anticipated this future together, but it was perfect. A little family that filled her heart, and this time she knew that it would last.

* * * * *

HARLEQUIN SELECTS COLLECTION

19 FREE BOOKS IN ALL!

From Robyn Carr to RaeAnne Thayne to Linda Lael Miller and Sherryl Woods we promise (actually, GUARANTEE!) each author in the Harlequin Selects collection has seen their name on the *New York Times* or *USA TODAY* bestseller lists!

⊕HARLEQUIN

HEARTWARMING

#379 CAUGHT BY THE COWBOY DAD
The Mountain Monroes • by Melinda Curtis

Holden Monroe and Bea Carlisle are hoping a road trip will give them time alone for a second chance—but it's a special Old West town they happen upon that helps them rediscover their spark!

#380 THE TEXAN'S SECRET SON
Truly Texas • by Kit Hawthorne

Single mom Nina Walker is shocked to see Marcos Ramirez again. Especially since her ex-husband has no idea he's a father to a son! Will the Texas rancher forgive her and finally claim his family?

#381 A FOURTH OF JULY PROPOSAL
Cupid's Crossing • by Kim Findlay

Former bad boy Ryker Slade came home to sell his father's house, then he'll leave. Instead he finds a connection with the pastor's daughter, Rachel Lowther. But Rachel also plans to leave town—unless Ryker gives her a reason to stay...

#382 THE MAN FROM MONTANA
Hearts of Big Sky • by Julianna Morris

Tessa Alderman has questions about her twin sister's death in a white water rafting accident, at the same time she's drawn to the man who may have the answers...Clay Carson.

HWCNM0621